CW00457417

MURDER
— *on* —
STAGE

BOOKS BY F.L. EVERETT

MURDER
— on —
STAGE

F.L. EVERETT

bookouture

Published by Bookouture in 2024

An imprint of Storyfire Ltd.
Carmelite House
50 Victoria Embankment
London EC4Y 0DZ

www.bookouture.com

Copyright © F.L. Everett, 2024

F.L. Everett has asserted her right to be identified as the author of this work.

All rights reserved. No part of this publication may be reproduced, stored in any retrieval system, or transmitted, in any form or by any means, electronic, mechanical, photocopying, recording or otherwise, without the prior written permission of the publishers.

ISBN: 978-1-83790-468-6
eBook ISBN: 978-1-83790-466-2

This book is a work of fiction. Names, characters, businesses, organizations, places and events other than those clearly in the public domain, are either the product of the author's imagination or are used fictitiously. Any resemblance to actual persons, living or dead, events or locales is entirely coincidental.

For Philip, the greatest gardener I know.

He had loved her all along, with a passion of the
    strong,
The fact that she loved him was plain to all.
She was nearly twenty-one and arrangements
    had begun
To celebrate her birthday with a ball.

> — 'THE GREEN EYE OF THE LITTLE
>   YELLOW GOD' *J MILTON HAYES*

It is remarkable how virtuous and generously
    disposed everyone is at a play. We uniformly
    applaud what is right and condemn what is
    wrong, when it costs us nothing but the
    sentiment.

> — WILLIAM HAZLITT

CHAPTER ONE

MANCHESTER, MAY 1941

'It's the absolute limit,' said Annie. She was standing in her Rayon slip, next to the bed, which was heaped with clothes. Shoes and suspender belts slithered gently down a mountain-side of dresses and cardigans towards the floor.

'None of these will last the month if clothes rationing comes in,' she went on, stubbing out her cigarette in the bedside ashtray – a lumpy pottery dish imprinted with *A Present from Clovelly*. She held up a withered blouse, its buttons hanging from threads.

'It's only a rumour,' I began. 'Perhaps we can brush up our dressmaking skills...'

'I'd need to have some in the first place for that. As if it's not bad enough having to queue for every blessed thing, begging for scraps from the butcher, trying to make a single cup of tea last a fortnight – now I'll have nothing to wear when I go dancing with Arnold.' She gestured hopelessly at the pile. 'I'll look like that beggar-woman on the town hall steps who's always covered in soot and pigeon droppings.'

I was far less smart than my best friend, but even I dreaded dressing by coupon. My meagre clothing budget barely stretched to a new handkerchief as it was. Being limited to whatever the old duffers at the Ministry thought women required was a horror too far, but according to gossip at the *Manchester Chronicle*, the newspaper where I worked as an obituary writer – rather than the crime reporter I aspired to be – June might see the end of fashion as we knew it.

I picked up a straw hat that had rolled to the floor and was trying it on when the downstairs doorbell rang.

'Mrs Turner's out,' said Annie. 'You go, I've no shoes on.'

It was always a relief when our beady-eyed landlady was at her sister's in Broadheath. She had a tendency to assume that all male callers were either impassioned swains, set on sullying the moral purity of her household, or white-slave traffickers determined to kidnap her 'ladies', and ship them to the Barbary coast.

I thudded down the stairs, hoping it wasn't a telegram boy. That was the worst thing about the war – bad news hovered like a swarm of flies, and at any moment, it could pour through the letter box or telephone wire, changing the course of your life in a moment.

It was a great relief to find our friend Lou on the step, holding the lead of his vast Alsatian, Marple.

'It's you!' I said.

'I was hoping for, "Good afternoon, Detective Inspector Brennan, do come in,"' Lou said. 'But I suppose "it's you" is at least factual.'

'I'm glad to see you. You can help me distract Annie from her clothing woes.'

'That's Arnold's job,' said Lou, following me as Marple's eagle-like talons clicked on the polished wooden floor. 'I saw him earlier at work, he said he might drop round later.'

'Oh, nothing too bad, I hope?' Annie's beau Arnold ran the family funeral business and, since the war started, he'd been working closely with the police and the ARP, moving bombing victims from the rubble, and 'giving them the respect they deserve', as he put it.

'Incendiary in Old Trafford,' said Lou grimly, throwing himself into his usual armchair. 'Destroyed part of the Metro-vicks building, and killed a night watchman. I hope Hitler's proud of himself. Young feller, doing no harm, probably thinking about his girl and what to have for breakfast. There wasn't a scratch on him, but...' He shrugged. 'Gone in an instant.'

I scratched Marple's head, and he flung himself to the rug with a sigh.

'Do you think the bombing campaign will carry on after Liverpool? The girls at work are all talking about it, saying it's bound to get worse again.'

'I doubt it,' Lou said. 'They'll always try for the odd raid if they can, I suppose, but I shouldn't think we'll see anything like that again.'

'I hope not,' said Annie. 'Edie and I have only just settled in here. And my mum's leg took months to heal properly after the garden wall fell on her. She's back volunteering again now, though; there's no stopping her. The entire front parlour's stuffed with knitted balaclavas. Those poor soldiers,' she sighed. 'Forced to wear Marjorie Hemmings' scratchiest offerings in high summer.'

'Most of the fighting seems to have moved abroad for now, if you believe the *Chronicle*,' I said, setting down the tea tray. 'They think that awful raid on the docks last week was the final fling. There's no biscuits, I'm afraid, Suki ate the last one when she dropped in yesterday.'

'She's like a squirrel, that one,' said Annie irritably. 'Cheeks bulging, storing other people's nuts for winter...'

Lou laughed disloyally, but I said, 'Annie, that's not fair. She's had a—'

'Horrible time, yes I know.' Annie poured tea into our

chipped cups. 'She just seems so *oblivious* to rationing. She'll eat anything that stands still long enough.'

I sighed. Annie had a point – my old friend Suki currently lived upstairs with Agnes Beamish, a motherly spinster who played in a string quartet. Suki had run away from her violent husband, Frank Sullivan, and in the weeks since there had been no sign of him.

I suspected Suki now ate partly because Frank had been very keen on his wife keeping her figure' – although she was naturally the size of a wren – and because, at the children's home where we grew up, the food had been doled out purely to keep us alive. Now, she was free and could eat what she liked – though 'eating other people's rations' was understandably high on Annie's list of cardinal sins.

I was about to offer our visitor some toast and jam instead of the missing biscuits, when the doorbell rang again.

'That'll be Arnold,' Annie said, and hurried downstairs to welcome him.

I heard her cry, 'Hullo, dearest!' swiftly followed by 'whatever's wrong?'

Lou and I exchanged a worried glance. He sat up from his slump.

'Haven't you heard?' Arnold appeared in the doorway. He looked even paler than usual, his white face in stark contrast to his bright red hair.

'Heard what?' My heart began to race. 'Is everyone all right? Clara...'

Our friend was now regularly flying Fairey Barracudas to aerodromes all over the country, and Annie and I lived in a constant state of concern about her.

'Clara's fine, so far as I know,' Arnold said. 'But it's pretty bad – I was at the police station at Newton Street, finishing off some paperwork on the deceased, when the news came in...'

'What news?' demanded Lou. 'Come on, mate, spit it out!'

'Sorry,' said Arnold. He looked quite wretched. 'It's London – there was a huge raid last night, the officer said they've never seen anything like it. Half the city's destroyed, apparently, bodies in the streets, the Houses of Parliament blown up, thousands of people homeless... it's like the end of the world.'

'My God,' said Annie. 'Quickly, put the wireless on.'

I was standing by the sideboard, and I did as she said, turning the dial frantically to get rid of the snowstorm of static. The clipped voice filled our little living room, detailing the bombing – six hours of non-stop bombardment from the sky, as the Luftwaffe relentlessly battered our venerable old capital city with their explosives. Many dead, entire streets collapsed into matchsticks, buildings that had stood for hundreds of years, folding and crumpling – 'the fire service has worked tirelessly throughout the night,' the newsreader continued, 'but still many of London's great buildings remain ablaze, and outside the capital's hospitals, relations gather to await news.'

My hand shaking, I switched it off and turned back to the room. Arnold had his arm round Annie's shoulders, but Lou was standing up, frantically patting his pockets.

'Has one of you got any change?' he asked. He looked peculiar – his usual faintly amused expression had been replaced by something like dread.

'Here, old man,' said Arnold, digging in his pocket and extracting a few coppers. 'What's up?'

'Marie,' said Lou. 'She's in London, she was going to the theatre last night – oh God, if anything's happened to her... Edie, where's your nearest telephone box?'

I pointed down the street, and he ran. Annie sank into his vacated armchair.

'Edie,' she said, 'Who's Marie?'

I was wondering exactly the same thing.

. . .

We sat in a confused and somewhat complicated silence in his absence. Like Annie, I had only ever been to London once, on a school trip to the Victoria and Albert Museum, but I remembered smart streets of tall houses, boats motoring busily up and down the Thames, huge, sooty buildings, the dazzle of Piccadilly Circus and Shaftesbury Avenue – and people. So many people, hurrying and hectic, all with things to do and places to go. The idea of all that life and energy reduced to stillness and smouldering ruins made me want to weep. Somewhere underneath the immediate sorrow, too, was a hot fury that I didn't want to examine too closely. Lou was my friend, and I thought I knew him – so why had he never even mentioned this *Marie*? He had told me more than once that after his fiancée, Lorna, was killed in the Spanish Civil War, he had sworn off love. But no, I thought bitterly, he had lied – did he think I was such a jealous little shrew I couldn't cope with him having a sweetheart? He was only a friend, why should I care – any more than I minded the obvious adoration between Annie and Arnold? Didn't he trust me?

The doorbell heralded Lou's return.

'I'll go,' said Arnold with relief. He was a dear man, but rather nonplussed by complicated female emotions.

Lou reappeared in the doorway. He looked anguished, and despite my feelings, it was dreadful to see him so upset.

'What's happened?' I asked, just as Annie said, rather accusingly, 'Who's Marie?'

Lou ignored her. 'She's in hospital,' he said. 'Bad concussion and her arm might be broken – she was just leaving the theatre, she loves musicals – I told her not to put herself in danger!' he added furiously. He was now pacing up and down the small area between the sofa and the sideboard, the three of us watching warily, like visitors at the zoo eyeing a puma.

'Her housekeeper answered the telephone, thank God, though why nobody's bothered to get in touch with me, or send a telegram, I cannot fathom. Her friend was fine, apparently, she's the one who rang up the housekeeper, but my poor Marie – of course, she'll have to come to stay with me, she can't recuperate alone...'

Annie glanced at me, eyebrows raised.

'London's in ruins, and Mrs Purnell said their basement area at Hampden Square took a nasty hit,' Lou went on. 'She's off to stay with her sister in Suffolk, and of course, the Luftwaffe could be readying for another raid tonight, that's if there's anything left...'

'Lou!'

'What?' He glared at me.

'We don't know who Marie is,' I said quietly.

'She's right, mate, we don't,' agreed Arnold. 'Is she your girl?'

Lou briefly closed his eyes, and opened them as if he'd snapped from a dream. 'You don't know?'

Annie shrugged. 'You've never mentioned her.'

'Oh, Lord,' he said. 'I thought I'd... sorry. She's my older sister. Lives in London – she looked after me when I came back from Spain. Two children, Clive and Frances, but they're spending the war in Devon with our mother...'

'Have you really got a niece and nephew?' I asked, astonished. Lou seemed to move through the world unencumbered, and it was deeply odd to see him recast as a doting uncle. Another part of my mind was contemplating the fact that Marie was not his great romantic love, and feeling a sense of relief. It was nice to know he hadn't lied to me, of course.

'Goodness me,' said Annie, 'I had no idea. You never mention her.'

'I don't talk about my family much,' said Lou. 'We're told to be careful in the police – if any of the people we arrest bears a grudge, you know...'

'They'd find the people you care for?' I asked. 'It's like a spy novel!'

He raised a shoulder. 'It's how it can be. In Spain, too. I never told anyone about Lorna. Much good that did me.'

Arnold stood and clapped him on the shoulder.

'You've had a nasty shock,' he said. 'More tea?'

'Oh, I think pub,' Lou said. 'I'll make arrangements for Marie to travel north as soon as she's out of hospital. In the meantime, a stiff drink might do the trick.'

I had a WVS canteen shift that evening, and Annie was on a late at the hospital. We waved them off, Lou looking slightly more his normal self in the face of Arnold's encouraging chatter. I heard him say, 'They can do wonders for concussion, you know. I knew a lad at school, terrible bonk on the bonce in a cricket match...' as they went down the path, and I smiled. Annie was lucky to have met someone with simple kindness stamped through him like Blackpool rock.

There was an atmosphere of industrious solemnity at the *Chronicle's* offices the following morning, but as I nipped to the lavatory, I heard stifled sobbing from one of the Victorian cubicles. I cleared my throat.

'Are you all right in there?' I ventured. 'It's Edie, do you need my handkerchief? It's quite clean.'

'It's all right, thanks,' quavered the occupant, and I realised that it was Gloria, head of the typing pool. She let herself out, and I noted that her normal glamorous make-up and coiffure were rather bedraggled.

'What's happened?' I asked, and she pressed a balled hanky to her eyes.

'It's my sister, Avril,' she said shakily. 'She's a dancer for

ENSA and was performing at the Prince's Theatre on Shaftesbury Avenue last night when it was hit. I had a telegram this morning to say her leg's badly broken. Dancing was her life, Edie, I don't know how she'll go on, she may never walk again...'

She collapsed over the cracked basin, her shoulders shaking. ENSA stood for Entertainments National Service Association, and mostly took variety shows and comedy plays abroad to perform for the troops at their bases. I knew they also toured in Britain, as we'd had a piece about it in the *Chronicle*, with a photograph of a local actress who'd volunteered. She was holding a large Chinese fan and showing a great deal of leg.

'Oh, Gloria,' I said, rubbing her back inadequately. 'I'm sure she'll be all right.'

I wasn't sure at all, and I remembered Lou saying that Marie had been at the theatre. I wondered if it had been the same one.

Back at my desk, with Gloria now surrounded by ghoulishly concerned typists, I was thinking of concocting an excuse to telephone Lou for news when the switchboard put a call through.

'Police,' said Olive, connecting the line.

'York, it's me.'

'Lou! I mean, DI Brennan, thank you for calling. How may I help?'

I had noticed our editor, Mr Gorringe, making his way through the office towards me and Pat, the head secretary, who was picking her wisdom teeth with the edge of a piece of blotting paper. I tried to alert her with my eyes, but it was too late. I saw Pat glance up, startle, and breathe in a scrap of paper, resulting in a dramatic coughing fit.

'York? Are you still there?'

'I'm here,' I said hastily, as Mr Gorringe stood in an agony of indecision over whether to whack Pat on the back or wait for the choking to stop. Thankfully, she gasped, swallowed and said, 'So sorry, sir,' and I tuned back in to Lou.

'Have you heard from Marie... marriage records at the town hall?' I improvised. 'I'm very interested in writing an obituary,' I added, as Mr Gorringe raised his head and stared beadily at me.

'I bloody hope not,' said Lou. 'I rang to tell you that I've had a telegram and she's out of hospital. But her house isn't habitable, there's a burst water main and it's flooded the street, everywhere's covered in rubble and plaster – long story short, she's coming to stay with me, and I thought she might need a pal up here.'

'Certainly I can do that,' I said carefully, aware of Mr Gorringe hovering. 'When would be convenient?'

'I assume you're tied up in a cellar again, and speaking in code,' said Lou, finally cottoning on.

'Very much so.'

'Right. Well, she's arriving tomorrow, so I'll be in touch with an arrangement once I see how she is. Stand by for further instructions. I think you'll like her.'

'Thank you very much indeed, sir,' I said, and replaced the receiver.

'Might I enquire to whom we shall be treated this week, Miss York?' said Mr Gorringe, blowing pipe smoke across my typewriter.

'I thought I'd write about Sir Jesmond Fitzwallace,' I said. 'He fought in the Boer war and was at Mafeking. Had quite a well-known collection of Georgian miniatures.'

'Ah, yes,' said Mr Gorringe. 'Although I believe Sir Jesmond was a confirmed bachelor, so quite why you were telephoning the archives about marriage records just now remains a mystery.'

A hot blush suffused my cheeks.

'Carry on, Miss York,' he said. 'And do mention his pet rat,

Ladysmith. He took her everywhere with him, I believe. The readers should enjoy that detail.'

The *Chronicle* was full of the London Blitz, and I felt rather useless as I bashed out my column on Sir Jesmond. Gloria was still sniffing intermittently, her head shooting up like a gun dog's whenever someone entered the office, and doubtless all of Manchester was full of people wondering if distant family and friends had escaped the worst of the bombing. Lou had been lucky to receive a telegram at all. I resolved to be a good friend to Marie, even if I didn't like her very much. If she was as abrasive as her brother, it might be hard going.

CHAPTER TWO

I didn't hear from Lou again until Wednesday. I assumed that Marie had arrived and was ensconced Chez Brennan, and that Lou, or his housekeeper, was busy looking after her. I arrived home that evening to find a postcard on the hall table:

> *Marie fully installed. Wants to meet you. Tried to warn her off, but she won't be told. Has theatre tickets for the Gaiety, TOMORROW NIGHT. Supper first. Will collect you from work. LB.*

It was so profoundly typical of Lou not to bother asking whether I was available that night, or even if I wanted to go to the theatre. I felt rather nervous at the idea of meeting his London sister, too. I suspected she'd be terribly smart, and I had absolutely nothing suitable to wear for a night out. I had no idea what was running at the Gaiety, either – it could be George Formby and his ukulele, or it could be *Titus Andronicus*, and I had no decent hats for either eventuality. I'd have to spend the evening pressing my least-worst dress... oh, damn Lou and his high-handed ways – I'd rather be pouring tea at the WVS canteen. At least I didn't have to dress up for that.

It was brave of the cast to pick themselves up and re-open in Manchester just days after almost being killed in the Blitz, I reflected, and they deserved all the support we could muster. I just wished I wasn't wearing cousin Helen's hand-me-down black satin dress, so old it had rubbed into matt patches on the seat and elbows, and my work lace-ups, more suited to tramping the Manchester streets than drifting through the Gaiety's powder-blue and gold foyer.

I waited in the *Chronicle's* lobby, adjusting my hat and waving to colleagues.

'You're a sight for sore eyes,' said Des, the retired-but-returned crime reporter whose job I coveted. 'Off out? Hold on, not a funeral, is it? Hope I haven't put my foot in it!'

'No, no, the theatre,' I reassured him.

'Ah! The ENSA thing at the Gaiety?' he exclaimed, stopping to light his pipe. 'Apparently, they got bombed out in London and they've come up here instead. Gloria was creating quite the fuss because her sister can't come with them. Lovely little item in the lead, mind you, Ginny something – quite enchanting. Mrs Des dragged me to something she was in just before the war, she's quite the ingénue. Good of her to hoof for the troops.

'And Leonard Lessiter, of course,' he went on, filling the lobby with acrid smoke. Des was like a steam train – you could always locate him in the office by the drifting plume above his head.

'Should I know of him?'

Des raised an eyebrow. 'Well, if you know anything about the theatre, my dear, I should think so. One of the greats, in his heyday! Ask not for whom the overture-and-beginners' bell tolls... He must be nudging his three score and ten, but on he goes, old trouper that he is.'

As he spoke, I saw a long shadow fall over the mat, followed by Lou wearing – to my astonishment – full evening dress. He looked more like a symphony conductor than the rumpled Inspector I'd become used to, and without Marple trotting at his side, there was a strangely austere aspect to his appearance. I felt rather nervous as I stepped forward, but before he turned to me, he slapped Des on the shoulder in greeting, and they immediately launched into a discussion about the black marketeers at Shudehill.

'George Chivers, you mark my words, he'll be at the centre of it,' Des said, and Lou nodded.

'We're hearing a lot about organised looting – reckon he's behind that? The Chinese gangs have been mentioned by top brass, but I'm not so sure...' On they went, musing and agreeing, while I waited silently, like the withered aspidistra by the stairs.

Eventually, Lou remembered that he wasn't in the Nag's Head, sinking pints with his pet crime reporter, but supposedly accompanying me to meet Marie for supper.

'York!' he said cheerfully, as Des finally raised a hand and puffed off towards Deansgate. 'I see you've scrubbed up. Though I'd best not take you to Lyon's Corner House, someone might mistake you for a Nippy.'

'I didn't intend to dress as a waitress,' I said crossly, and he laughed.

'You're quite right, you've no apron. Come on, we're late for Marie.'

I longed to point out exactly why we were late, but he was sweeping me along the pavements, past last winter's bombsites now verdant with weeds.

'Where are we meeting her?' I asked, as he stalked ahead on his tent-pole legs.

'Nowhere fancy. Kardomah,' he said, referring to the café

where I sometimes ate lunch with my friend Ethel. 'Think you
can cope, or will you be disappointed if it's not quails' eggs and
roast plover?'

'Sardines on toast is fine with me,' I said. 'How is Marie? Is
she feeling better?'

'Bit feeble still, but her arm isn't broken, just badly bruised.
She's more worried about her house – it could take weeks to
even start the repairs, and the Admiral's still at sea – she sent a
telegram, but he can't return at the moment, obviously.'

'The *Admiral*?'

'Her husband. Walter Archibald, a fine chap. But rather
busy at the moment.'

We had reached the piled sandbags and cheerful lights of
the café entrance, and Lou held the door open for me.

'There she is,' he said, waving at a slim, dark woman seated
at one of the best and largest tables. Ethel and I were generally
shoved under the stairs for our frugal lunches – perhaps this
was normal for more elegant customers.

As we approached, I could see that not only was Marie very
pretty – her face a softer, feminine version of Lou's sharply
angled cheekbones and narrow, dark blue eyes – she was also
dressed in the most exquisite pale-green silk dress and matching
jacket. I felt infinitely more suited to waitressing than to sitting
alongside this lovely creature, but it was too late. Lou was
already pulling my chair out and introducing me to his beloved
sister.

'I'm so delighted to meet you at last,' said Marie, after the
waitress had taken our orders. 'I've heard so much about you,
Lou never stops talking about yo—'

'How's your head today?'

He spoke across her, raising his voice over the sound of
clanking cutlery and the jazz band across the room.

'Oh,' Marie turned to him, 'much better, thank you. I took the liberty of tidying up a bit. Your Daily seems to have no idea that one can take dry socks down from the rack and actually put them away where they belong!'

She smiled at me. 'He's a marvellous detective, I know, but I'm not sure his skills extend to the home front.'

Lou sighed. 'Heard from the children?'

'Yes, a very brief letter from Clive – "all fine, don't fret so, Mum" – and a stream of consciousness from Frances that seemed to involve horses and a dream she had about an enormous sailor doll with teeth.'

I laughed. I was beginning to like Marie.

'I would have gone to recover down in deepest Devon with them, of course,' she told me, 'but our mother is insistent that I'll die without the city. She may be right, as I've never tried it. Even being bombed the other night hasn't put me off the theatre, it's just made me more determined that we must fight all the way, to keep our culture and cafés and cinema... what else begins with a C? Oh, cakes!' she exclaimed.

Lou regarded her patiently, as one would a rather excitable toddler.

'Marie,' he said, as the waitress arrived with our drinks, 'why is this table laid for an army?'

'Oh yes!' she said. 'I meant to tell you. I started talking to one of the ENSA lot while we were waiting to be rescued the other night – I must admit, thinking an entire theatre might collapse on you concentrates the mind and rather speeds up tentative friendships. They'd been signing autographs by the stage door, and I'd gone over there to try and find a cab...'

'And then...?' prompted Lou with exaggerated patience.

'Well, I found myself in a heap of grey dust and plaster next to Josephine Gardner, a lovely actress who'd been in the show – she was all right, luckily, just stuck under the door, it was blown clean off its hinges and, apparently, I wasn't making much sense due to the whack on the head. I think the sign that says "stage door" fell on me, as it was right next to me...'

Lou and I both winced in sympathy.

'Anyway, I ended up being carted off to hospital, and Josephine came to see me. She explained about the cast coming to Manchester, and when I said I was coming here, too, she very sweetly asked me and anyone I wanted to bring to the first night. They were all so kind, they sent flowers and cards, and I thought how lovely it would be to invite them all for supper before the show – they should be here any minute.'

'I see,' Lou said wearily. 'I thought you were going to have a nice chat with Edie, and instead, we're hosting a large theatrical event for people we've never met.'

'You never know, you might find at least one of them tolerable. Ginny Sutton is awfully pretty. He's such a perpetual bachelor, my brother,' Marie added, as though Lou wasn't there. 'Ever since Lorna, he seems to have taken a monk's vow. I'd love to marry him off. At the very least, I imagine a wife might know what to do with his socks.'

So might I, I thought, albeit my plan was rather more violent.

'Ah!' Marie suddenly signalled wildly with her working arm. 'Here they come!'

I looked up to see a crowd of people barrelling into the restaurant. The women wore stylish hats and jaunty scarves and high heels, and the men's suits were far from the sober civvies worn by most these days. The eldest chap – Leonard Lessiter, I presumed – wore a billowing linen ensemble and a Panama hat, with an emerald-green cravat tucked into his shirt, while a rotund, balding man in his fifties sported a hairy, yellow tweed costume that made him look like Mr Toad, despite the warmth of the day.

Marie stood to greet them, and they flocked about her like parakeets, exclaiming and declaiming. If they longed for attention, they had got their wish – most of the Kardomah's patrons were now craning round in their chairs to watch the glamorous commotion.

Ginny stood out immediately. She was exquisite, no more than twenty-one, with waved, shoulder-length ice-blonde hair (I imagined Annie whispering 'dye job'), and eyes that sparkled like a breezy blue day at the seashore. She was wearing a simple but very well-cut periwinkle blue frock, and she was nicely spoken, though her vowels still retained a hint of the ordinary Londoner.

'How do you do?' she asked, sliding into the chair beside me. 'Marie says you're a reporter, how fascinating!'

'Oh, only an obituary writer,' I said, 'not as interesting as being an actress. Have you recovered from the awful events last weekend?'

'As much as one ever can,' Ginny said, spreading her napkin over her slim thighs. 'It was awfully upsetting, as the stage manager was killed by a falling beam, and lots of people were hurt – but thank goodness, most of the audience had already left. I was in my dressing room, and we all shot out of the fire exit like greased rats. I had half a face of make-up still on, I must have looked very peculiar. Leonard came a bit of a cropper, though.'

Hearing his name, the older man leaned across the table.

'Does an angel speak of the devil?' he said.

His voice was deep, aristocratic, and resonated as if he gargled with gravel and honey. I exchanged a swift glance with Lou, whose expression read, 'what am I doing here?' in blinking neon lights.

'I'm just telling Miss York about your injury, Mr Lessiter,' Ginny explained, picking up a bread roll before reluctantly replacing it on the plate.

'Oh, my dear.' Leonard shook his head sorrowfully. He had the look of an ancient, noble bloodhound, with long jowls and deep creases in his cheeks, but he retained a full head of hair, white and springy as heather.

'I was in my dressing room,' he began, and the table fell silent at the sound of his words. I could imagine entire auditoriums hushed in anticipation of his performance.

'I had been preparing to go to Wiltons'. I'd reserved a table for a late supper with Monty Miller, enchanting little chap – aspiring actor, I was to help him with an audition. I was ridding my fizzog of Max Factor when our director Jack and I heard the siren, but I thought, "well, Leonard old beast, if the bomb's for you, may as well die in the arms of Mother Theatre, who has served you so elegantly all these years..."'

Lou looked faintly sick.

'Next thing I knew, there was the *most* ghastly crash, a roar like all my Meissen china collapsing at once – God forbid!' He shuddered. 'That was the roof falling in, and of course, I immediately determined to save as many souls as I could. I rushed out to find that the corridor was blocked by fallen bricks, and I began to dig my way out – but then...'

He paused.

'Then what?' asked the man across from him, who had been introduced to me as Guy Ferdinand. He was in his early thirties, classically handsome but with a rather sloping jaw. Annie was very suspicious of a Weak Chin.

'Yes, do tell,' put in Josephine Gardner, the character actress who I gathered was also Ginny's understudy. She was tall, with red lips, a mass of brunette hair and a small, expensive-looking silk hat.

'And I shall.' Leonard swept his gaze over us all. 'At that point, a light fitting plummeted from directly above me, missing my head by an inch, and pinned me to the floor.'

He nodded slowly. 'My upper chest was crushed – I feared I may not recover my voice, which is, of course, my instrument...' The waitress placed a steaming kidney pie before him, but he ignored her.

'Thankfully, the ambulance workers who winkled me out of my ghastly carapace were able to rush me to hospital, and despite my pain,' here he winced, rather convincingly, 'I sit before you today. Ready to perform once again, as are we all, for theatre runs like rich, red wine in our blood.'

Lou turned and muttered something into Marie's ear, and she suppressed a smile.

'He's quite the theatrical legend,' Ginny said to me quietly. 'He does know how to tell a story, and he's been terribly kind to me.'

At the far end of the table, the man I thought of as Mr Toad was regaling Josephine and Guy with a tale involving wild gesticulation and his own booming laughter. Marie turned to me.

'That's Stanley Kerridge,' she said. 'Have you heard of him?'

I shook my head.

'No, well,' she murmured. 'Comedian. He was very popular in the twenties, during the last days of the music halls. Used to do something amusing with a watering can and a top hat. I believe his act is rather more... vulgar nowadays.'

Stanley suddenly boomed, '—and I said, that's not a carburettor, madame, it's a clutch!'

Guy and Josephine laughed politely, as Stanley thumped the table.

Lou was talking quietly to the older woman beside him, who had been introduced as Florence Buchanan. She was in her sixties, and seemed spry and energetic, with a mobile face that veered between a wide, joyful smile and almost cartoon-like sadness as she spoke. I could see it would be a perfect face for the theatre as all her expressions would be easily discernible from the cheap seats at the back.

Ginny saw me looking over at her.

'Oh, Florence is wonderful,' she said. 'Such a mother to us all, always reminding us to take our medicine and go to bed early. She was quite famous at one point, she played the nurse in *Romeo and Juliet* at the Haymarket and had marvellous reviews, and she was the landlady in that film – what was it – oh yes, *The Chorus Girl*, about a girl who longs to be on the stage. I haven't seen it but, apparently, it was very good. She mostly teaches now, but like Leonard, she's returned to the boards for ENSA. Got to keep the troops happy!'

Ginny ate a tiny piece of fish. I imagined it was hard work remaining so sylph-like.

I spoke to her for a while about ENSA and what it was like abroad – they had been to France in the spring. 'Terrible food,' she said, 'and our digs were even worse than they are in London. Mind you, we've landed on our feet here. Good old Grafton Street.'

Grafton Street included a row of theatrical boarding houses near the hospital where Annie worked. They were old Victorian terraces with long gardens and crumbling but elegant facades, and amongst the cheap business travellers' hotels and old men's pubs, they provided a home for the actors and musicians who arrived on repertory and concert tours at the city's halls and theatres.

'How long are you here for?' I asked Ginny.

'Two or three weeks, polishing the new show,' she said. 'We've had to change quite a lot of it as our dancer, Avril, was injured. She's my room-mate in London, and we're all so hoping she'll be well enough to join us when we sail to Africa in June.'

'Africa?'

'I know.' Ginny smiled. 'It seems as far away as Timbuktu, but I suppose it *is* Timbuktu, so that explains it!'

I found I liked her very much. She had that indefinable charisma that marks people out as less than ordinary; someone destined for more than the quotidian life of the wireless and work and early-morning dustmen that most of us could expect. *Star quality*, Pat would call it. I was looking forward to seeing her in the show.

After the bill had been paid by Leonard, triggering rather empty protests and genuine gratitude, we followed them to the theatre and had a drink in the bar while they all rushed off to the dressing rooms.

'Well, Marie,' Lou said, looking highly incongruous on his spindly chair, 'that was a baptism of theatrical fire, and no mistake.'

'Oh, they're all so sweet, though, aren't they?' Marie said, laughing. 'Leonard, honestly. I imagine he gives the full Henry Irving to travelling salesmen when they come selling brushes. He can't stop himself.'

'Well, Florence certainly had a lot to say about Edwardian repertory,' said Lou rather testily. 'I feel I could find my way to her dear old dressing room at the Haymarket that just felt *so homely, despite all the flowers,* with my eyes shut.'

I snorted. 'I liked Ginny, though,' I added quickly, in case Marie was offended. 'She struck me as quite the shooting star.'

'Oh yes,' Marie said. 'She's a wonderful performer, already been noticed by film people, Josephine told me. ENSA are very lucky to have her.'

'I imagine there's a bit of jealousy towards her,' Lou said, lighting a cigarette and offering his case to us. 'A herd of clapped-out old-timers and a girl like that.'

'Louis, you really do always look for the worm in the bud, don't you?' said Marie. 'They all seem to get along beautifully. Besides, Josephine is hardly an old-timer, and nor is Guy...'

As she spoke, a bell rang, signalling the start of the performance, and we gathered our things and hurried to our seats in the stalls. I felt quite excited, sitting flanked by Lou and Marie as though they were my parents taking me on an outing. A red, white and blue curtain hung over the stage reading *Victory Gang Parade* while the auditorium smelled of scent and Turkish tobacco, with an undercurrent of dusty khakis from the various troops that had been bussed in from their bases around the city to see the show. They were loud and excited, and I heard one lad behind me saying, 'That Ginny Sutton, she's a bit of all right,' to his friend, who lasciviously agreed she was a 'very nice little piece'.

I forgot all about them as the lights went down and the show began. To my surprise, the whole cast was on stage in army uniform, looking almost unrecognisable from the chic assembly who had eaten with us just an hour earlier. They burst into a rousing rendition of 'Hang Out the Washing on the Siegfried Line', accompanied by a pianist in the orchestra pit.

'Look how miserable Leonard looks,' Lou whispered into my right ear. 'He's dying to have his big solo moment.'

I shushed him, but I thought he was right. Leonard's theatrical verve seemed to have deserted him, and he looked rather flat as Ginny and Josephine waved their arms and encouraged the audience to join in.

They ran offstage and Guy Ferdinand reappeared, wearing a crown and a sort of costume-party tunic, and launched into the victory speech from Henry VI that we'd learned at school. I remembered:

> *But if it be a sin to covet honour,*
> *I am the most offending soul alive*

Guy delivered it well. The soldiers behind me were whispering and guffawing, perhaps not quite so taken with Shakespeare as some of the audience, but they gave him a roar of approval, which continued with accompanying whistling, as Ginny and Josephine returned in tight black evening dresses and sang 'Lili Marlene' together. Ginny had a beautiful voice, pure as a crystal bell, and eventually the whole audience hushed and settled as she sang. I imagined her photograph up on billboards, her name in lights, cinema posters reading *Starring Ginny Sutton and Clark Gable*. Josephine, older at twenty-seven, was talented and attractive – but she didn't have 'it'. Ginny did, in spades.

Florence and Stanley came on dressed as charladies and did a sketch about baby Hitler in a washing basket, which got a big laugh, and then the lights dimmed, a single white spotlight beamed down, and Leonard walked onstage. The audience fell silent, and he stood for a moment, surveying us all. He was dressed in military uniform again, but his face was darkened to a deep tan with greasepaint and his white hair oiled flat. He looked like an elderly general who had been forgotten in a far corner of the Empire.

He gazed imperiously at us all, and announced, '"The Green Eye of the Little Yellow God".' It was a dramatic poem of the kind that Edwardian entertainers recited at supper gatherings. I vaguely recalled it – perhaps it had been on the wireless – but I hadn't heard it the way Leonard performed.

'There's a one-eyed yellow idol to the north of Khatmandu,' he began, a tone of slow-dawning horror to his words. The lads behind me were silent.

'There's a little marble cross below the town;

There's a broken-hearted woman tends the grave of Mad Carew,

And the Yellow God forever gazes down...'

He carried on, detailing the lovesick swain's stealing of the God's jewelled green eye for his love, the colonel's daughter. It was melodramatic doggerel really, but I felt a chill run through me as he intoned,

'He returned before the dawn, with his shirt and tunic torn,

And a gash across his temple dripping red...'

As he spoke the rest of the verse, Leonard put a hand to his chest, and kept it there, over his heart, as if he, too, were in mortal agony. He seemed to stagger slightly as he withdrew a shining dagger from his belt and held it up.

'*An ugly knife lay buried in the heart of Mad Carew,*' he declaimed, his voice breaking. "*Twas the vengeance of the... th... l'il... the yewl...*'

Leonard stopped speaking and stumbled. The dagger clattered to the stage and Marie turned to me, shock in her eyes.

Lou was up on his feet before anyone else in the auditorium, as Leonard folded sideways. Some thought it was part of the act and began to applaud, but from our position in the stalls, we had seen his face, grey beneath the make-up, and the sweat beading on his brow.

CHAPTER THREE

'Is there a doctor in the house?' Lou shouted, and a high, frightened chatter broke out amongst the audience as a man in the circle shouted 'Certainly! I am a doctor!' and began to pick his way past hats and handbags to the stairs.

The curtain now fell, concealing Leonard's prone form, and the jolly *Victory Gang Parade* looped across it now looked as horribly out of place as a party hat at a wake.

We snatched up our bags, and made our way out of the row of seats. Behind us, lads were exclaiming and shouting 'get the doctor up there, come on, mate!'

One woman in our row was still lugubriously eating sweets as she grudgingly moved her knees aside for us.

'Poor show, I call it,' she said through a mouthful of Romney's Treacle Toffee. 'Get him off, get the next skit on, I say. I like that Stanley Kerridge, he's very amusing.'

Her friend mumbled crossly in agreement, though fortunately her teeth seemed to be stuck together.

'Look at those two old Madame DeFarges, knitting at the guillotine,' said Marie loudly. 'Poor Leonard might be dead!'

Heads turned as we hurried towards the stage.

'Do try not to start a panic, Marie,' said Lou. 'Why not shout "fire!" while you're at it?'

As he spoke, the house lights came up, and the elderly stage manager rushed out, his bow tie trailing on one side.

'Ladies and gentlemen,' he said breathlessly, 'due to an unforeseen medical... that is, a medical emergency, that was unforeseen...' He took a breath as the audience shifted like an unquiet beast.

'I'm afraid the *Victory Gang Parade* is concluded for tonight,' he announced firmly. 'Please do write in if you require a refund. I must repeat, do not ask for cash at the box office, simply write with a stamped addressed envelope...'

The general muttering was now breaking into shouts of 'poor show!' and 'get on with it!' The little man almost ran off stage, and ushers began to herd the crowd towards the exits.

Lou mounted the stage and hauled us up behind him, before disappearing behind the enormously heavy curtain. I inhaled a mouthful of dust as the ancient velvet billowed back into my face, and was still coughing when it closed after me.

Leonard was lying prone, an arm half covering his face. Josephine and Ginny were clutching each other and crying as Guy attempted to resuscitate him, and Stanley hovered, muttering, 'Come on, man! Up you get!'

Florence was gesturing animatedly to an attractive younger man with brown hair in an untidy cowlick.

'I told him!' she said, 'I said he should rest after last week... all this excitement, what with all the bombing and the new show... it's all been too much.'

Guy suddenly sat back on his heels. 'Sorry,' he said. He sounded distant, and oddly calm. 'So sorry, everyone. I think it's too late.'

Florence unfastened the velvet cape from her shoulders and laid it gently over Leonard's face.

'Cover his face,' she said resonantly, 'mine eyes dazzle.'

'Come again, Flo?' Stanley barked. 'Man's lying dead, and you're making no sense.'

'It's a quotation from the *Duchess of Malfi*, in which I starred at the Haymarket in 1927,' she said, frost-coated.

'Excuse me, I'm a police officer...' began Lou, stepping forward.

'Good heavens, are you really?' cried Florence. 'I thought you were simply escorting one of these girls to supper!'

It all reminded me of a ridiculous farce – the body in the drawing room, the crowd of suspects, the heavy-footed police officer attempting to make sense of it all. But Leonard really was dead – his uniformed torso lay unmoving, his legs at a stiff, unnatural angle. Beside him lay the silver dagger – but there was not a mark on him.

'We should comfort the girls,' Marie whispered. I wished fervently that I'd brought my notepad, but it sat uselessly on my dressing table at home. This was a story for the *Chronicle*, without question – I'd simply have to remember it all.

The doctor from the circle finally arrived, clambering up to the stage, and was beckoned over by the cowlick man.

'Jack Webb – I'm the director,' he said. 'Thank you so much, Doctor, but I'm afraid it may be too late. Leonard is... well... he's not responding.'

The man, a tall, elegant sort in his fifties looked towards the body and saw Lou, who was already checking again for a pulse.

'Detective Inspector Brennan!'

'Dr Willoughby!'

It was like watching old school chums reunite after a boring holiday. They practically slapped each other on the back with delight.

Marie leaned in. 'That's the pathologist,' she said. 'Lou

thinks he's marvellous. He says Dr Willoughby has never had the cause of death wrong in his entire career.'

'Gosh,' I said, as the two of them glad-handed over the still body. 'Though I wonder how would one know, once they're buried?'

'Good point,' nodded Marie. She pulled me over to Josephine and Ginny as the girls wept.

'Oh, my dear girls,' she said, 'I'm so very sorry.' She opened her arms, and they slotted neatly in, one on each shoulder.

As Dr Willoughby bent to his task, Stanley turned away and lit a cigarette. I noticed he didn't offer the pack.

'Poor old bugger,' he said. 'That's what you get for messing about with cursed statues.'

'Stanley!' shrieked Florence. 'How could you? You'll have the girls hysterical!'

They seemed to be getting there all on their own, judging by Marie's damp silk shoulders, which I noticed with a wince were now stained with greasepaint. The auditorium was now silent, everyone had gone, and finally, I girded myself to ask questions like a proper reporter, rather than standing about in my waitress get-up like a walk-on part.

The cold, white spotlight was still beaming down on poor Leonard, the rest of the stage in shadow, and I turned away. I was sure he wouldn't want his earthly remains to be stared at – but at least he had died on stage. He would probably have wished for that.

'Miss Buchanan,' I said gently. Jack Webb seemed to be vainly attempting to reassure her. 'May I have a word?'

'For your newspaper?' She swivelled, gazing at me beadily.

'Well – I realise it's rather soon, but of course, we'd want to break the news in the first edition...'

She pursed her magenta lips. 'One would rather have thought,' she said, 'that a loss of this magnitude would run in the paper of record. *The Times*,' she added, in case I had no idea what she meant.

'I'm sure it will,' I said, 'but as it's happened here in Manchester... just a word or two on Leonard's... theatrical legacy.'

Florence clamped my wrist in her stiff-boned hand. Its skin was like ruched silk, and liver spotted – up close, she seemed much older than I had thought.

'I cannot stand here contemplating poor Leonard's remains,' she said. 'We'll go to my dressing room. My God, to think we were standing together in the wings, not twenty minutes ago... one can hardly bear it.'

'Was there any sign that he was suffering?'

'Well, Leonard makes such a meal of everything, it's hard to tell,' she said waspishly, before remembering that he was dead.

As we passed through the wings, almost tripping over the charlady's washing basket prop and a large wooden placard reading 'sing up!', I heard quick steps on the wooden boards behind us, and turned to find Ginny.

'Please,' she said, 'Edie, if you're writing something about Leonard – oh, do let me say something, too!'

Her voice broke on a sob. She was still wearing her evening gown, and in the dim light she looked like a beautiful ghost, purple shadows under her heavily made-up eyes.

'Of course,' I said, and we hastened after Florence, down passages lit with dim bulbs that cast a peculiar, aquatic light and sent long, slim shadow-selves hurrying alongside us.

Florence's dressing room, when we finally reached it, was not at all as I had imagined.

In my mind, *backstage at the theatre* was an image borrowed from Hollywood films, with banks of first-night lilies, mirrors framed by Arctic-white bulbs and silken negligees slung carelessly over chairs. Florence's dressing room more closely resembled the living quarters of a rather slovenly gypsy.

There was a mirror, half-obscured by a fringed paisley shawl, a scatter of make-up amongst half-drunk cups of tea and a sherry bottle, and a fold-out card table covered in a crimson brocade tablecloth, which held a well-thumbed pack of medieval-looking illustrated cards. A rack in the corner bowed under the weight of Florence's costume changes, high-heeled shoes were strewn across the floor, and the armchair was piled with discarded clothes, including, I noticed queasily, a rather grubby-looking girdle. A small, dim lamp illuminated the scene – perhaps it should have been charming, but I found it squalid and depressing.

'Have a seat,' she said. Ginny perched on a fold-out chair and Florence subsided onto the dressing table stool, which left me the armchair. Gingerly, I poked at the teetering clothes pile and created a small space to insert myself. The room smelled of greasepaint and wax, with a faint undertone of damp garments that needed a good laundering.

'I'm so sorry about what's happened,' I began. 'He seemed such a...'

'He was,' Ginny interrupted, her voice breaking again. 'An utter darling. He was so terribly kind to me, he sent me first-night flowers because nobody else... well,' she paused, 'I mean, they weren't able to.'

It seemed an odd way to say it, and I mentally filed her phrasing away for later.

'He was such a wonderful actor,' she went on. 'He was marvellous tonight of course, but what you saw was nothing compared to what he was capable of – he once played Hamlet...'

'What are your memories of him?' I asked. 'Were you close? I don't mean...'

Ginny smiled sadly. 'Oh, I know you don't,' she said. 'That would never have been a possibility, even if he wasn't old enough to be my grandfather.'

'Ginny!' objected Florence.

'Well, he was. But he was generous with his time and his knowledge. I met him when I starred in *Hedda Gabler* at Drury Lane, just before the war. He was playing George for the third time, and I was so in awe of him, I was a little nobody and he was so famous...'

'You weren't a nobody for long,' said Florence drily. She turned to me.

'Rave reviews in every newspaper, stage door queues a mile long, roses from admirers arriving every ten minutes. And a standing ovation on the last night.'

'Oh,' Ginny batted at the air like a cat with an invisible toy, 'that wasn't *just* for me.'

'Nevertheless,' Florence said. 'If I hadn't enjoyed my own long moment in the sun, I might have been quite envious of Miss Sutton.'

'Your own career has been simply stellar!' cried Ginny.

I felt I needed to cut through all this mutual flattery and pleasant reminiscence.

'Look, do tell me something more about Leonard,' I said. 'Was he funny? Honest? What did he like to do when he wasn't acting?'

Ginny leaned her elbows on the card table, and it wobbled alarmingly. 'He's always said he should have retired long since, but the stage kept drawing him back.'

'Dear Mother Theatre,' agreed Florence fondly.

Where was Lou? Suddenly, I felt I badly needed a dose of his abrasive tone.

'But I do remember, he once said he had plans to run an antiques shop,' added Ginny, sniffing back tears. 'In fact, I think he used the word *emporium*. He thought he might go back to Knutsford, his home village, and set it up there with his friend Cedric.'

'Who was Cedric?' I asked, interested.

'Oh, a pal from his days in rep, I think,' said Ginny vaguely.

'He always said Guy rather resembles him. In fact, where is Guy? Should we go and find him?'

'Oh, he'll find you, my dear,' said Florence. 'He's never far away, is he?'

Ginny shot her the briefest glance, but it was enough to make Florence turn away and fiddle with some cottonwool.

'I should go and get the others,' Ginny said, 'they must all be so upset...' She rose unsteadily to her feet.

'Flo, will you read for me later?' she asked the older woman. 'I feel so distraught, I can't see how we can all go on after this.'

'Of course,' said Florence. 'I shall have a quick word with Miss York, and I'll see you back here.'

'All right,' Ginny said. I heard her murmur, 'Oh, it's all just unbearable,' as she vanished down the gloomy corridor, and Florence sighed.

'Poor little creature,' she said. 'She'll find this very difficult. Of course, it's dreadful, but when one's an old hand, one gets used to our exits and our entrances, the brief hour upon the stage...'

I tried to think of a way to ask subtly, but it was not easy. 'Miss Buchanan,' I said, 'do you have any idea how Leonard might have died? I don't suppose... you don't imagine foul play? Nobody was jealous or angry with him?'

'Good gracious!' she said. Her face was chalk white, and her eyes glittered like jet beads in the candlelight. 'I cannot fathom a single, solitary circumstance in which anyone would hurt our dear Leonard. It's impossible to imagine. No.'

She put her hand over her face and quavered 'no!' again, presumably in case the first time hadn't been dramatic enough.

'It just seems so sudden,' I went on. Leonard had seemed remarkably well during our supper. But surely Florence was right – nobody would bear a grudge against the venerable old thespian. Or if they did, not one powerful enough to kill him onstage in front of hundreds of people. Perhaps a heart attack or a stroke had felled him.

I was about to ask Florence for her own recollections, when loud voices and footsteps drifted in through the open door. I heard Lou saying '... be a matter for the coroner,' and a male voice replying. Ginny reappeared, followed by the rest of the troupe, Lou and Marie. It gave me a small jolt to realise that Leonard would not be with them.

There was a hubbub of noise as they all poured in. Josephine had been crying, and had black trails down her pale cheeks, while Guy looked shell-shocked. He went straight to Ginny, and spoke rapidly into her ear. Marie came to me, and said, 'The ambulance has gone now, Dr Willoughby went with it. He said there'll be a post-mortem and the pathology lab might want a look. But I can't imagine it was anything but natural causes, can you?'

Stanley was helping himself to Florence's sherry while Guy attempted to comfort Ginny and Josephine.

The roar of conversation was halted by the sound of a teaspoon tinkling on a glass. Ginny was standing up, and we quietened.

'Look,' she said tremulously, 'I know how shocked and devastated we all are, and how much we shall miss Leonard. And I know,' she went on, her voice stronger now, 'that it might be tempting to cancel the run, and simply mourn our dear friend in private. But I say, the show must go on!'

'Hear, hear,' said Guy, and cleared his throat.

'I say, we hold a show that's a tribute to Leonard,' Ginny continued. 'All of us can learn one of his best-known scenes, or his monologues, and perform them instead of the *Gang Parade* for one night. Audiences will flock!' she said.

'I'll have to square it with ENSA...' said Jack Webb doubtfully, and Ginny gave him a contemptuous look.

'What kind of organisation would say no?' she demanded. 'He was our star, of course they'll agree!'

'It's just, they might feel that the troops won't know very much about Leonard's...'

'So what?' cried Ginny. 'They can learn, can't they? I say we pay homage to him by devoting ourselves to our tribute show, and Edie can write about it!'

'I'll do my best,' I said, worried. Would Mr Gorringe want a lengthy theatrical tribute to an old Shakespearean in the paper? It was seemingly now my job to persuade him.

'Wonderful idea, darling!' said Florence warmly. 'I shall perform his *Hamlet* soliloquy.'

'Hold on, I rather thought I might...' started Guy.

'I'll do the climactic scene from *Hedda*,' said Ginny. 'Guy can take Leonard's role...'

'How about I put up tonight's monologue?' asked Stanley. 'Last time I recited, it was *The Lion and Albert* at the Winter Gardens for a horde of kiddies. It's time I had a crack at something decent.'

'The... do you mean *The Green Eye*?' asked Jack Webb. He looked horrified. 'It's... that was his final performance.'

'And?' asked Stanley bullishly. 'What's your point, man?'

'I think, perhaps... look, we're all shocked and upset. Let me think about it,' said Jack, and Stanley subsided. I rather admired Jack's tact.

Lou signalled to me and Marie.

'I think it's time we left them to it,' he said. 'It's been quite an evening.'

As we said our goodbyes, Ginny said, 'You must all come to the tribute. Jack will leave tickets on the door, and we'll have supper afterwards.'

We thanked her – how could we refuse? As I bade farewell to Florence, whose recollections I had completely failed to extract, she said, 'Can you take them all away with you? I must do Ginny's private reading before we go back to Grafton Street, the landlady doesn't like it.'

'Reading?'

'Tarot,' said Florence. 'I learned it from a gypsy in France during the last war. It's quite an art. I'm famous amongst the actors for my intuition.'

Lou was beckoning irritably from the doorway.

'Ginny relies on my readings,' Florence went on. 'She says she won't make a decision unless it's in the cards. She's terribly superstitious, all actors are. She won't move without her lucky bracelet. Takes it everywhere.'

I mouthed 'all right!' at Lou, who was violently tapping his watch, and finally took my leave. After the night's horrors, I felt I never wanted to set foot in a theatre again. Unfortunately, I didn't need Florence's cards to foresee that I'd be returning within days. What I couldn't have known was quite how disastrous that next visit would prove to be.

CHAPTER FOUR

'We had the results back from the post-mortem.'

Lou had telephoned me at work first thing, and I was holding a hurried conversation with him while Pat was in the Ladies, after a lengthy chat about her problems with slugs eating the lettuces she was growing to 'help see Hitler off.'

I stiffened. 'Was it murder?'

'No, you ghoulish spectre. They think it was probably a blood clot, caused by the beam that fell on him during the Blitz, but it took a few days to kill him. Sad, but not criminal, unless you blame Hitler. Sorry to disappoint.'

'Oh, stop it,' I said, though a small part of me remained unconvinced. Leonard seemed so well until the show began – the grey face, the staggering and slurring, had made me wonder if he had been poisoned somehow. On the other hand, they were such a tight-knit bunch, I had quailed at the idea that Leonard's death might have been unnatural.

'Guy said the funeral will be in a couple of weeks in London,' said Lou. 'So much for a gentle old age of antiques with Cedric. Anyway, now we know, so you can do your obit of the old plum, and I can get back to Chivers and his mysterious supply of furs and nylons. See you in the foyer at seven tomorrow, for the Leonard show,' he added. 'Marie's beside herself with excitement, my sister loves a drama almost as much as she loves solving literary crimes. You're made for each other.'

The theatre was heaving when I arrived on Saturday evening. That day's *Chronicle* had carried a large advertisement for the Gaiety's tribute performance, with a portrait of Glinny looking particularly winsome. Clearly word had spread, as there was a long queue at the box office waiting for returns. Perhaps Leonard Lessiter was not Mr Gorringe's cup of tea – I knew my editor was a passionate and high-minded opera lover – but he had certainly been a hit with ordinary theatregoers.

'I remember seeing dear Leonard in *Arms and the Man*,' said one well-spoken woman behind me, who was wearing an enormous fox-fur stole, despite the warmth of the evening. 'He made a glorious Captain Bluntschli, awfully dapper.'

'That marvellous face,' agreed her friend. 'It just *spoke*, didn't it? Shame he never married again.'

'I expect plenty would have liked to get their hands on his money,' observed the fox-fur woman. 'Wise of him to resist.'

They passed by and up the stairs to the circle. The *Victory Gang Parade* posters had been changed to banners showing a very flattering sepia portrait of Leonard in his youth, with black writing announcing the one-off tribute.

I was standing beside one of them, scanning the foyer for Lou and Marie, when I heard a hiss.

'Miss York! Over here!'

I spun round but couldn't see who had called me, until there was a rustling from behind a vast potted fern, and Josephine Gardner peered out.

'I can't let the punters see me,' she whispered. 'I've been lurking, looking out for you and DI Brennan.'

She was wearing her Lili Marlene evening gown and white elbow-length gloves. I was in my unfortunate waitress costume again, as a consequence of owning nothing else suitable.

'Please, come with me,' she said, 'I need to speak to you privately.'

She took my arm in a firm grip.

'I can't!' I said, as the crowds milled towards the auditorium. The air was thick with heavy scent and sorrowful murmuring.

'They won't know where I've gone, and Lou needs to collect the tickets...'

'I've got them.' Josephine handed me a white envelope and tugged gently at my elbow. 'You must come, it's important.' She had a lovely voice – low and what Agnes Beamish, Suki's flat-mate, would call *contralto*. 'We're on in twenty minutes,' she added, still concealed behind the fern. 'There's no time to waste.'

I gave the foyer a final scan and, with a jolt of relief, saw the doors open to admit Lou, once again in his incongruous eveningwear, and Marie looking ravishing in a striped satin dress-suit, her tightly belted waist only slightly larger than a wedding ring. I wondered how she'd cope with clothes rationing.

'Lou!' I called, and they hurried over.

'Sorry, sorry,' he said. He seemed to be in a furious temper, though for once it wasn't aimed at me.

'You see, Marie, *some* women are able to get out of the door on time,' he said tightly. 'Not everyone has to engage in a "hat drama" or launch into hysterics about the "wrong colour of handbag"...'

'I couldn't find my bottle-green ostrich feather clutch!' she insisted. 'I could hardly bring that old brown lizard thing to the theatre... hullo, Edie dear.'

'Look,' I said, 'Miss Gardner's here, she needs a word with us.'

Josephine's heavily made-up face emerged from the ferns again.

'Detective Inspector, Marie,' she said, 'please come – I need to talk to you all, but not here.'

With a sting of nerves, I suddenly wondered if we had done something wrong – an objection to my obituary plans, perhaps, or a complaint over how Lou had handled Leonard's death. Josephine pushed through a discreet door behind the staircase painted the same colour as the walls, ushered us up a rather stark flight of stairs and, once again, we found ourselves backstage in the strange underwater glow of the wall lights.

'Quickly,' said Josephine. 'The beginners' bell will be ringing any second.'

'Where's Ginny?' asked Marie, but Josephine said nothing until we reached her dressing room. She herded us inside and closed the door behind us.

'Look,' she said, 'sorry about all the cloak-and-dagger business, but I don't want to put the wind up the others yet.'

'About what?' asked Marie, perching on the arm of a little couch. Josephine's room was far less personal than Florence's travelling caravan. A good luck card depicting a black cat stood on the mirrored dressing table, alongside a neat little box containing her make-up. A red dressing gown hung from the door, but everything else was arranged on the rail.

Josephine lowered her voice again. 'It seems quite mad to ask, I know – but have any of you seen Ginny?'

'Today?'

'Yes, today – just now, this afternoon – any time at all!'

'Why would we have seen her? Isn't she here?'

'No!' Josephine sank into the chair at her dressing table and clutched her head. I felt rather worried that the greasepaint would stain her white gloves. 'Nobody can find her,' she said. 'We've been all over the theatre looking – no message, nothing! And the whole evening was her idea, she was so excited about it all – she's been rehearsing her speeches day and night. Ginny's young, I know, but she's a real trouper, she'd never leave us in the lurch!'

Lou now looked uncharacteristically concerned, and Marie asked, 'Does she ever suffer from stage fright?'

'Never!' said Josephine. 'Everyone else does, particularly with a new show – Stanley can barely speak beforehand, and Guy has a little private reciting ritual he has to go through, but Ginny is the same onstage as she is off. I've never known her to be afraid. She once told me she feels most fully herself when she's performing.'

'When did you last see her?'

'This morning, about eleven, at our digs,' said Josephine. 'Sybil, our landlady, was out in the garden and Ginny had been chatting to her. She came in, we had a cup of tea together and talked about tonight. I had to come in early to rehearse my piece with Stanley, he simply can't get it right,' she added crossly. 'If it doesn't have raucous jokes about pies and pints in it, he's not interested. Ginny said she'd be at the theatre about three o'clock for our song rehearsal, but she didn't turn up.'

'Does your digs have a telephone?' asked Lou.

Josephine laughed. 'Hardly. We barely have running water. It's just so unlike Ginny,' she went on. 'She's never let us down yet.'

'Could she have been taken ill?' I wondered. 'Was she feeling quite all right when you saw her?'

'Never better. Upset about Leonard of course, but she was glowing with health and strength, as ever. It's quite sickening.' Josephine smiled briefly. She seemed fond of the younger woman.

Marie leaned forward. 'JoJo, might she have fallen out with someone in the cast? A row of some sort? Who was with her last, do you know?'

Marie was good at this, I thought admiringly. Straight to the point, like any successful fictional detective.

'I don't know,' admitted Josephine. 'I know Stanley was here in the afternoon, of course, because we were together rehearsing, and I heard Florence arrive at about three o'clock – but I don't know where Guy was, or Jack.'

A bell rang loudly above the door.

'Oh lawks,' she said. 'I'm on. Look, I've got to go, and I suppose I'll have to sing our duet of "Someone to Watch Over Me" on my own, which makes a mockery of the whole thing. Honestly, when she turns up, I swear I'll give her what-for.'

She whisked a white fur stole and evening gloves off the rack, and turned to leave the room.

'See you afterwards for our supper,' Marie said. 'I'm sure she'll have turned up by then.'

'Who knows?' Josephine hurried away, and we looked at each other.

'How very odd,' I said.

Marie nodded. 'I'm inclined to think something's befallen her,' she said. 'Unless it really is a lover's tiff and she's sulking.'

'What lover?' Lou stared at her, puzzled.

'It's perfectly obvious,' said Marie. 'To me, at least. Ostentatiously not touching each other, the way they crackled with electricity whenever they were near... I feel quite certain there must be some feelings there. Such a shame for poor Ginny.'

'What's a shame?' Lou was now looking at her as though she was explaining a complex mathematical theorem in Russian.

'Oh, of course, you don't know – I forget how much idle theatre gossip I have tucked away in my head,' said Marie. 'You see, he's married, to Rosemary Court-Chambers, as was, eldest of the Sussex Court-Chambers sisters, of course.'

Like Lou, I had no idea who she was talking about.

'She's terribly aristocratic, and I think he's rather used to the high life by now. He'll never leave her, no matter what he feels for Ginny. I imagine her father was furious when she took up with a penniless actor, but it must be ten years now.'

'Who are you talking about, Marie?' Lou interrupted her chatty monologue, and she looked surprised.

'Well, Guy, obviously.'

I thought back to how carefully they had stood apart. Even as he'd comforted Ginny and Josephine, I remembered, Guy had held Ginny slightly away from himself, as though she were an unexploded bomb.

'Do he and Rosemary have children?' I felt horribly unsophisticated. I seemed to spend a great deal of my life trying not to look shocked by other people's peculiar arrangements.

'No,' Marie said. 'It was not to be. Besides, Rosemary's so busy with her charities and good works, where would she have fitted them in?'

'We don't know if you're right, Marie,' put in Lou. 'Or, if you are, whether these fond "feelings", as you so delicately put it, have become anything more than that.'

'Oh, I strongly suspect they have,' said Marie, standing up and brushing down her skirt. 'Of course, I don't know him, I only have an acquaintance with Rosemary through her various charity events and concerts and so on, but one hears gossip...'

'You don't think Rosemary could have found out about whatever was going on with Ginny?' I asked.

Marie gave a small shudder. 'One hopes not.'

'None of this wild speculation is locating Miss Sutton,' said Lou. He, too, rose to his feet. 'I'm going to find a telephone box and ring the station, see if any accidents have been reported.'

'But the show's starting!' As Marie spoke, the second bell rang.

'I suspect I'll live without Stanley's finest monologue,' said Lou. 'I'll meet you in the bar during the interval for a debrief. If Ginny turns up on stage, come and find me.'

Marie took my elbow, and we hurried back the way we'd

come, down the grimy stairs and out into the warmly lit, gilded foyer, which was now empty but for a cigarette girl tucking her blouse into her skirt.

'It's starting,' she whispered to us. 'Best hurry!'

We did, and slid into our seats in the front row of the circle just as the curtain rose and Guy appeared onstage to give a short, moving speech about Leonard.

As the show progressed, it was impossible to tell that the rehearsal time had been so brief. Josephine's scene opposite Stanley was polished, and Florence was touching and dignified.

It was all rather flat, however – and it was evident that someone was missing.

'Where is she?' hissed a woman behind me. 'I only came for Miss Sutton.'

In the interval, Marie and I made our way to the circle bar, where we found Lou lurking at the back, away from the crush.

'No sign,' I said. 'She's not turned up. Any luck?'

He shook his head. 'No accidents to speak of unless you count an unexploded incendiary near Stockport swimming baths, which I rather doubt is related. I spoke to Ferdinand, though.'

'And?' demanded Marie. She was so much more blunt with him than I would ever dare to be, and it was quite enjoyable to watch him putting up with it.

Lou raised his voice above the noise. It always struck me that if people all agreed in advance to converse at a normal volume in a crowd, they wouldn't need to bellow at each other.

'He's worried,' he said. 'He claims he saw her last just after lunch – he'd had some soup and was heading straight to the theatre to rehearse the monologue in costume, he said, and she was going to set off there later in the afternoon.'

'What was she doing until then?' Marie and I asked in unison.

'He didn't know,' said Lou. 'Rehearsing alone? Knitting? Whatever women do when they're by themselves, I assume.'

'Do you think they *had* fallen out?' asked Marie.

Lou shook his head. 'Guy didn't mention anything. But this is the trouble with actors, isn't it? You can't always tell when they're acting.'

Lou joined us for the latter part of the show – although he insisted on calling it 'the second half' – and still, Ginny did not appear.

The applause after each scene or recital was genuine, but it was clear that many members of the audience were puzzled, judging by the murmurs.

The final performance was Guy's. He walked onto the darkened stage dressed in a modern army officer's uniform, and stood beneath the chill, white spotlight. I tried to forget that Leonard had lain on the same boards just a couple of days ago.

'*There's a one-eyed yellow idol to the north of Khatmandu...*'

His delivery was very different from Leonard's. Guy sounded weary, almost doomed, as if he were telling a tale that had happened to somebody he knew, and still felt the bitter sadness of it. At the climactic moment, when Leonard had staggered and collapsed, I involuntarily held my breath, and I felt Marie tense alongside me.

Guy drew the dagger from his belt and held it, weighing it thoughtfully as he spoke the words. He recited the last lines.

'*There's a broken-hearted woman tends the grave of Mad Carew, and the Yellow God forever gazes down.*'

He laid the dagger on the stage and bowed his fair head, in tribute to Leonard.

Even I felt quite moved, and I could see bobbing hats and flashes of white amongst the stalls, as women extracted handkerchiefs and dabbed away tears. There was a roar of applause, and I leaned towards Marie.

'He really is a good actor, isn't he?' I murmured, and she nodded slowly, her eyes on the stage.

There was a table set for nine waiting for us at the St Clements Grill down the street. The restaurant offered an 'after-theatre supper', which turned out to be a small serving of grilled fish or an indeterminate meat dish with peas and chipped potatoes, but amongst the red-shaded lamps and damask tablecloths, it was still quite easy to forget the war.

We arrived first, and Lou instructed us. 'Edie, you quiz Guy and Jack, using your womanly wiles.' I bristled. 'Scant as they are,' he added. 'Marie, you probe Florence and Josephine and I'll take Stanley. Between us, we need to find out what they all think has happened – and whether something really has befallen Ginny.'

'Shouldn't we all be out searching for her, rather than eating...' I consulted the menu, 'casserole a la crème?'

'God alone knows what's in that,' muttered Lou. 'Snoek, I shouldn't wonder.'

Marie shuddered. Snoek was a particularly vile cheap tinned fish that had gradually replaced tinned salmon in the grocer's. Ethel had recently likened it to 'boiler lagging with a touch of rock-pool'.

'And no,' Lou said to me. 'The best thing we can do is get to know the cast better. Then if she's not at home when they get back to their digs, and there's no news of her returning to London, they can report her missing and I can begin a proper investigation. But for now, let's hope she's simply had an attack of stage fright.'

'She doesn't suff—' began Marie. As she spoke, there was flurry of activity at the entrance. The others had arrived, still with traces of stage make-up giving them an oddly doll-like appearance. Guy waved over at us, though his expression was grim. There was a rather awkward dance round the chairs, as Marie and I contrived to sit beside our designated interviewees, but eventually, they all settled like exotic aviary birds on their perches.

'We'll all have the casserole,' Stanley told the waiter, 'unless you lads want to stump up extra for steak.' I was between Guy and Jack, who shook their heads.

'I'm not sure I can eat at all,' said Guy. His skin was still a peculiar shade of tan. 'I'm so dreadfully worried – I think I should go back to Grafton Street and check for her there.'

'Well, have a quick bite first,' said Jack sensibly. 'We're all starving, I imagine. I'm certain she'll be waiting for us all and there'll be some silly explanation.'

'But she adored Leonard,' said Guy, fiddling with his table knife. 'She'd never have missed our tribute.'

Based on what little I knew of Ginny, I agreed with him. Jack leaned in to speak to me.

'It *is* rather odd,' he said in a low voice. 'I expect this sort of thing happens all the time when you're a reporter, but it's quite new to us.'

'Oh no, it doesn't!' I said. He had a kind, clever face, with a lock of thick brown hair that kept escaping its oil and falling over his hazel eyes. He didn't look old enough to be a director.

'It's just, Ginny's always been so reliable,' he went on. 'You don't often get that quality combined with talent like hers, but she hates the idea of letting people down – a theatre troupe is a team, she says, and it won't succeed unless we're all playing as best we can.'

How earnest she sounded, I thought. Not at all like the flighty actresses of my imagination.

Our casseroles arrived – thankfully they didn't appear to contain anything fish-like, though as I poked out a piece of greyish meat, Jack said, 'probably someone's pet cat, if rumour's anything to go by.'

Horrified, I returned it to my plate, and he laughed. 'I'm joking,' he said. 'But I don't suppose that chicken had much of a life.'

Guy shot him an injured glance. 'I'm not sure how you can joke at a time like this,' he said. 'Leonard gone, Ginny vanished... it's like a curse. Even as I spoke the poetry tonight, I thought perhaps we'd invoked something... '*Twas the vengeance of the Little Yellow God.*'

'Oh, come on, man,' said Jack. His tone was more bolstering than mocking. 'I know Ginny and Florence are our resident Gypsy Rose Lees, but surely you don't believe in that sort of nonsense!'

'Oh, I don't, really,' said Guy, prodding unhappily at a bit of carrot floating in its oily sauce. I had the sense that Lou was looking over at me, but I ignored him. I was clearly failing to conduct my interviews in the approved police fashion.

'What about you, Mr Webb?' I said. 'When did you last see her?'

'Not at all, today,' said Jack. 'I saw her at rehearsals yesterday, then I was holed up in my room, going through the script and I didn't see anyone until I got to the theatre at lunchtime. I think our landlady, Sybil, was gardening, and I don't know where her sister Daphne was. We can ask them later if they saw Ginny.'

'Look here, I really feel I must get back,' said Guy. 'I'll hail a cab. I'll wait up for you if there's any news.'

'Are you sure?' Jack looked concerned, but Guy was already signalling to the waiter for his hat. Clearly, someone else was expected to foot the bill for his uneaten meal.

The others stayed put, and the conversation across the table seemed lively, though I sensed Lou was struggling with Stanley.

'No idea, pal,' I heard him say. 'Probably trying to make

somebody jealous. These young girls, they're all daft as brushes...'

'When you say "somebody"...?' asked Lou. Stanley glanced about theatrically and leaned in. I saw him mouthing something, but Lou's reaction was obscured by the waiter arriving to gather our plates.

'Do you know Guy well?' I asked Jack as the silver coffee pot arrived.

'Well, we weren't at school together or anything like that,' he said. 'I was a plain old London grammar bug, but I directed a couple of plays at Oxford and then went into rep, where I worked with him a couple of times. I met both Leonard and Ginny on *Hedda Gabler*.'

'She must have been awfully young to play the role,' I said, and he nodded.

'She was. But a pretty, talented nineteen-year-old actress turns a lot of heads,' he observed.

'Any heads in particular?' I asked, hoping to sound casual.

'Come now.' Jack laughed. 'I'm sure you can imagine there were strings of hopeful suitors. Stage-door Johnnies and lounge lizards,' he joked, in clipped, Edwardian tones, and I smiled. Evidently, he wasn't prepared to indulge in gossip about his own company. We talked instead about his ambitious plans for ENSA in Africa – assuming all was well with Ginny.

'As well as the *Gang Parade*, I thought perhaps we could do *Hamlet*, in tribute to Leonard,' he said. 'The Dane himself. Not sure what the troops will make of it, but imagine that glorious poetry, with the sand dunes rising behind the stage, and the setting sun a crimson ball of fire... it'd be memorable at least!'

Jack's ambitions as a director clearly lay somewhere far beyond Stanley reciting *The Lion and Albert* to a ribald crowd.

Guy signalled for the bill, and Marie finally leaned away from Josephine, with whom she'd been talking earnestly, and said, 'Anyone need a lift? We could share a cab.'

Lou looked irritated – it was late, and I suspected he wanted to get home to Marple, who didn't enjoy being left to his own devices and had a tendency to shred upholstery.

The others shook their heads, and it transpired that Stanley had his car parked near the theatre and would 'cram them all in.'

'Had some errands to run,' he said. 'Otherwise, I wouldn't bring her into town – too much risk of damage to the old girl, ruddy rusty nails and glass all over...

Lou's face suggested that he was more concerned about quite how many glasses of post-show champagne Stanley had drunk, but he said nothing.

He turned to Josephine.

'This is my number,' he said, extracting a small card from his pocket and handing it to her. 'Could I ask you to find a telephone box and ring me at work in the morning, to let me know of any news? I'll be there from eight, and you can reverse the charges.'

Josephine nodded and slipped it into her evening bag.

'You want to watch that one!' boomed Stanley, leering at her. 'Giving you his telephone number, but is he as innocent as he appears?'

'I'm a Detective Inspector,' said Lou coldly. 'I might ask the same of any of you.'

Stanley looked shocked. 'Didn't mean anything by it, pal,' he blustered. 'Bit of a joke was all, JoJo's a pretty girl...' He turned away with relief as the waiter brought his hat.

Our goodbyes were subdued – it was clear that as the moment of reckoning approached, the cast felt increasingly uncertain as to whether they'd find Ginny waiting at Grafton Street. They hurried away, and Lou hailed us a passing cab.

'Well, that was *not* the evening I expected,' said Marie, as the driver pulled away. 'Poor Leonard was quite overshadowed.'

The blacked-out streets had turned them both into silhouettes beside me.

'What did you get out of Josephine and Florence?' Lou asked.

Marie lowered her voice.

'JoJo told us all she knew earlier, but Florence said she left for the Gaiety at lunchtime, and that Ginny seemed worried when she saw her this morning.'

'Worried in what way?' I asked, as the cab bumped over potholes. I assumed I'd be dropped off first, and wanted all the information I could extract.

'Florence is so *vague*,' said Marie crossly. 'I'm sure she puts it on, to enhance her spiritualist nonsense, but she said, "I had a sense that all was not well with her." I asked what she meant, and she said something about a *dark aura around her*. I mean, for heaven's sake.'

Lou was shaking his head. 'These people,' he muttered. 'Did she remember anything useful whatsoever?'

'She said that Ginny wanted to talk to her later on about something important,' said Marie. 'She did the tarot card reading for her the other night, but she wouldn't tell me what it said.'

'Did it say, "don't pay any attention to psychic piffle peddled by a woman old enough to know better"?' asked Lou.

'Actors are very superstitious,' said Marie. 'But I agree, it does all seem a little unlikely. And JoJo said that Ginny seemed in glowing health and perfectly well this morning, so that doesn't add up, either.'

'I suppose they may yet get back tonight and find her in bed with influenza,' I said. 'We don't know for sure that anything's happened to her.'

'Sybil would have telephoned the theatre if she was ill,' said Marie. 'JoJo told me, they have an arrangement at the digs

where, if anyone's indisposed, the landlady will go to the telephone box down the road and let the stage manager know.'

We were nearing my road. As I fossicked in my handbag for
the door key, I asked, 'What can we do?'

'With luck, I'll hear from Josephine in the morning,' said
Lou. 'Then I'll be in touch, Edie. I might need you to do me a
favour.'

I thought, absurdly, of Lou's socks, drying on the rack.

'What sort of favour?'

'If Ginny hasn't come back, and she's reported missing, I
need you to go to Grafton Street and speak to them all. They'll
talk to you.'

'I could...' began Marie eagerly.

'Edie has the excuse of working for the *Chronicle*,' Lou said.
'I doubt you shouting "let me through, I'm a nosy parker," will
be quite so effective.'

'Though perhaps it won't be necessary,' I said. 'Ginny may
be back by now.'

'Perhaps,' said Lou, as the cab pulled up outside Mrs Turner's lodging house and he got out to open the door for me. As I
walked up the dark path to the front porch, I thought of vibrant,
talented Ginny, and the absence where she should have been on
stage. I thought of Florence saying '*a dark aura*,' and though I
knew it was silly, I found myself shivering, despite the warm
night air.

CHAPTER FIVE

After consulting my map and applying lipstick, I set off for Grafton Street. The morning was warm, and late tulips and wallflowers were blooming in suburban front gardens, though I noticed that several of the little pocket-squares had been given over to vegetable-growing. Women were out with their hair tied into scarves, watering and digging their miniature crops. One even had a trug piled with strawberries. A little girl was sitting on the doorstep, hulling one and eating two while her mother's back was turned.

As buses rattled past and people strolled to church, it was impossible to imagine that anything sinister could have happened to Ginny, but Lou had been adamant. 'JG telephoned, GS not back,' read the note delivered by a messenger boy over breakfast. 'Please go as agreed.'

I was hot and extremely thirsty by the time I arrived at number twenty-three. It was a tall, red-brick Edwardian house, soot-blackened and with flaking paint on the windowsills, but there was a pot of bright pink cyclamens on the scrubbed stone doorstep and a clean lace curtain behind the glass panels of the door. In the window, a typed sign read *Manchester's best-loved theatrical boarding-house for players and thespians*, and a small pair of painted theatre masks dangled above. A poker-work sign hung in the other side of the box bay window, reading *All the world's a stage*, and beneath that, a large white cat sat on the sill, fastidiously licking one paw.

I climbed the steps, and rang the bell, half expecting it to play an overture. Instead, it emitted an unpleasant, drill-like note that caused the cat to leap off the sill and vanish into the shadows of the room beyond.

'Good morning!' cried the short, plump woman who opened the door. She had blonde curls pinned into an old-fashioned bouffant, and I guessed she was approaching forty. Her face was pinkly soft, and she had the sort of dreamy smile that suggested she began each day with a saucer of cream and a ribboned gift.

'Are you here about the vacancy?' she asked. 'We haven't got round to putting up a sign yet, as it's just the one room available, and normally you all come as a pack, don't you?' She laughed. 'I always say, rooming a single actor is like spotting a lone magpie – rather bad luck! Still, you don't look as if you'd bring anything but good luck along with you, in your lovely yellow dress. Like a little piece of sunshine! What's your name, dear, and where are you playing this week? Let me just get the ledger...'

'Oh – no,' I said, as she turned back to the hallway. 'I'm not an actor. I've come to speak to the ENSA cast about...' I paused. Did this motherly, fluttering butterfly know that one of them was missing? If she was the landlady, she surely must.

'About Ginny Sutton. And where she might have got to,' I finished.

She stopped and turned back to me.

'Are you a friend, dear?'

'Sort of,' I said. 'Edie York. My friend Marie met the ENSA cast recently, and we saw them last night – they said she was missing.'

The woman heaved a great sigh.

'Come along in,' she said to my relief. 'Those poor darlings. I'm Daphne, by the way. I've run the place with my sister Sybil since I was widowed. I can't imagine what they must all be going through – Ginny is such a dear, so pretty and neat, like a little songbird, and none of us can quite believe it...'

She continued her breathless monologue as she led me through a hallway lined with framed playbills dating back to the 1890s. Tasselled lampshades shielded old-fashioned gas lights on the walls and a mahogany banister curved upwards, leading to the cast's bedrooms. Everything gleamed with polish, and the air was scented with lavender wax, which almost entirely disguised the faint, underlying smell of cat.

I felt surprisingly at ease as Daphne, still chatting, opened a door and showed me into a cosy little wallpapered room that led onto a large kitchen. More framed illustrated posters for long-ago plays covered the walls – I noticed *Hamlet*, and *Hindle Wakes*, and a couple of scroll-encrusted, antique-looking advertisements for plays I didn't know – *I Called You Mother* and *Make Haste, My Love*, which looked like the sort of melodramas that would have Lou guffawing.

'Have a seat, dear,' said Daphne, indicating the little green velvet couch. Like everything else in the house, it was a well-cared for Victorian relic, with polished, turned legs on castors and enormous, tasselled silk cushions embroidered with birds and flowers. It was hard to remember the year was still 1941 – I could easily have been transported back in time by a century or so. A large, ornate clock ticked loudly on the mantelpiece, and the white cat wandered in, gazed at me with its translucent, sea-glass eyes, and backed out again, looking disgusted.

'Thanks,' I joked.

'Oh, don't mind Bernhardt,' said Daphne. 'She's a terrible flirt, she only likes men. You should see her with Guy and

Leon... oh!' She broke off. 'My goodness, I'm so sorry – it's so hard to remember that he's not still with us.'

'Did you know him well?'

'He stayed with us often,' said Daphne. 'His wonderful anecdotes...' She looked up and away to the gilded mirror behind the clock as if Leonard's spectre hovered somewhere in its silvery mists. 'I know people call actors' accommodation "digs",' she went on, 'but we prefer to think of it as opening our home to fellow players, creating a happy community of theatricals...'

I shifted slightly against my cushion.

'But Ginny!' cried Daphne, suddenly returned to the present. 'Our little bird! There's been no sign of her as far as I know – unless she came in terribly late of course and is still asleep.'

It was almost half past ten and I wondered if the rest of the cast were asleep, too.

'Do you remember what time you saw her last?'

Daphne consulted the depths of the mirror again.

'I suppose it must have been early afternoon,' she said. 'Yes, that's right, the others had mostly gone off to rehearsals, but Ginny likes to go through her part at home. She was rushing about, reciting bits of her scenes, and getting ready.'

'Did she seem worried, or agitated at all...?'

'Not at all,' said Daphne. 'Quite happy, a dear little buzzing bee. I believe... let me think... I went out to the grocers' at about half past two, Sybil likes me to collect the breakfast rations for the week on Saturdays. I don't remember seeing her as I left, so I think she must have gone by then. I didn't hear the door, but of course, I don't anymore.'

I wondered whether she was deaf, and must have looked puzzled, as Daphne said, 'I just mean, it slams all hours of the day and night, you see. People let each other in, or pop out for a bit, and we often give our regulars a key – it's Noises Off, we simply don't pay any attention to the constant comings and goings.'

I had sunk so far into the billows of cushioning that I felt quite disadvantaged and struggled painfully upright again.

'Is your sister here?' I looked into the kitchen, a comforting space with primrose-yellow walls, a huge kitchen table covered in a gingham-printed oilcloth, colourful china arranged on a vast Welsh dresser, a gleaming Aga and bright rag rugs dotting the tiled floor. It was the sort of kitchen I had dreamed of as a child, growing up at the home, eating my relentlessly dull bowls of porridge and soup and gristly stew at long, scratched trestle tables in a white-walled dining hall, which was forever freezing, even in August.

'Sybil? I expect she's about somewhere,' said Daphne vaguely. 'But you'll want to see your friends – and I haven't even offered you a cup of tea! Heavens, what a dreadful hostess I must be. I'll go and fetch the cast, and then I'll pop the kettle on. Unless you'd prefer something else? I think we have some biscuits somewhere, unless Stanley's scoffed the last one...'

She was poking hopefully round the shelves when Jack Webb appeared in the doorway.

'Hullo again,' I said. 'No sign, I take it?'

He shook his head.

'What happened last night when you got back?'

'Well,' said Jack, flinging himself into the button-backed chair. It was far too small for him, and, with his rangy frame and ruffled hair, he rather resembled a jack-in-a-box.

'We all had a good look to see if she'd left a note, but there was nothing. Guy wasn't up, so we had to assume she wasn't back. Everyone's exhausted after a performance, and with the emotion of the tribute show... I think we just wanted the day to end. When I got up, I went down to tap on her door in case she'd been out very late, but there was no answer.'

'Didn't you check inside?'

'Well, no,' said Jack. 'I'm not the sort of man who—'

'But Josephine or Florence could have perhaps—'

'Speak of the devil,' said Jack with some relief. There were light footsteps in the tiled hallway, and Josephine entered the little room. She wore a navy linen dress, and her hair was curled and set in soft, dark waves, as though she'd been to the salon.

'Edie!' she said warmly. 'I'm glad you're here. It's too worrying, there's not a sign of her.'

Josephine took a gold cigarette case from her pocket, offering me one. I saw there was a dedication etched beneath the lid, but I couldn't read it from where I sat. I declined, but Jack took one and she lit it by holding them both in her scarlet-painted mouth as she inhaled. Jack took the cigarette and placed it between his own lips, in a gesture that seemed oddly intimate.

'I barely slept for thinking about her, Edie. I know people will believe she's just run off or had an attack of stage fright, but I know her,' Josephine said. 'She wouldn't.'

'Was there... is she going out with anybody in particular?' I asked, as the kettle shrieked. Daphne poured boiling water into a Cornish-ware teapot and loaded the pot and cups onto a raffia tray. As she searched for milk in the pantry, the back door opened with a click, and another woman came into the kitchen. She was in her fifties, I guessed, with fox-red hair piled onto her head and held in place with green Bakelite combs. She wore leather boots, mud-stained twill slacks like a land girl and a cotton blouse, with several incongruous strings of bright wooden beads round her neck. She had a faded, melancholy beauty that must once have been mesmerising.

'Syb,' said Daphne, 'we've a visitor.'

Sybil washed her hands at the sink, then pulled out a kitchen chair and sat down.

'Whatever are you all doing crouched in the snug like little nocturnal bats?' she asked. 'It's a glorious day, we should all be *inhaling* this sunshine before it goes!'

She was well-spoken, with what my school choir mistress would have called 'perfect diction'. I wondered if Sybil had ever taken elocution lessons, as there was not a trace of Mancunian vowel.

'At least come and sit at the table with me,' she said. 'I don't want to get grass and twigs all over the good furniture. Daphne, dear, where are those biscuits?'

Daphne pulled various tins from the dresser and rummaged, while we gathered round the table.

'Now,' said Sybil, extending a long, slim hand for me to shake, 'who is this little thing?'

'This is Miss Edie York, Syb,' said Josephine. 'She's an obituary writer for the *Chronicle*, she's been writing about Leonard, and we've all come to know her a little – she's a friend of Marie, who I told you about.'

'And I was at the tribute performance last night,' I said. 'I'm so sorry you've lost a friend. Were you there?'

Sybil shot a glare at Daphne, who was decanting a set of misshapen, seed-scattered biscuits onto a thick blue plate.

'I'm afraid not,' said Sybil icily. 'Though we'd very much have liked to honour the memory of darling Len, Daphne developed one of her *headaches*, and I was required to minister to her.'

'I'm so sorry,' said Daphne to the room at large. 'They come on very suddenly – it's a sort of *clenching* pain that starts in my temples, and if I don't lie down quickly, it can be quite crippling. But by this morning, thankfully, it was more or less gone.'

'I tell you over and over,' said Sybil, 'you simply must make another appointment with Dr O'Connor, Daphne. And don't let him brush you off this time.' It was clear as gin that Sybil was the elder sister.

Daphne offered the biscuits around, which on closer inspection were full of caraway seeds, perhaps my least favourite taste in the world. I hoped she wouldn't think me rude for refusing.

'Edie's also been very concerned about Ginny,' said Jack. 'As are we all.'

'Did you see her, Syb?' asked Daphne, settling into a chair as she crunched. 'It's awfully peculiar, and none of us can quite remember when we last caught sight of her.'

'That's just it,' said Sybil. 'I didn't see her at all after mid-morning – I was out in the garden all day, digging and weeding. Ginny popped out for a chat about the show, she knew I was *so* looking forward to it, and we discussed her opening monologue – I advised her to start in a hushed tone, and let it build. Then I think I had a word with Guy before he left – he brought me a cup of tea, the dear thing – but I had hoped to get all my gardening finished early, to get ready for the show...' She glanced irritably at Daphne again. 'So, I was pottering about out there when everyone left.'

'So they were all gone by the time you came indoors? When was that?' I asked.

'Well, I suppose it must have been about four,' said Sybil. 'Yes, it was, because the wireless was still on, and the BBC concert was just ending – I was rather annoyed because I adore Brahms, you see, and it was his violin concerto, the one he wrote for his friend Joseph Joachim, and one does love it so...' She tailed off and took a sip of tea. I noticed Sybil wasn't eating a biscuit, either, which probably explained her rangy, model-like figure, in contrast to Daphne's more comfortable proportions.

'The house was empty?' I persisted.

'Well, yes, I believe so,' said Sybil, dragging herself from the glory of Brahms. 'I shouted upstairs to check, but answer came there none.'

A thought struck me. 'Has anyone actually looked in Ginny's bedroom?' I asked. 'Is it possible she was taken ill, went to lie down and has been asleep all along?'

They looked at one another. 'Well... no,' said Josephine. She looked embarrassed. 'We tapped on her door when we came in, but you see...' Her cheeks were bright pink.

'I'm afraid I'm lost,' I said.

Jack mouthed something at Josephine. 'I can't... not with us all here,' she said. She had entirely lost her composure. 'Edie, could you come with me, and we'll go and check together?'

I was baffled as to why she couldn't simply check herself, but I rose from my seat and followed her into the hallway.

'Look,' whispered Josephine, 'it's an open secret amongst the cast, but Ginny would so be terribly embarrassed if anybody else knew. You *mustn't* put it in your newspaper, Edie, promise me.'

'I won't tell anybody,' I said. I immediately wondered whether I could keep my glib promise, if it transpired that the 'open secret' had a bearing on Ginny's disappearance.

'Well, she and Guy... they're having a... they're sort of... together,' she said. 'At least, Guy is married so nothing can come of it, but they're both awfully smitten...'

'Oh, I see!' Marie had been correct. 'You mean, Ginny might be in Guy's bedroom?'

'Quite,' said Josephine. 'That's sort of how they... well, her own bedroom is used more as a dressing room.'

She bent down to stroke Bernhardt who had wandered into the hall, and her face was hidden by a curtain of hair.

'Guy came back before the rest of us last night, if you remember,' Josephine added, straightening again. 'He was in bed when we came in, and we still haven't seen him.'

'Surely if Ginny's back, he'd have let you know?' I asked. 'If they're together, he'd want to reassure everyone.'

'Not if they were both asleep, perhaps. Honestly, I'm relieved you're being so sanguine about it,' said Josephine. 'Sybil and Daphne don't know – or perhaps they do, but we certainly haven't said anything. Sybil prides herself on running a respectable establishment, she won't have players from the burlesque revues or anything like that staying here, so she might frown rather on their little... liaison.'

My recent experiences with the bohemian artists' colony up in Lancashire had somewhat inured me to what Annie called 'shenanigans and carry-on' amongst creative types, and besides, I thought, Ginny and Guy had almost been killed in the London Blitz – perhaps it was no wonder they had fallen into one another's arms, particularly after the shared shock of Leonard's death. It was even possible that the aristocratic Rosemary Court-Chambers might turn a blind eye, as generations of well-bred wives had done before her, so long as nobody was rocking the marital boat or producing illegitimate heirs.

'I won't breathe a word,' I said. 'But surely it's worth knocking on Guy's door to make sure.'

'I suppose we should, before we send out the search parties. Come with me, won't you?' Josephine asked. 'I shall feel very embarrassed if he's alone, and even more so if he isn't.'

I followed her up the stairs, which were carpeted in a faded flowered pattern. Gilded mirrors hung amongst the playbills above.

'Guy's in bedroom four,' said Josephine quietly over her shoulder. 'Florence always bags three, she says it's her lucky number. I wonder if that's because it overlooks the nice quiet garden, rather than the noisy street.'

I laughed. 'Superstition will get you everywhere.'

'Leonard was in bedroom one,' added Josephine more sombrely, as we passed the closed mahogany door. 'It's empty now. Stanley's in number two, I'm in five on the third floor, Ginny's in six – well – that's her room, at least, I suppose. Jack's got the attic room, number seven. It's much bigger than ours, but you whack your head on the ceiling whenever you stand up. He rather sweetly offered to take it, to save me and Ginny seeing stars every morning. Sybil and Daphne are opposite him. They share a room.'

She paused outside the door, which held a small brass plate with the number four etched into it in Victorian-looking script.

She took a deep breath and knocked lightly.

There was no response.

'Guy?' I called gently. 'It's Edie. Are you in there?'

There was silence, followed by a muffled groan.

'Guy?' called Josephine more urgently. 'Are you all right?'

'Hold on,' came Guy's croaking voice from within. 'Let me get my gown on...'

We heard the sound of splashing water, and footsteps.

Guy peered round the door, wearing monogrammed leather slippers and a paisley silk dressing gown over duck-egg blue linen pyjamas. If Jack had looked tired, Guy appeared as though he hadn't slept a wink.

'Guy, are you all right?' asked Josephine. 'Has there been any sign of Ginny? We thought you might have news.'

He slumped against the door frame.

'God,' he said. 'Oh God, this can't truly be happening.'

'What is it?' I asked fearfully. Had he heard something dreadful about her fate overnight?

'I just... I thought perhaps if I stayed in bed all morning, I'd come downstairs and she'd be back,' he said. 'It was almost a bargain with God, that if I didn't go looking, she'd appear. I couldn't face joining you all without Ginny. When I heard the doorbell, I hoped... I so desperately hoped... but it must have been you, Edie. Besides, she'd have a key, of course. Oh dear God.' He shuddered. 'I didn't sleep all night. I still haven't. I just lay here, waiting, waiting, waiting... but she's gone.'

He leaned his face against the frame, breathing heavily.

I glanced at Josephine.

'We thought she might be with you,' admitted Josephine, but he shook his head.

'If only she had been.'

'Perhaps,' I said tentatively, 'we could have a look in her room. See if she's taken any of her things with her.'

'You think she's run off?' asked Guy. 'Oh, but she wouldn't. Not my – not Ginny.'

'I've written to Avril,' Josephine told him. 'It won't go until tomorrow, but I've asked her to contact us as soon as she can.'

'I can ask her sister, Gloria,' I said suddenly. 'I work with her. She says they speak every day, so she's bound to know by Monday if Ginny's turned up back home in London. Run to the box and telephone the *Chronicle* switchboard just after nine o'clock in the morning, and I'll have news.'

'Brainwave,' said Josephine. 'I'll post my letter anyway, just to be sure. I shall feel dreadful, poking about in Ginny's room,' she added. 'We spend so much time thrown together on tour, our rooms are our sanctuaries. We tend to respect one another's privacy, but...'

'Needs must,' I supplied, and Josephine nodded unhappily.

Guy turned back to his room, presumably to get dressed and renegotiate his bargain with God, and Josephine led me up another flight of stairs.

'Here's our eyrie,' she said. 'It's quite a cosy nook, but it does get awfully stuffy in summer.'

Josephine paused outside the door, her elegant fingers on the handle.

'Good God, this makes it feel real,' she said. 'As if we really should be worried sick.'

She turned the handle quickly, and pushed open the door. I inhaled a waft of light, floral perfume and stepped inside. The curtain was open, sunlight illuminated the faded Persian rug, and it was clear the bed hadn't been slept in – though that wasn't surprising, I remembered, as Ginny had been sharing Guy's bedroom. I wondered suddenly if someone had found out about the affair and was blackmailing Ginny. A married man, and a younger woman... it wasn't unheard of, but it would certainly cause a scandal and damage her career, perhaps irrevocably, if it reached the newspapers. I'd talk to Marie about it later, I decided. If they wanted money, though, of course they would be targeting Guy. Perhaps someone had threatened to tell Rosemary, and demanded payment for their silence – but who? The cast all seemed so close, even Stanley with his bluff remarks, and Florence with her old-fashioned, gypsy theatricality.

The room was small, with raspberry-pink striped wallpaper, a little basin in the corner with a round mirror, and an inlaid cherry-wood wardrobe. A small fireplace with a fan in the grate faced the door. There was a fringed, pink-shaded lamp attached to the wall above the single bed, and beside it was a chest of drawers with a few personal things scattered across the surface.

Josephine opened the wardrobe door. Ginny was tidy – her clothes were hung up, pairs of shoes lined up neatly on the shelf beneath. A stiff, leather suitcase was stored tidily above the wardrobe. Evidently, she hadn't intended to leave for long.

'Odd,' said Josephine. 'Her hat's still here.' She lifted a smart, black straw hat from the top shelf. 'I suppose she sometimes wears a scarf around her hair, but if she's going to the theatre, I can't see her leaving without a hat, unless she went in a tearing hurry. Oh, and look,' Josephine pointed to a box hanging from the door hook, 'she's left her gas mask. Although I suppose she didn't always remember it...'

'What about her handbag?' I asked. 'Where would she keep that?'

'On the bedpost, same as I do, I'd imagine,' said Josephine. 'Or on the chair?'

A peach silk dressing gown was draped over the wooden chair by the window. I lifted it, but there was nothing beneath save a few pages of script. It seemed to be a scene from *Hamlet* with notes scribbled beside Ophelia's speech – 'quieter here', 'passionate!' It was jarring to see Ginny's vibrant handwriting amid the heaviness of her absence.

'No bag,' I said. The window looked onto the street, where a smartly dressed couple was walking by, arguing about something. He was raising his arms in a gesture of furious helplessness, and she was saying something agitated – '... *your flaming mother*' floated up through the still air as they passed.

I turned to Josephine.

'Do you think she and Guy could have had a row?' I asked. 'That might have made her run off, if she was very upset.'

Josephine was studying the line of shoes.

'They've only been together a few months, so far as I know, and Ginny told me it was love at first sight,' Josephine said quietly. 'They seem positively entranced by one another, strictly *entre nous*, so I'd be very surprised if anything had gone wrong between them. Ginny was so upset about Leonard – well, we all were – and Guy was being simply lovely to her. It's very queer,' Josephine added, 'but none of her things are missing that I can see, except for her handbag. Both her jackets are here, and all the frocks she brought with her, I think. Of course, she may have packed something I haven't seen, but we tend to travel pretty lightly on tour, and we were all in a something of a hurry to escape the Blitz.'

'It was a warm day yesterday,' I said. 'Perhaps she felt she didn't need a jacket when she left.'

I crossed the room and studied the things on the bedside table. A hairbrush, a travel book about Africa, though judging by the placement of the bookmark she hadn't got far with it, a glass of water, now furring lightly on top, and a brown glass jar of Vimm's vitamin pills.

'No appointments diary,' I said.

'No, and no note saying, *I've run away, here's where to find me*, either,' said Josephine. 'More's the pity. Look, I'll go and post my letter to Avril so it goes first thing tomorrow. I suggest you have a chat with Guy. He was the last person to see her.'

'I shall,' I said. 'Though if she took her handbag, she must have left the house after he'd gone.'

'But the little red purse she keeps her wages in is here, and her powder compact and lipstick,' said Josephine, checking the bedside drawer and finding them beneath a folded nightgown. 'She may have gone somewhere in a hurry – though whether she was intending to go straight to the theatre afterwards, we can't know.'

I thought of beautiful Ginny, running down the front steps on a sunny Saturday afternoon, her head full of speeches and rehearsals – where else would she have been going? But despite her apparent intentions, Ginny had never arrived at the Gaiety Theatre. If she wasn't back in London, it was beginning to seem that the young actress had vanished into thin air.

CHAPTER SIX

Back downstairs, Guy was up and dressed, morosely drinking tea. Florence and Stanley had also emerged and sat at the table, eating crusty toast made by Daphne on the Aga plate. I longed for a piece, but nobody offered.

Florence dusted the crumbs from her hands, and made to stand.

'Before you go,' I said to her, 'could I have a word in private?'

She looked startled but nodded.

'We'll go in the drawing room,' she said. 'If that's all right, Sybil?'

Sybil nodded. 'Of course. *Mi casa es su casa*,' she said grandly.

The drawing room was the one with the box bay window facing the street, and Bernhardt had made her way back in. She was sitting on the lacquered upright piano, lightly patting the coloured beads on a lace doily.

'Bless her,' said Florence fondly, sinking into a tufted, pink brocade sofa. This room was pleasantly cool after the heat and bustle of the kitchen, with yet more framed posters and playbills hung over the walls. I had assumed they were all souvenirs of guests' productions, but one for *The Taming of the Shrew*, at the Palace Theatre in October 1904, caught my eye, as it featured a portrait of a delicately beautiful woman who looked oddly familiar. I peered at the printed words beneath.

Starring Miss Sybil Charnwood as Katherina.

'She was terribly good-looking,' I observed.

'Oh, she was the best of us,' said Florence reverently. 'The most wonderful stage presence, the loveliest face and voice.'

'Why did she stop acting?'

Florence's misty look of recollection changed to wariness with a blink. 'She doesn't say. But I know she prefers not to be asked about it.'

I thought it rather odd to have a large, framed poster of something you didn't want to be asked about in the front parlour, but I nodded.

'Florence,' I said, 'I know tarot readings are private, but it's beginning to look as though something may have befallen Ginny. Did she say anything at all during your reading the other night that might suggest she was upset or in some sort of trouble?'

Florence widened her already large eyes. It was rather like interviewing an ageing Disney cartoon – everything about her was slightly exaggerated.

'I'm afraid I wouldn't tell you if she had,' said Florence. 'A reader and her client enter into a sacred contract.'

'But Miss Buchanan, surely you see that if Ginny was worried about something, it could help us to find her?'

She pressed her lips together. 'I'll say this, and this only,' she said. 'Ginny was concerned about matters of love. That's what she asked about.'

'And what did the cards say?' I asked, glad Lou wasn't listening in.

Florence shook her head. 'Nothing that would help anyone to find her.'

'Where do you think she's gone?'

'I have no idea,' said Florence. 'But I sensed a darkness in her cards. That's all.'

I bit back a sigh of frustration 'I'm afraid I don't know quite what that means.'

'It was a feeling,' said Florence haughtily. 'I cannot explain it beyond that. A sense that all was not well. A veil cast over the future.'

'A *veil*? What sort of vei—'

Florence rose. 'I'm afraid I have other business to attend to,' she said. 'I'll bid you good morning. I shall look forward to reading your obituary of dear Leonard.'

'Did you tell Ginny what you saw?'

Florence looked at me. 'Of course I did,' she said.

Back in the kitchen, Guy was still slumped at the table talking to Jack. Sybil had gone outside again – I could see her through the open back door, carrying a trowel and a wooden crate over to an impressive-looking vegetable patch. There were bean rows and cold frames, and along the back wall I could see the serried tops of raspberry canes.

'What a bleeding carry-on,' said Stanley loudly, casting aside yesterday's *Daily Sketch*. He had finished his toast and was now ploughing steadily through the remaining biscuits. I worried for Daphne and Sybil's rations.

'Whatever do you mean?' Guy asked coldly.

'Well,' Stanley settled back in his chair, his hands folded over his stomach as if he were about to take a nap, 'it's obvious, isn't it, lad? She's had enough.'

'Enough of what, exactly?' Guy asked. There was an edge to his voice like a stiletto blade.

'Don't...' began Jack, but it was too late.

'Enough of being treated like a second rate bit o' fluff,' said Stanley. 'She's a nice lass, and she wants respecting. Not a bloody *affaire* or *liaison*,' he adopted a ludicrous French accent, 'or whatever you posh types call it. I've heard her crying, you know, when she thought nobody was listening. Dressing room next to mine, you'd be hard pushed not to hear her weeping and wailing. Make your mind up, lad, I say, or leave her be, because she's nobbut half your age and you've spoiled her for anyone else.'

Guy appeared to be struck dumb with rage, but Jack said, 'Now look here...'

''E knows I'm right, though, you see,' said Stanley, standing up. 'I'm off. You think on,' he added, pointing at Guy's white face, like a vengeful Dickensian ghost.

He stumped out of the room. Daphne busied herself at the Aga, though there was a quiver about her shoulders that suggested she'd heard every word. Guy turned to me.

'That's rich coming from him. He's a bloody old stirrer,' he said furiously. 'Yes, all right, I'll admit that Ginny and I have a... we're... well, we've fallen in love, I suppose. I'm in hell, and while I don't expect any sympathy for my situation...' I heard Annie in my head saying, *'That's lucky, because you won't get any.'*

'... I haven't slept with worry. I've gone over and over the last time I saw her – she was perfectly all right, we kissed each other goodbye, I went off to the theatre, she said she'd be along a bit later, and that was it. She wasn't upset, or worried about anything – apart from her grief over Leonard of course.'

'Could that have driven her away, do you think?' I asked. 'Did she know any of Leonard's family, someone she might have wanted to visit urgently?'

'That's rather a good point,' murmured Jack.

Guy shook his head hopelessly. 'Why would she have kept such a visit a secret? And besides, Leonard was a lone wolf – his friend Cedric's back in London, I believe he's organising the funeral, but apart from him... no, he never mentioned any family.'

'When did you see her last?' I asked.

'Just after lunch,' said Guy. 'She was drifting about, chatting and drinking tea.'

'Do you remember what she was wearing?'

He closed his eyes. 'Yes. She had on wide, navy linen trousers, and her green silk kimono top – she wore it a lot, it was an emerald colour that looked wonderful with her eyes. Excuse me,' he said, and stood, but not before I realised that his own eyes had filled with tears.

He left the room and I remained at the table, thinking fast. Suppose Florence had told Ginny that the affair with Guy had run its course, I thought, or that he'd never leave Rosemary. Perhaps one of her stage-door admirers, or someone she'd met in London, had whisked her away – and Ginny had been only too happy to leave behind her grief about Leonard, the motley cast and her cowardly lover?

She must have known she'd let the cast down, but maybe she no longer cared. She was young and perhaps impetuous – even as we searched and worried, was she holed up in a comfortable hotel with someone who adored her?

'Jack, Stanley,' I said, 'could we have a chat?'

'Of course,' said Jack. 'Let's go outside, while the weather's nice.' He stood to usher me and Stanley out of the back door, which was propped open by a terracotta plant pot full of soil.

Now I could view the garden properly, I realised how charming it was. A thrush was singing in the magnolia tree by the door, and a broom bush released its exquisite scent into the sooty city air.

The flower beds were given over to the growing of vegetables, and sunlight glinted on the cold frames. Sybil had left her spade in the ground near the metal air raid shelter and a robin now perched on the handle, like an illustration from *The Secret Garden*.

'Have a seat,' said Jack, offering me a green wicker garden chair. Stanley heaved himself into another, with a tapestry cushion supporting his broad back, and groaned in relief.

'My flaming twinges,' he said. 'Oops, should mind my French in front of the ladies. Then again, you working women... can we call you ladies these days?'

He guffawed, and Jack shot him a look of irritation.

'I'm here to find out a bit more about Ginny's disappearance, if that's all right,' I said. 'We're just trying to put it all together, DI Brennan and I, and of course, Marie is terribly worried.'

'Don't know why,' said Stanley. 'Actresses run off all the time. I tell you what, love, Clacton pier, nineteen twenty-five, we had a right one. Little blonde thing she was, with very fancy tastes. Myrna Montgomery was her stage name. Her real name was Bertha Birtwhistle, you can see why she changed it.'

He paused for uproarious laughter, and I smiled politely.

'Anyway, she's starring in *A Caravan of Summer Fun*, I'm top of the bill, of course—' Jack winked at me imperceptibly '— and Myrna, Bertha, whatever her name was, she's late every night, rushing off before curtain call... we thought she had a bad bout of shellfish poisoning.'

Pause. I smiled again, though my cheeks hurt.

'Turned out,' Stanley lit a cigarette and exhaled a dragon-roar of smoke and laughter, 'she was only having it away with the manager of the Grand Hotel on the front! We found her out when me wife went to look for her and stumbled upon her, sitting up in the master suite four-poster, bold as brass and naked as the day she were born, with her silky drawers draped over the lampshade.'

'Stanley!' Jack snapped.

'Give over, she's a reporter, she's heard it all,' said Stanley, still choking with laughter.

'I didn't know you were married,' I said, to change the subject.

'Long gone, love,' he said. 'And good riddance. Between Mrs Kerridge and her mother, I was more henpecked than a sack of dried corn. I'm not saying my mother-in-law's fat...' he began.

Jack leaned forward determinedly. 'She's here to talk about Ginny, Stan,' he said. 'So let's do that.'

'She asked!' he said, mock-injured. 'All right, Lady Reporter, what do you want to know?'

'I wondered if you could tell me what you know about Ginny's life outside the theatre,' I said. 'Did she have other friends? Boyfriends, even?'

'Boyfriends!' said Stanley. 'Depends if you count those long streaks of p—'

Jack gave him another look.

'Stage-door Johnnies, we used to call 'em,' Stanley amended. 'Lounge lizards. Course, before the last war it was all top hats and carnations and supper at the Ritz. Now it's Tommies in uniform, barely old enough to shave. Ginny wouldn't look twice at 'em, I can tell you that.'

'How do you know?'

'She's another one with fancy tastes,' he said darkly. 'Too fancy for the likes of me.'

I almost laughed at the idea of beautiful twenty-one-year-old Ginny being charmed by a bluff, rotund comedian in his fifties. Jack was gazing intently at a bumble bee that had landed on the azalea beside us.

'Asked her out once,' Stanley said. 'Back in London.

Thought she might appreciate an evening uptown on the arm of somebody famous, entry to the best restaurants, known on the door at every club in Belgravia. But no. *She makes it a rule not to get too friendly with the cast*, apparently. Funny that, because when it comes to a certain Mr Ferdinand, she seems to have abandoned her rules altogether. Yet there's not even a peck on the cheek for old Stan here.'

Stanley, I now knew, was a bitter and rejected man, suffering from the delusion that his fading fame should render him exquisitely desirable to every beautiful young woman in his orbit. It hadn't occurred to me that Stanley could have been the source of her distress – but what if he'd tried to 'jump on her' as Annie termed it? She and the other nurses had a code for certain doctors with wandering hands – NSIT. 'Not safe in taxis.' Stanley could very definitely be filed under that category.

'When did you last see her?' I asked.

He blew his cheeks out. 'Now you're asking. Saturday morning, was it?' He turned to Jack.

'You left for the theatre quite early,' Jack reminded him.

'I did, I did. That's right. Probably at breakfast.'

'Did she seem all right?' I asked. 'Troubled about anything?'

'I was more interested in Sybil's bacon butties,' said Stanley. 'I can't recall.'

'Did you see her at the theatre that evening, or hear anyone going into her dressing room?'

He screwed up his fleshy face. 'I did hear summat,' he said eventually. 'Must've been the door clicking, something like that. I'd nipped out between acts to have a smoke, and I'd left me fags in the dressing room. I remember I thought, "oh, she's back, like a bad penny", but she wasn't, was she? So it must've been someone else.'

'Did you hear anything else?'

'Like what? Fairy music? Bagpipes?'

'Footsteps,' I said. 'Male or female footsteps.'

'Some of these theatre lads are very light on their feet,' he guffawed.

I waited.

'I couldn't say,' he said. 'But maybe I fancy I did hear high heels – could have been. Or it could have been Flo or JoJo going to their own dressing rooms for something.'

'And that was all?'

'That was all, Officer.' He saluted comically 'I wouldn't turn it into a melodrama, love,' he added. 'As I say, actresses aren't known for their reliability. Fluffy little pretty heads, and no sense in any of 'em. I remember in nineteen-seventeen, there was...'

'I think Miss York probably wants to talk to the others, too,' Jack said. I smiled at him.

'Well, that's me told.' Stanley lifted himself painfully from the wicker seat. 'I know when I'm not wanted. I shall be off to my quarters.'

He ambled indoors, and I heard him shout, 'Any more of those bickies, Daph?'

I felt quite flattened.

'God, look, I'm sorry,' said Jack. 'He's always like this, but he gets even worse when he's talking to a pretty woman.'

I didn't know whether to acknowledge that remark but felt a sudden heat in my cheeks.

'I honestly don't think Stan is likely to be any use to you,' Jack added. 'But I suppose as far as you and the DI are concerned, we're all under suspicion until she's found.'

'Jack,' I said, 'what do you think has really happened to Ginny?'

He sighed heavily. A cloud had slid over the sun and the garden lay in shadow.

'I wish I knew. I suppose I assumed she was having a wonderful time in the show – that was certainly the impression she gave. She came with a superb reputation, marvellous reviews – I felt so lucky to have such a cast to work with, particularly given the circumstances. I was all set for the call-up, though rather dreading it, I admit.' He smiled wryly. 'But then ENSA got in touch, and it seemed such a providential way to do one's bit. I'm far better at directing than I ever would be at fighting.'

'You said you knew Ginny before the war?'

'Oh yes.' Jack nodded. 'I directed her in *Hedda Gabler*. Ginny was so young, but so good. It was a joy to work with her again – even if a "gang show" isn't quite what I'd hoped to be doing.' He laughed.

I smiled at him. Jack was likeable and seemed remarkably straightforward compared to the opacity of the rest of the cast.

I leaned forward. 'Look,' I said, 'between us, do you think Ginny and Guy had a row before she vanished?'

Jack lit a cigarette. 'It's certainly possible. Florence hinted that something was wrong – I dismissed it as her witchy nonsense, but perhaps Ginny had confided. You should probably talk to her.'

'I've tried,' I said. 'Apparently, tarot readers take the Hippocratic oath.'

He laughed again, properly this time.

'She does take her powers terribly seriously, I'm afraid. Perhaps your detective friend can get the truth out of her. Edie...' He suddenly looked embarrassed. 'Or is he... I mean, it's none of my business, of course, I just wondered...'

A pink flush stained Jack's cheekbones.

'Are we together?' I asked.

'I suppose... yes. I just wondered... Ignore me, none of my business, so sorry...'

'No, we're not together,' I said. 'Just friends.'

'Oh!' He ran a hand through his thick hair, and smiled up at me. It was rather contrived, but I smiled back.

'In that case... I don't suppose you'd like to come for lunch or supper with me one day? I don't mean to embarrass you...'

'That's very kind of you,' I said. 'I think perhaps when we find Ginny...'

I felt proud of myself for being so measured, rather than helplessly grateful that a handsome man wanted to buy me a sandwich. I'd learned that lesson the hard way, and I'd never forget it.

'Of course, of course.' Jack nodded violently.

'I'm sorry to ask,' I went on, 'but did you and Ginny ever... I'm not sure how close you are.'

'No,' said Jack. 'She's a darling, but she's not my type. Besides, as a director, I've never thought it wise to involve myself with the actresses in my productions. It can cause all manner of ructions – beginning with jealousy about "preferential treatment" and ending with people storming out.'

'Do you think Ginny stormed out?'

Jack stubbed his cigarette out on the little terrace. 'It would be terribly unlike her. She's such a trouper – not the hysterical type at all.'

'So something has happened to her – in your opinion?'

He paused for a moment, then he looked at me. 'Yes. I hate to say it, Edie, but I really think it has.'

'Good day!' Florence jangled down the steps into the garden, necklaces clashing, breaking the tense silence.

'Hullo, Edie,' she said. 'Still here, I see.'

'I'm worried about Ginny,' I said. 'I expect we all are.'

'I'll leave you to it.' Jack stood up. 'It was lovely to see you, Edie.'

He gave me what Annie would call 'a significant look' and squeezed my shoulder lightly as he passed. I wasn't sure how I felt about Jack. He was handsome, intelligent, thoughtful and he seemed to like me. He was also, I reminded myself, a suspect in Ginny's disappearance – and perhaps in Leonard's death, too.

Florence lowered herself into Jack's vacated seat and rearranged the limp, flowered cushion behind her back.

'Terrible,' she said resonantly. 'Not a word, not a sighting. That poor child.'

'Miss Buchanan,' I said, 'whatever you and Ginny discussed might be very important. Do you think perhaps you could tell me, in confidence?'

She fixed me with her dark eyes.

'I cannot,' she said, 'for supposing Ginny were to come back and discover that I had shared her secrets – whatever would she think of me?'

'But she might have come to harm.'

'Not as a result of anything she told me, I assure you.'

She was a brick wall.

'Perhaps you could tell me something else,' I said. 'How did Ginny get along with the other men – Jack, and Stanley?'

Florence drew in a long breath. 'Well,' she said, 'there was certainly no bad blood with Jack.'

'But...?'

'I believe she and Stanley were not... in sympathy.'

'In what way?'

'He was rather overly keen, I'm afraid. You see, dear,' – she leaned forward, confidingly – 'us older actresses know how to deal with men like him. One simply slaps away a wandering hand and remains friendly. No harm done. But Ginny...' She shook her head.

'What did she do?'

'Well, when Stanley... pressed himself upon her during rehearsals in London, she was terribly cross. Told him exactly what she thought of him, and rather humiliated him in front of the rest of us, I'm afraid.'

Bloody good for Ginny, I thought.

Florence saw my face. 'No, it's no good you see,' she said in a peremptory tone. 'It's all very modern, I'm sure, but a cast is a tight-knit bunch – we simply cannot work properly when there is dissent and bad feeling between us. Ginny should have turned a blind eye and carried on.'

'But she didn't.'

'No, I'm afraid she didn't,' said Florence, 'and whether she was right or wrong,' – I struggled not to interrupt – 'the fact is, she and Stanley were on rather poor terms afterwards. He would not apologise to her, and she utterly refused to let bygones be bygones. I believe Guy had a word with him, and he agreed to leave Ginny alone, once he realised they were... well, you know. *Amants secrets.*'

'And did he?'

'I assume so,' said Florence. 'But if you want to know more, you should probably talk to Sybil. She's known Stanley for many years, she may be able to shed some light.'

'Thank you,' I said. 'I shall.'

'But for goodness' sake, don't make the mistake of thinking poor Stan would hurt anyone,' she added testily. 'It's not a sin for a man to hope, is it?'

As she gathered her fringed wrap around her shoulders, I wondered whether a man might, however, commit a sin when hope was thwarted.

CHAPTER SEVEN

Lunchtime was looming, and as I thanked Florence and made my way back into the kitchen, I found Daphne, monitoring a large frying pan on the Aga. Sausages were spitting in the fat, and the comforting scent made me long for a couple, ideally tucked into a soft bread roll with a dash of English mustard.

'Hullo, dear,' said Daphne, turning and prodding the meat. 'I'm doing a quick lunch for the cast. Want a couple?'

'I can't take your rations!'

'Well, we've got extra at the moment,' she said. She looked embarrassed. 'It's not as if Ginny and Leonard are eating theirs.'

It seemed rather heartless, but she was right. I accepted the offer gratefully, and sat down at the table as the others trickled in, accompanied by the cat, drawn by the unmistakable smell of frying meat.

Sybil appeared last, taking her seat at the head of the long table and the desultory chat turned to clean-up efforts after the London Blitz.

'I feel awfully lucky to have escaped without a scratch,' said Josephine, who sat opposite me. 'Poor Avril – I telephoned, and the doctor said it was a tricky break. They don't know if her leg

will heal properly. She may never be able to dance profession-
ally again.'

A murmur of horror ripped through the cast.

'Ghastly,' said Sybil. 'Without the stage, what can those like
us live for? Though I suppose I've had to manage since my own
days of treading the boards came to an end.'

I wondered why they'd ended, and whether it would be
terribly rude to ask. After all, Florence still acted, despite being
several years older than the landlady. Before I could frame my
question, Guy spoke up.

'Ginny always says the same – that the theatre is everything
to her.' He gazed pensively into the remains of his sausages.

'She told me she wanted to be on the stage from the
moment she was born. Her talent was so enormous – nobody
gets reviews like that at her age, it's quite astonishing how much
the critics lov—'

He was interrupted by a sudden clatter. Daphne had acci-
dentally knocked her plate with her elbow and the last
remaining sausage had dropped to the floor. A streak of white
fur disappeared into the garden, bearing the spoils off to a safe
spot beneath the magnolia.

'Oh, that blasted cat!' she cried, but everyone was laughing.

Under the cover of general hilarity, I turned to Sybil. 'I
wondered if we could have a quick chat,' I said. 'There's something I'd like to ask you about.'

She looked surprised. 'I don't see why not. But I'm afraid
we'll have to do it while I bash the ivories in the front parlour,'
she said. 'I've promised to accompany a young singer we know
at a local fundraiser next week, and I'm terribly rusty. One must
practise.'

'That's quite all right,' I told her, and as the cast began to
disperse back to their rooms, or to soak up the warmth in the
garden over their smokes, she led me through to the room I'd
first seen from the window, and seated herself at the piano.

Sybil launched into a hymn-like tune that I recognised as 'The Ash Grove'.

'Do you sing?' she called over the crashing chords.

'Not really, I—'

'Shame. One should always be able to sing, dance and recite competently – not only does it entertain others, it means one is never bored.'

'I wondered...' I glanced nervously behind me. It seemed the height of bad manners to be airing my suspicions with everyone still in the house. I lowered my voice. 'Do you think perhaps Stanley...'

'What?' she shouted, building to a crescendo. I waited until the final note had died away. Sybil turned to me.

'Stanley,' I said quickly. 'I've heard that he and Ginny were at odds. I believe you know him quite well, and...'

Sybil looked thoughtful for a moment, and her gaze drifted towards a framed *Hamlet* poster, with a drawing of a large and terrifying-looking man and a frail woman in a white dress quailing before him. '*Starring Mr William Currie as The Dane and Miss Sybil Charnwood as Ophelia,*' read the curlicued Edwardian lettering beneath.

'Stanley Kerridge,' murmured Sybil. 'Does anyone really know him? One wonders, frankly. Yes, I have been in proximity to Stanley for many years – he is a regular guest of number twenty-three, most of his work is in the North nowadays, and he has been nothing but loyal...'

She drifted off again.

'But...?' I ventured.

'Well, one doesn't want to cast nasturtiums, as we gardeners say.' She smiled unexpectedly, and the full beauty of her face was suddenly clear – she must have been ravishing in her youth, I realised.

'But... let's just agree that Stanley has an eye for the ladies. I'm too old to appeal to his sort, fortunately, but that's not the

case for little Ginny, I suspect. Reading between the lines, there
was no love lost there – if he entered a room, she'd leave. I
wondered quite how they got through each show, but I assumed
she simply avoided him.'

'Do you think he might have harmed her?'

Sybil gave a long, shuddering sigh, and clenched her hands
on her lap.

'One truly hopes not,' she said eventually. 'But it is peculiar.
In all the years we've been hosting our theatrical guests, not one
has ever disappeared mid-run. And yet, within a week, first
Leonard collapses, and then Ginny vanishes. It's as if the
production is cursed.'

Not another superstitious actor, I thought, but I said, 'I do
hope not. Did Stanley seem quite his usual self to you on
Saturday?'

'I think so,' she said. 'Although he did take his car to the
theatre, which was unusual for him – he doesn't like to leave it
unattended in the town, it's rather his pride and joy.'

Newton Street police station looked unusually cheerful in the
May sunshine, and I was glad I'd decided to come and see Lou
straight after my visit to number twenty-three. The
surrounding bomb damage had been patched up a little, and as
I ran up the steps, I sincerely hoped the gossips were wrong in
their conviction that it was our turn for another battering by the
Germans. 'Britain can take it' was all very well as a slogan, but
actually doing so, yet again, was a prospect that seemed
unbearable.

Though such a blue and shining day outside, it seemed the
weather inside Newton Street remained forever November, and
I shivered in my cotton frock as we passed the barred gate
leading to the cells.

Lou ushered me into his office and took his seat behind the

desk. It was hard to remember, suddenly, that we were friends – here, he bristled with authority.

I told him what everyone had said, and Lou took swift notes in his tidy, copperplate handwriting. When I had finished, he sat back.

'Well,' he said, 'who did you think was lying?'

I laughed in surprise.

'Why do you assume any of them are lying?'

'They're actors,' he said. 'They know how to be convincing. A very young woman on the cusp of dazzling success has seemingly run away, for no apparent reason. She left the whole cast in the lurch on an important night, which she was instrumental in organising, she gave no warning, and she hasn't sent a message, even to her friend Josephine, to let them know she's safe.'

He lit a cigarette and inhaled.

'So either she wants to punish every last one of them, or something's happened to her,' he said through a plume of smoke. 'Personally, having met her, I'm leaning towards the latter explanation. She doesn't seem the vengeful type.'

'But if she and Guy had a row...'

'Which nobody heard? Besides,' said Lou, 'even if they did, she's the sort to turn up to work and take him to task afterwards. I can't see her ruining the evening for everyone, she's a real *show must go on* type.'

I nodded. 'What about the things Florence told her? The darkness around her, all that business?'

'I'd have every bloody charlatan fortune teller in Lancashire arrested if I had my way,' said Lou furiously. 'Have you any idea how many of them have popped up since this war started, peddling lies and mystic bilge to the bereaved? Taking their hard-earned money, promising to contact their little Jimmy who was killed at Dunkirk? *"I've got someone here wearing a uniform, he says he misses Mam, and sends a special pat to the dog. Don't cry, dear, he's happy now."* It's disgusting,' he almost bellowed. 'Exploiting grief, making money from these poor...'

'Lou!' I said. 'I know, it's awful, but Florence isn't one of those people. She thinks she's helping, she doesn't charge.'

'No, she just tells them they're surrounded by darkness and terrible things will happen,' he said. 'And Edie, if you're going to come up with some twittering female rubbish about *"maybe the cards know something we don't"*, you can leave my office, ideally by the coal chute.'

'Of course I'm not!' I felt my temper rising. 'But clearly Ginny believes it – maybe she was so upset, she ran off.'

'Maybe,' said Lou. 'In which case, Miss Sutton has plummeted in my estimation. And anyway, why wait two days? If she was that worried about being engulfed by ectoplasmic doom, she'd have gone that night.'

'Perhaps you're right,' I said. 'I can ask Gloria for news first thing tomorrow. What can we do till then?'

'Wait,' he said grimly, 'and hope she turns up in the meantime. Because if she doesn't, I'm beginning to wonder whether she'll be found alive or dead. And don't – *don't*,' he went on as I opened my mouth to reply, 'quote that ridiculous poem at me. It's not the green eye of the little yellow God that's done for Ginny. More likely the roving eye of the little pan-sticked sod.'

I laughed, and Lou reached for his hat. 'Come on,' he said. 'There's something else I want to talk to you about. I'll stand you a pot of tea if you're game.'

At Bob's Caff nearby, the tiny space was as crowded as ever, and we hovered in the doorway until a helmeted worker stood up, freeing a minuscule marble-topped table. We crammed ourselves in, and over the crashing of plates in the sink and Bob singing 'Someday I'll Find You', which his tone rendered more threat than promise, Lou leaned forward.

'I saw Arnold this morning,' he said. 'He was passing on his way to the mortuary, and he stopped by for a chat.'

Lou broke off to shout our order at Bob, and got a thumbs up.

'Have you heard about his latest... scheme?'

'*Scheme?* No. What do you mean?'

'Right,' Lou sighed. 'I thought as much. Presumably Annie's got no idea...'

'No idea about *what?*'

'Look, don't say anything to her,' said Lou, 'but as you know, our lad Arnold is head over heels for Miss Hemmings. I assume the feeling's mutual.'

'Of course. They're perfect for each other, it's lovely, they're so...'

'Yes, indeed. Well, you'll never guess what Arnold whisked out of his breast pocket to show me. Clue – it belonged to his late grandmother.'

My mind was unusually blank. What, I wondered, could Arnold's dead relation possibly have – then I realised.

'A ring!' I shrieked. 'An engagement ring! Oh, how wonderful! When's he planning to ask her?'

'I suspected you'd react like this,' said Lou mutinously, as Bob banged down our mugs of brick-coloured tea.

'Happily?'

'Excitably. Hear me out, though,' he said, jabbing the air with a teaspoon. 'Is this really the best thing for them both?' He ticked off the points on his fingers. 'Firstly, they've barely been back together for a month. I know it's wartime, but Arnold's in a reserved occupation, there's no rush. Secondly, if they marry, where will they live? Over the bodies in Arnold's family business up in Burnage with his mother? I've met her, and I can tell you, she's not the sort to take kindly to a glamorous young rival for Arnold's affections. Thirdly,' he took a gulp of scalding tea, 'that leaves you high and dry, without a flatmate to share the rent. And also...'

'Hold on,' I said. 'Marriage and children are what Annie's always wanted. And they love each other.'

There was a small part of me, admittedly, feeling both shock and sorrow at the idea that Annie would no longer be living with me, chatting over our meagre dinners and sharing clothes and advice. I had never thought beyond our current situation, and the idea of moving into some 'third girl wanted' set-up with strangers, with forests of stockings drip-drying over the bath and jealously guarded bits of bacon in the pantry, made my heart sink to my boots.

'That's as maybe,' said Lou. 'But the fact is, I think he's rushing into this...'

'Well, if he is, Annie is too,' I said. 'People get married all the time, and they've known each other since last year – I don't understand why you're so against it. Annie was engaged to Pete within weeks of...'

'Exactly!' said Lou as if I'd solved a cryptic crossword.

'Hold on,' I said. 'Are you suggesting that Annie is somehow untrustworthy, simply because she agreed to marry her then-boyfriend, who was about to risk his life?'

'Are you suggesting it wasn't a bad idea? They agreed to go their separate ways long before he was killed.'

'That's nothing to do with it!' I wanted to fling my remaining tea at his fat head.

'Anyway, it's not just that,' said Lou. 'Let's face it, she's a lovely girl, and I know she's your best friend, but she's quite flighty. I don't want to see my pal hurt—'

'Why would she hurt him? She adores Arnold!'

'For now,' said Lou. 'But what about when the next hand-some patient or seductive soldier comes along? Then what?'

'So your objections are nothing to do with it being too soon, or where they'll live,' I said, my heart pounding with rage. 'You simply don't trust Annie, who has never given Arnold the slightest reason to doubt her!'

'It's not a matter of *trust...*' he began.

I dug into my handbag and threw a scatter of coins onto the table, where they bounced and rolled to the floor. 'I'll pay for my own tea,' I snapped. 'Good luck finding Ginny.'

'Edie, come back...' I heard him say, as I flung myself out of the tiny café, but I ignored him and let the door slam behind me, setting the bell jangling like a fire engine. Hot, angry tears stood in my eyes, and I blinked them back so I could find my way to the bus stop.

How dare he? Lou didn't understand Annie's heart, but I had grown up with her, and I knew that all she'd ever wanted was a kind man who truly loved her, and the chance to have lots of babies. Who cared where they'd live, or what Arnold's mother thought, I raged as I stamped through Back Piccadilly. If Annie didn't mind living above the chapel of rest with her mother-in-law, what business was it of Lou Brennan's? My life would change, too, of course, but I wasn't so *damned selfish* as to try and put a spanner in the works of Arnold's proposal. Evidently, Lou had hoped that by appealing to my self-interest, I'd persuade Annie to turn him down. Well, he could whistle. I wouldn't say a word against it, and when Arnold did sink to one knee, proffering the heirloom ring of the Whitings, I would celebrate with Annie, entirely as a best friend should.

'Look!' called Annie, waving a postcard at me as I walked through the door. 'It was pushed under the mat, I only found it when I went down this morning.' It depicted an intricate water-colour of an aeroplane, and I took it from her as I unpinned my hat one-handed and read.

Hullo you two!

Flying going swimmingly – or perhaps I should say airily – and I'm nipping back for Mum's birthday this weekend. May I pop round for tea and chats at about four o' clock on Sunday? No matter if you're out! If in, do feel free to invite half the neighbourhood – I miss seeing people out of WAAF uniform!

With affection,

Clara.

'Oh wonderful!' I exclaimed. 'I'm so glad she's all right. We've still got an hour or so, we'll have to use up the margarine and make some ginger biscuits. We can ask Suki, and I'll nip and telephone Ethel – and what about Joan?'

'Do you think she'd get on with the others?' Annie looked doubtful.

'I think Clara would like her very much,' I said firmly.

Joan, an artist formerly ensconced in a colony of pacifist bohemians, had just moved from the Peak District to Manchester. After Lou and I had found the killer of sculptor Jean-Luc, the remaining artists had packed up and gone their separate ways. Joan had explained that she would be moving to Manchester to live with friends for a while, and we'd agreed to stay in touch.

I had heard from her the previous week – she'd sent a postcard with her address and telephone number, and a small pen and ink sketch of her new home.

'Keep that, it might be worth a fortune one day,' Annie had said.

I ran to the telephone box, and Joan sounded delighted to accept our last-minute invitation. Ethel, too, was greatly relieved to have reason to escape Mother and her vicious parrot, Nelson.

I wanted to invite Marie but couldn't think how to do so

without involving Lou. He was the blockage in every sink, that man, I thought furiously.

By the time I'd been upstairs to see Suki – Agnes Beamish was in, and they were playing Canasta, so I felt I must invite her, too – we had a full complement of guests and a certain dearth of ginger biscuits.

'Well, we'll just have to fill up on soup,' sighed Annie. 'There's a whole sack of lentils going begging in the pantry. I don't think the weevils have got them yet.'

'Gosh, it's just like the Moulin Rouge in *fin de siècle* Paris.'

'You magic fancy buns out of a top hat, then,' she said. 'We haven't even got the coupons for the hat.'

As we laid out our meagre plate of biscuits and stirred the vat of lentil soup on the stovetop, Annie nipped out to the telephone box. Returning, she said, 'Arnold says he'll ring Lou and tell him to ask Marie to join us. I thought you seem to like her, so she must be nice.'

'I'd have invited her myself, but I'm not talking to...' I began, then remembered the reason why, '... to many people at the moment,' I improvised. 'Work's been so busy.'

Annie gave me a curious glance, but said nothing, and to my relief, as I poured the milk into a pottery jug, the doorbell rang.

Ethel was on the step and thrust a bunch of white peonies into my arms. 'I'm so grateful you've got me out of the house, I've brought you a cake, too,' she said, pecking my cheek. She held up a large cream-coloured tin. 'Eggless Victoria sponge, not terribly exciting, but Mother wilfully refuses to eat margarine, so I used up our ration.'

Marie and Clara both arrived at once, and I was required to perform a flurry of introductions.

'How absolutely jolly!' Clara cried. 'I didn't suspect there'd be so many of you marvellous ladies around, we're all so busy these days. What a thrill to talk to people who aren't dressed like Biggles,' she added, squeezing my arm, and Marie, who was wearing a red summer dress tailored to her exquisite figure, laughed in delight.

As we all scrambled upstairs, talking at top volume, the bell rang again, and I pushed back through the *melée* to let Joan in. She looked magnificently stylish in tweed trousers and a short-sleeved white blouse, her bobbed hair swept back into a flame-orange silk scarf.

'Edie!' she cried. 'In much happier circumstances than the last time we met! I'm so glad you asked me to come, look, I've brought a big jar of meat paste and some wonderful bread that my friend Elizabeth has made, she's a superb baker.'

Joan handed me the still warm, fragrant loaf wrapped in its white cloth as reverently as if she were passing over a swaddled new-born, and I took it just as carefully and clasped it to my bosom.

Upstairs, Annie had wound the gramophone, and a brass-heavy tune was playing, while Suki had arrived downstairs with Agnes and was pouring sherry into teacups.

Our table was suddenly heaped with food. Ethel's sponge cake, the meat paste, the loaf, a large tin of toffee and a pile of decadently sugared buns had joined our shrivelled biscuits.

Annie and I glanced at the food and each other, gleeful as five-year-olds. The atmosphere was light and giddy with the joy of women together, talking and laughing.

'Clara,' I said, over the music. She had gravitated to the window and was chatting animatedly to Annie. 'I'd like you to meet my artist friend.' I steered her over to where Joan was deep in conversation with Agnes and Suki.

'Joan,' I said, when Suki turned to reach for a bun, 'meet Clara. She flies aeroplanes!'

Joan looked round, an expression of polite greeting fixed on her elegant face. She took in Clara's beaming grin, her height, her wild curly hair, and her social smile fell away as their eyes met. I stepped back. As I'd later tell Annie, I really didn't want to get in the way of a moment they would both always remember.

Two hours later, the tea party was still in full swing, and I was perched on the arm of the sofa talking to Ethel.

'I do like him so,' she was saying, 'I just wish it wasn't all letters, and we could spend some proper time together. Mind you, he should get leave in a few weeks, he thinks...'

A few weeks earlier, Ethel had met Ian Carmichael, an officer with the Scots Guards, and was now embroiled in a long-distance letter-writing romance.

She had, she'd just told me, put a deposit down on a 'shoebox couple of rooms' in West Didsbury, and Mother was having conniptions.

'Telling her was probably the worst thing I've ever had to do,' Ethel shouted over the blare of horns coming from Count Basie on the gramophone. Suki was jigging round the rug with Annie and Marie, her hair falling out of its combs, shrieking with laughter. I thought of how she had looked when she'd first arrived on the doorstep after escaping her violent husband Frank, and my heart lifted.

I was getting up to make a fresh pot of tea when the door-bell rang again, its shrillness cutting through the music.

'I'll go!' said Agnes, who had sunk several teacups of sherry and was now swaying happily and clicking her fingers, despite her classical quartet background.

A few moments later, she returned, looking puzzled.

'Edie?' Agnes called. 'This lady says she knows you, I expect it's all right to let her in?'

I turned round, the teapot in my hand, to see Josephine Gardner standing in the doorway, her skin pale against her crimson lipstick.

'Josephine!' I said, startled. 'Come along in! I think there's still some paste and toast, and a bit of sherry in the—'

'I shan't stay, Edie,' said Josephine. 'DI Brennan told me where to find you. I've not come to gate-crash, I promise, but I need to tell you something important, and I don't think it can wait until tomorrow. It's about Ginny.'

CHAPTER EIGHT

I led Josephine through to our little kitchen and put the kettle on the hob, then I sat opposite her at the tiny fold-out table and kicked the door closed. Beyond it, a raucous sing-song had started up, and something that sounded alarmingly like the beginnings of a conga. 'Join on, team!' I heard Agnes shout, followed by the grinding scrape of furniture being shoved aside. I felt deeply thankful that Mrs Turner was at her sister's.

'What's happened?'

Josephine shook her head. 'I'm so sorry to barge in like this, I didn't know what else to do.' She took a long, shuddering breath. 'I don't know what to think about it, but it makes a nonsense of the idea that Ginny ran away.'

I sat forward in my chair. 'Tell me.'

In the living room, somebody shouted 'to the left, girls!' and there was a great, centipede-like thunder of feet.

'I've just been to the theatre – there's no show on a Sunday, but I needed to get out of number twenty-three, there's the most appalling atmosphere. Stanley and Guy are barely speaking, Florence seems to be in a fugue state, and without Leonard or

Ginny, it's simply miserable.' She sighed and put her hand against her head.

'Anyway, the cleaner recognised me and let me in, and I went backstage, just wanting to be on my own for a bit,' she went on. 'I passed Ginny's dressing room, and I thought, supposing she's taken something from there – I had a queer feeling that her clothes might all be gone, and I should check.'

'But she was last seen at the digs,' I said, confused.

'I know. I can't explain why I looked, really. Perhaps I just felt I ought to be doing something more to try and find her. Anyway, that was when I saw it.'

She paused.

'All her clothes were there, her bits and bobs, her make-up... nothing was gone. But something extra had appeared.'

'What?'

'Her bracelet,' Josephine said. 'The charm bracelet Ginny never, ever takes off – she's convinced bad luck will befall her if she does, and the only time she doesn't wear it is on stage, because it tinkles so – well, it was on her dressing table. None of the charms seemed to be missing, and it wasn't broken. So, Edie, tell me – am I going quite, quite potty, or does it suggest to you that Ginny left number twenty-three as intended, arrived at the theatre – and then something inexplicable happened to her?'

I stared at Josephine. 'When you say she never takes it off...' I began.

'I mean never. She added a charm to it recently, I think Guy had given it to her, and she said, "Honestly, JoJo, I truly believe it brings me luck. I hate even taking it off to go on stage." She's a wonderful girl, but very superstitious – silly, I know, but it's not uncommon with actors. A performance can go so wrong, and be so terrifying, we lean on these little comforts to help us through the nerves.'

'But Ginny wasn't nervous, you said,' I observed. 'I thought she never suffered from stage fright.'

'She doesn't,' said Josephine. 'But perhaps she has other things to be worried about.'

'Guy?'

She shrugged. 'All I know is that she would never have willingly taken it off unless she believed she was about to go on stage.'

'Did you look to see whether her stage clothes for the first scene were gone? Or if her green wrap, the one that Guy said she had on, was hanging up?'

'No, her stage clothes were there, but her wrap wasn't.'

'Can you remember exactly where you found the bracelet?'

'It was in a little trinket dish, just by her make-up box,' said Josephine. 'As you know, she's quite tidy – nothing was out of place, but it was where she always puts it while she's on stage. Then she fastens it back on when she's dressing after the show.'

'Could she have forgotten? She was awfully upset about Leonard, and you were all in and out of rehearsals all day on Friday...'

'Well, that's what I thought at first,' Josephine agreed. 'But you see, Florence told me that Ginny was wearing her bracelet on Saturday morning. They were talking about the tarot reading she'd had, and Ginny said, "Well, at least I've got this," and lifted her wrist to show Florence.'

'Did Florence say what the reading was about?'

'No. "Love" was all she'd tell me. It's not hard to work out, though, is it? Ginny was obviously hoping that Guy would leave Rosemary and run off with her. I suppose Florence must have told her that he wouldn't.'

'Would that be reason enough for her to run away?'

'But where to?' Josephine asked. 'Her father's dead and I know she can't bear her mother. Unless she's back with Avril in London, I can't imagine where she'd go, and ENSA wages don't stretch to an hotel.'

I nodded. 'And she didn't take anything but her handbag.'

'But she left the bracelet,' said Josephine. 'Oh, it's such a ludicrous puzzle!' she added furiously. 'I feel quite cross with her, putting us through all this. I hope to hell she's got a decent explanation when she finally turns up.'

'If she does,' I said gently.

Josephine's eyes filled with tears. 'I know,' she said. 'It's just easier to be cross with her than to think the worst. I can't bear it otherwise.'

I laid my hand over hers.

'I promise I'll do everything in my power to find her,' I said, as the kettle whistled violently.

Josephine stood up.

'I know you will,' she said, 'and I trust DI Brennan, too, and Marie. Between us all, surely we can find her.'

She pulled her gloves back on, and shook my hand.

'Thank you, Edie,' she said. 'It's a relief to have told somebody.'

I saw her out and returned to the party, fresh worries swirling in my mind.

To my frustration, Gloria was slightly late for work the following day. She slid behind her desk at five to nine, meaning I had no chance to speak to her before Mr Gorringe's morning rounds. I scribbled a note, and as he led the troops into morning conference, I threw it haphazardly at her desk. Puzzled, she glanced at me, then unfolding the paper, gave a swift nod. Five minutes later, we were huddled in a cubicle in the Ladies', Gloria reeking of Arpège.

'Go on, then,' she said. 'What's the big mystery?'

I explained what had happened – that Ginny was missing, and we thought she might be with Avril, back in London. Gloria's riveted expression reminded me of cinema-goers watching the climactic shoot-out, and it occurred to me that the story of Ginny's disappearance would be all round the news-room within minutes.

'Keep it under your hat,' I added belatedly. 'We don't know for sure that she's actually vanished yet.'

'Well,' Gloria breathed, 'sounds like she might have. Our Av rang up last night and she said she was wondering whether to let out Ginny's room as she's going straight on to Africa after the Manchester shows. She was worried she'd be letting her down, but I said, well, if she's not using it, make a few bob, Av, to pay the doctors you need, and chuck 'em out when she's back.'

'So she definitely wasn't there last night.' I felt a heaviness settle on me. 'I think it's time to get the police properly involved.'

My next onerous task was to telephone Lou, and I had no choice but to do it while Mr Gorringe and Janet Paulson were safely trapped in conference.

Closing my eyes, I asked Olive on the switchboard to put me through, and waited to hear his irritable tones in my ear.

'Morning, Edie,' he said, when the call connected. 'Before you say anything else, I must apologise. I was being judgemental and unfair, and I wish I could take back the things I said. I'm very sorry, and I truly think Arnold will be lucky to have Annie as his wife.'

I was so taken aback, it briefly crossed my mind to wonder whether this was somebody doing a clever imitation of Lou, while the real version was tied up in a cell, shrieking for help through a gag.

'What's brought this on?'

'Marie gave me a good dressing down when I told her you'd stormed out of Bob's,' he admitted. 'Told me I was being pig-headed and patronising and that both you and Arnold know Annie far better than I do. When my sister came in last night, apart from reeking of crème de menthe and forgetting where the bathroom was, she was extremely voluble on the subject.'

I laughed, despite my lingering anger. 'She's right, Annie is a gem. And Arnold knows that, even if you don't.'

'I agree,' said Lou. 'I hope you can forgive me. I don't want our friendship ruined because of my idiocy – and more importantly, I need you to help me find Ginny.'

It was business as usual, then. Nevertheless, I was vaguely aware of my spirits lifting, as though a curtain had been drawn back to let light pour in.

'I forgive you,' I said. 'Although you *were* thoroughly obnoxious. Your sister is much nicer. And she can Lindy-hop.'

'I must work on my technique,' Lou said. 'Now, tell me what you've discovered.'

I rattled through an explanation of Josephine's visit and the doubt cast on both Guy and Stanley, uncomfortably aware of Pat ear-wigging at the next desk, and Gloria ostentatiously shuffling papers beside her. As I looked round, the door of the conference room opened, and Mr Gorringe emerged, glancing keenly across the office to make sure all was well in his kingdom.

I placed my hand over the receiver as the editor appeared by my desk.

'Leonard Lessiter,' he said. 'Your obituary is due today.'

'Yes, sir. It will be with Janet this afternoon.'

He nodded. 'Very good. I trust it will illuminate the full panoply of his career on the stage.'

'Edie?' Lou shouted into the receiver. 'Are you there?'

Mr Gorringe looked at me. 'Somebody appears to require an urgent discussion,' he said. 'I shan't keep you.'

'Can you bunk off work this afternoon?' Lou said loudly, as my editor strode off. 'Until she's formally reported missing, I can't open an investigation – besides, Sergeant O' Carroll's got his hands full with George Chivers and his merry men. I need your help.'

I longed to revel in Lou finally admitting that I was useful – that, God forbid, he might even need my skills.

'You need to get to the theatre and have a good poke about,' he said, 'before I go back to Grafton Street and read the riot act to our fragile thespians.'

'What am I looking for, exactly?'

'Anything that suggests Ginny was at the theatre on Saturday night, before the tribute show. Speak to the stage-door feller, anyone hanging about, the manager – you can say it's for an article. Try not to put the fear of God into them, though. I don't want it all over the papers until we know more.'

I had already decided to tell any suspicious colleagues that I was out interviewing for a new obituary. I pushed the thought that I really might be to the back of my mind.

When I arrived at the theatre, a light rain falling, it seemed to be closed – the doors to the foyer were locked. I made my way down the side of the building, to the sign reading 'stage door', and knocked lightly. There was no answer, but I spotted a bell half-concealed behind the frame, presumably to deter eager fans, and pressed it.

The door was opened by an ancient man dressed in a powder-blue uniform encrusted with gold frogging, fringed epaulettes and a peaked cap. He looked as though he should be in a Gilbert and Sullivan operetta, playing the Major-General of Moldovia.

'Yes?' he said, peering at me.

'I'm Miss Edie York,' I said. 'I'm from the *Manchester Chronicle*, I'm just writing the obituary of Leonard Lessiter, and I – we – were hoping to have a word with theatre staff about their reminiscences of the great actor.'

He stared at me beadily. 'Might you be a "fanatic", attempting to gain entry under false pretences?'

'No!' I felt insulted. 'I was here when Leonard collapsed, and I'm a reporter...'

It was only half a lie, I told myself. 'If I could perhaps come in, I'm quite happy to find my own way about...'

'I'm sure you are,' said the man. 'Mr Wallis Middleton, stage-door manager since eighteen ninety-seven. I've met a great many reporters in my time, Miss York, and very few of them look like you.'

'There's a war on,' I said. 'Women are doing all kinds of jobs.'

'More's the pity,' he muttered.

'If you won't let me in, I shall have to let my editor, Mr Gorringe, know,' I said. 'He won't be at all happy, as he's expecting a full piece on Mr Lessiter. I was hoping to interview you, in fact.'

'Me?' He looked startled.

'You must have seen some marvellous performances over the years,' I said. 'Your own recollections could make the piece.'

I waited, as his desire for attention wrestled with his need to enforce the rules.

'You'd best come in, then,' he said. 'But don't be bothering the cleaners, they've a job to do.

'I know the stage manager, Mr Tremlett, is in a meeting for the next half-hour,' he said. 'I can ask him if he'll speak to you after that. I've some business to attend to.' He indicated a ledger of spidery writing on his small desk. 'In the meantime, I suggest you make your way to the foyer. There's another lady there, waiting for her husband to arrive. I trust you shan't disturb her.'

He pointed down a corridor towards the stairs. In the foyer, the harsh overhead lights were switched on, entirely robbing the area of its lamp-lit evening romance, and a cleaner in a flowered apron and hairnet was running a carpet-sweeper over the blue pile, creating stripes worthy of a royal lawn and humming tunelessly to herself. The box office was closed, but there was a small cluster of Art Deco armchairs beside the stairs, shaded by the large fern where Josephine had concealed herself, and in one of them sat a blonde woman who glanced up from her book as I approached. I saw that she was reading *Greenmantle* by John Buchan, an adventure story I'd thoroughly enjoyed some years before.

'Gripping, isn't it?' I asked, taking a seat opposite her.

'Mm. I suppose so.'

Her voice was clipped and carried the strangulated vowels of the upper classes. She could only have been in her early thirties, but she was dressed in the style of a much older woman, in a camel-coloured fine woollen suit with a glinting diamond brooch pinned to the collar, a very expensive-looking felt hat and cream, kid-leather shoes. From what little I knew of fashion, her handbag appeared to be a gleaming, crocodile-leather Hermés.

Her demi-waved hair was the natural blonde of the Scandinavians, and her eyes were blue, but in contrast to Ginny's fair loveliness, this woman had a sour downturn to her vermilion lips, and her pencilled eyebrows had been plucked into little peaks of angry surprise.

'How d'you do? I'm Miss Edie York,' I said. 'I'm writing an obituary of Leonard Lessiter for the *Chronicle*. Awful, isn't it?'

'Dreadful,' she said, turning a page without reading.

'Are you waiting for somebody?' I asked.

'I am,' she said.

I felt interviewing a blood-filled stone would be easy in comparison. 'Might I ask, is it one of the ENSA cast?'

'I suppose you might. It is, as a matter of fact. Do you know them?'

'Yes, I do, I met them recently, through a friend of mine, Marie Archibald.' I noticed that my vowels had become slightly elongated, as though her own aristocratic accent was engulfing my own.

'Oh, Admiral Archibald's wife?'

Her entire manner altered, and she laid her book aside. 'Such a *charming* woman. I believe she was injured in the appalling bombing in London. I do hope she is quite recovered now?'

'I saw her yesterday,' I said, deciding not to mention that at the time, Marie had been scoffing a sugar bun and limbo-dancing under a walking stick held aloft by Annie and Agnes Beamish. 'She is very much improved, thank you.' I wondered how long I could continue speaking like a character in an Austen novel, and whether she'd notice if I stopped.

The woman leaned forward, proffering a gloved hand.

'Rosemary Ferdinand, née Court-Chambers,' she said. 'Well, Lady Court-Chambers, strictly speaking, but one's title seems rather *de trop* in wartime, I feel.'

She was Guy's wife – and she had fallen straight into my lap, like a poisoned apple.

'You're waiting for Guy?'

'Yes, that's correct,' she said, 'I came up after reading about Leonard's death in *The Times*. I knew Guy would be distraught, and I felt I must visit.'

'Are you staying at Grafton Street?'

Rosemary gave a huff of disparagement.

'Hardly. Have you been? According to Guy, it's the absolute end – he strongly advised me not to bother.'

I bet he did, I thought grimly.

'No, I've taken a room at the Midland Hotel,' she went on. 'I've been here since Friday, I drove straight up when I heard the awful news, but of course, Guy's been so terribly busy with the tribute show, so I motored over to Alderley Edge to see my dear friends, the Clissinghams. Do you know them? I used to hunt with Pinky Clissingham. They have a rather lovely Queen Anne manor – Holmesworth Fold – where they breed racehorses. I believe the King came up to visit their stud-farm before the war, he was rather impressed, apparently...'

I nodded along as if I knew the first thing about the Clissinghams or racehorses, but my mind was on a different track entirely. If Rosemary had been in Manchester since Friday, she could very easily have seen Ginny at the theatre on Saturday.

'Did you come to the tribute?' I asked. 'Marie didn't spot you in the audience, but then, it was packed...'

'Oh no, I'm afraid I didn't,' said Rosemary. 'It's the most dreadful confession, but I simply cannot bear the theatre. I know one's supposed to enjoy it, but frankly, it bores me rigid. All those idiots striding about in fancy dress, solemnly pretending to be someone else, and we're all meant to go along with it. Give me a gleaming horse and a pack of hounds any day.'

'But Guy...'

'Oh heavens, I know.' She rolled her eyes. 'Acting keeps him happy, and I suppose ENSA cheers the troops up nowadays. But no, my dear, I did not marry him for his acting skills.'

I wondered why she had married him, but she was not forthcoming.

'I dined at the hotel last night,' she added. 'Rather good, surprisingly. One doesn't imagine that an industrial Northern city like this would offer reasonable food, but it was remarkably edible.'

I bristled silently.

'Anyway, my plan now is to meet Guy here, have a late lunch somewhere, and rescue him from the horrors of Grantham Street, albeit briefly,' she said, flicking open a mirrored compact and examining her lipstick as she spoke.

'Grafton,' I corrected, thinking of Sybil's carefully framed playbills and sweet peas, and Daphne's lovingly made lumpy biscuits.

'Hardly matters what we call it,' she said. 'He can stay in my suite this evening and enjoy a few luxuries if he likes. I find it rather ludicrous that he pretends to muck in with the young hoofers in "digs", don't you? The man has monogrammed slippers, for goodness' sake.'

I almost said, 'I know'. I wondered whether Rosemary suspected his feelings for Ginny.

'Did you hear that Ginny Sutton has gone missing?' I asked.

Rosemary did not say, '*Who?*'

'Missing?' she repeated. 'Whatever can you mean?'

The cleaner was now banging her Ewbank into the chair legs near us and singing 'Boogie Woogie Bugle Boy' in a cheery warble. Rosemary gave her a look of such froideur, she immediately backed into the giant fern.

'Perhaps you could do that somewhere else,' said Rosemary.

'So sorry, madame,' she whispered.

I tried to catch the poor woman's eye with a silent apology, but she had disappeared behind the stairs.

I told Rosemary, briefly, what had happened – that Ginny had not turned up for the tribute performance on Friday night, and that there had been no sign of her since.

'Good Lord,' she said. 'These flighty girls, I do wonder they manage to get work on the stage at all. They're so appallingly unreliable.'

'Oh no,' I said. 'I don't believe Ginny is like that. In fact, it's beginning to seem that something may have happened to her. Josephine Gardner thinks she returned to the theatre on Saturday, just before the show. She left something of hers in the dressing room, but then she vanished.'

Rosemary stared at me. Her unmoving eyes reminded me of glass marbles.

'Charm bracelet?'

'How do you know?'

She smiled tightly. 'Guy asked my advice on where to buy a good luck charm for her. I told him to try Liberty's. I hardly imagined the great jewellery houses of Bond Street would offer such things.'

Rosemary had seen my expression. 'Oh dear, yes, I suppose it is all terribly unromantic and practical to a young woman such as yourself, who I imagine dreams of stardust and moonlight trysts,' she said. 'But I'm perfectly aware that Guy enjoys certain... liaisons when he's away on tour. He's a typical male, I'm afraid, and there will always be some tawdry little actress making cow-eyes at a handsome and well-connected man. It's pure flattery, nothing more.'

I decided to ignore her remark about moonlight trysts. 'So... you know about Guy and Ginny?'

'What is there to know?' She extracted a long cigarette from a slim gold case, and as she flicked it closed, I noticed a delicate inscription inside the lid, a looping G. It looked oddly familiar.

'A little *cinq-a-sept affaire* is nothing,' she went on. 'As long as she's sensible enough not to try and trap him, the tour ends, Guy comes home, the caravan moves on and the girl goes back to her squalid "digs" with, one presumes, a few happy memories to keep her warm. My only concern is blackmail,' she added. 'But I trust that Guy isn't foolish enough to engage with the sort of classless tart who might resort to that kind of thing.'

I tried to move my face normally. 'Do you never worry that... well, if one of them were to have a baby...?'

'Good Lord, no,' she said. 'Guy knows perfectly well that if any little gold-digger comes crawling and the child is his, he'll be cut from my inheritance faster than you could snip a ribbon. One assumes he takes that into account.'

'I see,' I said. 'And you've never met Ginny?'

'I may turn a blind eye,' she said, 'but I do choose not to fraternise with these types.'

As she tapped ash from her cigarette, the door to the stairs opened and a tall, suited figure appeared.

'Darling!' he cried, seeing Rosemary, then he halted as he saw me and realised that I was talking to his wife.

I smiled in greeting, and he recovered himself and bent to kiss her cheek. But I had seen the fleeting expression that crossed his face – and it was one of dread.

CHAPTER NINE

After five fruitless minutes with stage manager Mr Tremlett – 'No, I don't recall seeing the young woman at all after Friday rehearsals, I was engaged in a very important meeting with our lighting engineer...' – I made my way back downstairs before something struck me. I only had Josephine's word for it that the charm bracelet had been left in the dressing room on Saturday, and her recollection that Florence had seen Ginny wearing it that morning. But memory was unreliable, I knew that. Perhaps Ginny had in fact forgotten it after Thursday's performance or Friday's rehearsals, due to the shock of Leonard's death. I turned and ran back up to the foyer. Rosemary and Guy had left, but the beleaguered cleaner was now polishing the chrome posts of the staircase. She had stopped humming.

'Excuse me,' I said, 'may I have a quick word?'

She turned, the cloth in her hand.

'Sorry I troubled your friend earlier,' she said flatly. 'If I may, miss, could I very kindly ask you not to complain to the manager, it shan't happen again, and I need this job...'

'Oh gosh, no, it's not that at all,' I said. 'It's just – I wondered, do you clean the dressing rooms?'

'I clean everywhere,' she said. 'It's just me and young Doris now, we do the lot.'

'Might you have cleaned Ginny Sutton's dressing room in the last few days?'

'The little blonde thing what's missing? Odd, isn't it? I'm Norma, by the way.'

'Edie. I'm looking into her disappearance for the *Chronicle*.' In fact, I was looking into it unpaid, and risking my job yet again, for Lou Brennan.

'Ooh, the newspaper?' She leaned against the stair post. 'I had a deaths announcement in there last year, for our Mam. *The Lord looked down and whispered "come", the gates, they opened, and in walked Mum.* Beautiful, isn't it?'

'Lovely,' I lied. 'I wondered if you could remember whether you cleaned Ginny's dressing room on Friday and Saturday?'

'I did that,' she agreed. 'We dust round daily. Polish the mirrors. You wouldn't believe some of the rubbish these actors leave lying about.'

'Did you clean Leonard Lessiter's after...'

Norma shuddered. 'No,' she said. 'I don't like to intrude in the circumstances. I'll wait for instructions, and Doris won't go near it, she swears it'll be haunted now.'

I nodded solemnly. 'Norma, when you cleaned Ginny's dressing room on Saturday, what time was it?'

'It'd be early afternoon,' she said. 'We do the main public areas, then the backstage area. I do the dressing rooms. So yes, about two or so.'

'Do you recall seeing a charm bracelet on Ginny's dressing table?'

I held my breath.

'It's funny you say that,' she said. 'It wasn't there then, that I do know. I give all the dressing tables a good polish at the end of the week, they're always stained with greasepaint and bits of cottonwool and I don't know what. So I'd have noticed, but it was all tidy as usual. Not like Miss Buchanan,' she added. 'You can't find the bleeding surfaces to clean them in her hovel, 'scuse my language. I popped back in today late morning, as there's no show on Sunday, we get round quicker Mondays – everything was just as I'd left it, but there was a little silver bracelet by the mirror. So I thought she must've been back.'

She shot me a nervous glance. 'It's not gone missing, has it? I'm not a thief, miss.'

'Oh no,' I said, 'nothing like that.'

'I hope she turns up soon,' said Norma. 'Never known an actress leave in the middle of a run before.'

I thanked her, and retreated the way I'd arrived. Wallis Middleton was lurking in his tiny cubicle by the stage door.

'Get what you needed?'

'I did,' I said. 'It was very useful.'

'I've been considering my own recollections,' he said. My heart sank, anticipating an exhaustive litany of the great and good's stage appearances over the past century.

'Miss Sutton,' he said. 'She always came in the stage door, like the others. Actors sign in and out, you see, in case of fire or air raids, then we know they're backstage.' He held up the spidery ledger.

'Been looking through this. She signed in on Thursday, see,' he pointed to a page, and I saw the neat signature – *G. Sutton, 4.10 p.m.*

'Signed out for supper, then again after the show when Mr Lessiter passed away, 11.35 p.m.' He pointed. 'She was with Miss Buchanan, I remember. And then Friday, rehearsals in the afternoon, and Saturday, nothing.' He flicked the pages as if to prove he was telling the truth. I saw Guy's own signature from earlier on, the looping G and F.

'That's very helpful,' I said. 'But would you have been here all the time? Could anyone get in if you'd nipped out for a minute?'

'Nobody,' he said with satisfaction. 'The stage door is never unattended when unlocked, miss.'

'She could have come in at the front, with the public?'

'Why should she do that?' he asked. 'She's no reason to, when she can come this way.'

I walked back to the office, passing a gaggle of fire wardens hosing down the smoking crater from a small incendiary on Corporation Street. I was so used to stray bombs now, I barely noticed. My mind was filled with questions over Ginny and her bracelet.

If she hadn't been back to the theatre on Saturday, as Wallis Middleton insisted, then somebody else had left the bracelet there – but why? And if she had, why would she enter and leave through the main doors, only to then sneak backstage, avoiding everyone? Perhaps she had left something important in her dressing room, I thought, and needed to snatch it up without being seen before she left. But if she had secretly come by the theatre, why leave her precious bracelet? Unless... Guy had bought her the last charm it held, I remembered. A black cat. Perhaps this was Ginny's way of telling him it was all over.

I had to find out whether Guy and Ginny had rowed on Saturday. He said not, and nobody had heard them – but a row could be quiet as well as loud. I remembered the terror Mr Pugh at the home had struck into us, when we were beckoned to his office. His Welsh accent would grow stronger, but the volume would decrease the angrier he became, until he was almost whispering with furious contempt.

When I returned from work that evening, I heard the upstairs door bang and Suki calling, 'Edie, is that you? Can I come down?'

'Of course,' I yelled. 'I'll stick the kettle on.'

She skittered downstairs and threw herself into an armchair. 'No Annie?'

'She's on nights,' I said, 'I think she's just left.'

'Oh, that's good,' said Suki. 'Have you any toast?'

'Bit stale, but if you're game, I am,' I said, lighting the grill. 'Why's it good that Annie's out?'

'I need to talk to you privately.'

Not another private chat, I thought. I was getting very tired of being urged to keep other people's secrets.

I made the tea and toast with the last scrapings of the meat paste, and joined her.

'What's up?'

'Oh Edie, I feel silly even saying it, it's been weeks, I know...' She sighed. 'I just keep thinking I've seen Frank near Madame Faye's. I nipped out for a cigarette the other day, and there was a man turning the corner who had just his build – those big shoulders and little muscly legs. You don't think it *was* him, do you?'

She took a bite of toast, and crunched at speed, her huge brown eyes fixed on me.

'I hope not. How would he know where you were, Suki? He never even knew I'd been to see you, let alone where I live. And I doubt he'd ever think of looking in all the hair salons in Manchester.'

'I know,' she said, 'but when we were married, I once told him that Madame Faye had offered me a job, and perhaps he remembered. It was during a row,' she added. 'He said I'd starve without him, and I said Madame Faye wouldn't let me starve because she said I could have a job any time... I wish I'd kept my big gob shut now, I can tell you.'

I felt a pulse of fear. Frank Sullivan was surely the type to store personal information that he could one day use to his advantage.

'Even if he does come in,' I said, more bravely than I felt, 'Madame won't let him near you. Surely he wouldn't cause a violent scene in a hair salon.'

'Wouldn't he, though? You haven't met Frank. I don't know, Edie,' she said. 'I just have a sense of unease all the time, as though he's watching, biding his time. I can't settle.'

'Will you see about a divorce?'

'I wouldn't know where to begin,' she said. 'Solicitors and people in wigs and forms to fill in... I wish he'd just drop dead, I really do.'

'Here's hoping,' I said. 'But Suki, if you feel afraid getting the bus to work, one of us will go with you to the stop – and I'm sure one of the others at the salon will see you home.'

'Oh, Agnes has already offered,' said Suki. 'She's a saint, that woman. But I can't turn everyone's lives upside down because I've got a vague feeling. I'm just being daft. Anyway, guess what?'

I put my cup down. 'What?'

'Agnes has got a sewing machine, and I've been running up a few things for her on it – she showed them off to the ladies in the classical quartet and now they want me to make their dresses, and they'll pay me!'

I beamed. 'Suki, that's wonderful! I had no idea you were so talented at dressmaking.'

'Well, I had to be,' she said. 'Frank wouldn't give me money for nice things, but he always wanted me to look like a Holly-wood starlet when we went out.'

'Could you make clothes for me and Annie?' I asked eagerly. 'Of course, we'd pay. It's just a matter of finding the fabric... soon, we may hardly be able to get anything at the draper's, so I don't know...'

'Ah,' Suki said, 'fear not, Agnes has masses. She's got all her old sheets and pillow slips from before the war, and a whole wardrobe of twenties dresses she says will never fit her again. I can easily rework them.'

I ran to get Annie's copy of *Vogue*, and we were poring over the latest 'Wartime Modes' when the doorbell rang.

In the excitement, I had entirely forgotten my offer to tell Lou everything.

'I'm off upstairs anyway,' Suki said. 'Aggie's doing fried kippers in oatmeal. Come up soon, and we'll try on the dresses. I'll get my pincushion out!'

I waved her off and went to let Lou and Marple in, feeling rather like the arrivals board at London Road Station.

There had been no sign of Mrs Turner for several days now, so I beckoned them upstairs, and filled the kettle again, donating the very last of the stale bread to Marple, who swallowed it in a single gulp.

I filled Lou in on all I'd discovered, which took far longer than I'd imagined, because he kept interrupting with questions and expressions of disgust.

'I've no idea why people think the aristocracy is something to aspire to,' he said. 'Most of the time, they behave like a Hogarth painting come to life.'

'I can't imagine Rosemary Court-Chambers on Gin Lane,' I said. 'Sherry Avenue, perhaps.'

Lou laughed.

'I think Josephine was telling the truth about the bracelet,' I added, 'but Rosemary was a bit terrifying, frankly, and I do wonder how she really feels about her and Guy's little "arrangement".'

'I expect Marie will have chapter and verse on her deepest emotions,' said Lou. 'She's like the Preston forensics laboratory when it comes to other people's marriages. Talking of which, she wants to buy you lunch, to thank you for the "simply marvellous party". When are you free? I'll let her know.'

'How's tomorrow?' I asked. 'I can ask her more about Rose-mary and Guy.'

'Done,' said Lou. 'Lyons' Corner House, one o'clock?'

'Fine. But I won't have ages...'

'Marie is quite capable of talking at double speed, so no trouble there.'

He clicked his fingers to Marple. 'We're off. Oh, by the way,' he said. 'Arnold informs me he's booked a table for two at Les Frères de la Côte on Saturday night. You might want to tell Annie to practise her "thrilled" expression for when he does the deed.'

'Oh! It's really going to happen!' I cried. 'This is wonderful! I shan't say a word, I'm quite sure Arnold would want his proposal to be a surprise.'

'I agree,' said Lou, manoeuvring a reluctant Marple onto the landing, 'Though I imagine his knocking knees might give it away.'

Marie was already tucked into a corner table when I arrived at Lyons' Corner House, dressed in her glorious striped silk suit. I wondered whether she would enjoy using Suki's dressmaking services. As I approached, she was finishing off a long letter, which she signed with a flourish, blotted and tucked into an envelope in one seamless movement.

'Edie!' she cried, 'What perfect timing you have, I've just finished my weekly letter to the children. I've been telling them all about Ginny, and the ENSA cast – they'll love to read about all the mystery. Well, Clive will,' she added, seeing my doubtful face. 'Frances will only be interested in the dancer with the broken leg. Honestly, she's obsessed with the ballet. Springing off the furniture night and day, pirouetting into the bath...'

She sighed. 'Gosh, I do miss them. But it's a comfort to

know they're safely tucked away in Devon, rather than dodging shrapnel with us lot.'

The 'nippy' waitress handed us menus. Her uniform really did look quite similar to my eveningwear, bar the frilled cap.

'I think a fish mayonnaise for me, please,' said Marie, 'and a pot of tea.'

'I'll have the same.'

Marie leaned towards me, raising her voice over the sound of the three-piece band thumping away on the small stage.

'Tell me everything,' she said, and I attempted to *précis* the previous day's revelations over a ponderous rendition of Ernest Tubb's 'Walking the Floor Over You'.

'Oh, Rosemary can be tricky,' Marie sighed, when I reached my meeting in the Gaiety foyer. 'She's a funny one... so many good works, but terribly difficult to get on with. It doesn't surprise me, I must admit. She was hopelessly in love with Guy, by all accounts, so I think she'd put up with almost anything to keep him.'

'Anything except a threat to her inheritance,' I said, as our food arrived. 'Or so she implied.'

'Ah, yes,' said Marie. 'I doubt the Court-Chambers family would take kindly to an illegitimate heir.'

I put my cutlery down.

'Marie, you don't think... could Ginny have been...?'

'Having a baby? It hadn't occurred to me. I suppose it's possible,' she said thoughtfully, 'although one always imagines men of that class to be terribly careful about such things. It wouldn't be the first time an accident had happened, though... and while Rosemary's first ABC book was Debrett's, perhaps Guy isn't quite up to snuff on the rules.'

'If Ginny was pregnant,' I said, 'supposing Rosemary found out? Perhaps Guy told her, or at least somebody did.'

'Or Ginny told Guy, and he couldn't risk a scandalous

divorce and no inheritance,' said Marie. 'A weak man could panic in that situation.'

'He seemed so upset, though, when she was missing!'

We stared at each other.

'But he's an actor,' we said in unison.

'Do you think she might have confided in Josephine?' I asked. 'They seem quite close, though I believe Avril was – is – her best friend, and she hasn't heard a word from Ginny.'

'I don't know JoJo terribly well, of course,' said Marie, 'but I went to the theatre last night, to see her before the show. I wanted to wish her luck, see if she'd heard anything.' She laughed at my sceptical expression. 'Oh, all right, I was being nosy. She seemed off, somehow – she's now playing all Ginny's roles, as Jack thinks it's not worth rehearsing another actress before they start work on the Africa show. So perhaps she was nervous. But every time I mentioned Guy, or Ginny, she almost flinched.'

'Perhaps because she's worried about her friend? Or doesn't trust him?'

Marie sighed. 'I don't know... it might be nothing.' She looked uneasy. 'And please don't tell Lou I did this, or his rage will make the Blitz look like a bee sting.'

'I won't,' I promised, intrigued.

'Well, before the performance, Josephine went to the Ladies' – and I had a look inside the good luck card on her dressing table.'

'And?'

'Hold on,' she said, 'I jotted down exactly what it said.' She fished in her handbag and extracted a small leather-bound notebook.

'You really should be doing Lou's job.'

'I know,' Marie said. 'I taught him everything he knows. Ah, here we are.'

She unfolded a pair of tortoiseshell reading glasses. 'Blind as a bat... Yes, it had a black cat on the front, and inside it said, *Darling JoJo, wishing you all the luck in the world.* "*She walks in beauty, like the night/of cloudless climes and starry skies/and all that's best of dark and bright/meets in her aspect and her eyes*", and then there was a sort of squiggled initial that could be a G if you squint, or perhaps a Q, a J or an F. Even a rather tortuous S,' she said, holding the card away, then bringing it close to her face.

'Crikey,' I said, craning to look. 'G could be Ginny, though,' I said. 'Or F for Florence.'

'Yes, but does that sound like a female friend to you? I'd say something like, "break a leg, old sausage", not all that flowery poetic business.'

'I probably wouldn't quote Byron to Annie, no,' I agreed. 'And, of course, there's the choice of a black cat.'

'What about it?'

'Ginny's charm,' I said. 'Guy bought her a black cat for her bracelet.'

'Curiouser and curiouser,' said Marie. 'If Guy was seeing Josephine behind Ginny's back...'

I suddenly remembered where I'd seen the gold cigarette case with an inscription, just like Rosemary's.

'Well then,' said Marie. 'If Guy gave JoJo a gift... perhaps they were involved.'

'But she seems genuinely upset and puzzled by her disappearance,' I argued. 'She showed me Ginny's room and checked the bedside table...'

Marie raised an eyebrow. 'Perhaps Ginny confided in Josephine, not realising that she and Guy were having a fling, and Josephine was terribly jealous.'

'Yes, but being jealous and... well, getting rid of somebody are very different things, aren't they?'

'Very,' agreed Marie. 'And you'd think JoJo'd read Guy the

riot act, rather than Ginny, if so – which puts our handsome
blonde thespian back in the dock.'

'It's so hard to imagine him harming Ginny, though,' I said.
'He really seems to adore her.'

'Perhaps he adores every attractive woman he meets, until
they start being difficult,' said Marie. 'Or find themselves having
his child.'

CHAPTER TEN

I was idly glancing through my postbag an hour later and thinking about Rosemary, when Mr Gorringe opened his door and looked over. He was holding a few pages in his hand, and, with a queasy sensation of dread, I realised it was the obituary of Leonard that I'd completed the previous afternoon, dropping the pages into Parrot Paulson's in-tray as I left.

'Miss York,' he said, 'may I have a word?'

In Mr Gorringe's office, the frantic bustle and clack of the newsroom was entirely muffled. It was a haven of peace and drifting pipe smoke, but as I perched on the leather chair opposite his desk, my heart was banging so hard I was sure he could see it leaping under the lawn cotton of my blouse.

'Miss York, this is a matter that requires great discretion,' he said. 'I trust you can reassure me that this will go no further?'

I nodded blankly. I had no idea what he was about to say, but the obituary pages were now laid in front of him, and I saw he had circled a section in his trademark blue pencil. He tapped a finger twice on his desk, a sign of unease well known to his staff. I held my breath.

'On Saturday evening, I attended a Rotary Club dinner, and was seated beside the coroner,' he said.

It was not what I had expected him to say, so I rather idiotically blurted, 'Did you?'

'Talk turned to Lessiter's demise,' he went on. 'I believe you were in the audience. And, word has it, on the stage afterwards.'

I nodded. 'Yes. My friend knows the ENSA cast – we went to see if—'

He held up a hand. 'Miss York, as a lifelong newspaperman, and also as an ordinary citizen concerned with justice, I must ask this unfortunate question. Are you quite certain that the death was natural?'

I must have gaped like a cod, as he added, 'I do not expect you to proffer medical insight, Miss York, but we will need to employ caution when describing the event. You write here, '*although undoubtedly a shock to his legions of admirers both within and far beyond the Gaiety Theatre, they may take some comfort in knowing that the great actor's life came to a natural close on the stage, a final curtain call worthy of a legend...*'

I had been rather proud of that, but Mr Gorringe laid down the papers and sighed. 'A rather more junior pathologist was on duty that night, apparently, and after several Hors d'Age cognacs, Sir James admitted himself somewhat dissatisfied with the man's conclusions. He hinted to me, in confidence, that there may be a case for re-examining the body.'

'Really?' Pins and needles tingled through me, and I felt faint. I gripped the smooth arms of the chair and took a deep breath.

'This is, needless to say, entirely off the record and strictly confidential,' added Mr Gorringe. 'I trust you shall respect the obvious reporting strictures, Miss York, but please do remove the circled paragraph. Should more details be vouchsafed, I shall inform you.'

'Of course.'

He nodded a dismissal, and I made my way, on shaking legs, back to my desk.

'Are you all right?' Pat asked. 'You look as though you're to be shot at dawn.'

'Fine,' I murmured, winding a fresh sheet of paper into my typewriter. As I sped my way through the new version of the obituary, I went over it in my head. Leonard's collapse, the body on the stage, the weeping actors... Ginny had been there, and Josephine, Florence, Guy, Jack and Stanley... we had all been with him before the show at supper, and the cast had been with him backstage before his death. Could one of them really have intended to harm him? And if so, could one of them have killed Ginny, too?

A brief call to Lou while Mr Gorringe was in a meeting did nothing to reassure me.

'This is strictly confidential,' I whispered into the phone, 'but I need to tell you some news about Leonard...'

'What about him?'

I explained what Mr Gorringe had said.

'I've not heard a word about this.' Lou sounded aghast.

'And you'd better not breathe one, either, or I shall lose my job.'

'I won't, you know that. But if it's true, this casts a very different light on things.'

'As in, they may both have been killed?' I asked.

'Perhaps. Or Leonard was killed, and Ginny ran away after killing him. Or...'

'Surely she can't have done,' I said. 'Ginny adored Leonard. And besides, she had the idea for the tribute show. It was Ginny who made it happen, she'd never have left just before it began, and I can't imagine her harming a bluebottle.'

Lou sighed. 'What we can imagine and what happens when

a crime is committed can be very different. But I agree she's an unlikely murderer. We don't even know for sure that Leonard's death was suspicious, just because the coroner got tight on brandy and criticised a junior... Maybe it *was* the Blitz injury that saw him off.'

'Maybe,' I said. 'But do you remember, he looked pretty dreadful during the monologue? It was my understanding that a stroke comes with no warning. Like Hitler.'

'That's an interesting point,' Lou said. 'He was quite grey, wasn't he?'

'Yes. Not himself at all.'

He sighed. 'Just when I think I'm free to finally pin some evidence on bloody George Chivers' lot, half of Shaftesbury Avenue turns up, murdering each other.'

'And what about Ginny?'

'I'll pull some strings with the pathology lab, see if I can get the new results on the quiet. Meanwhile, I'll send someone down to the Gaiety to speak to the box office staff and the door-men, see if anyone saw Ginny coming in on Saturday evening, though I don't hold out much hope – the crowds were like a Wembley cup final.'

'What about Stanley?' I asked.

'What about him?'

'Well, don't you think he might be a suspect? He was thwarted over Ginny...'

'If every thwarted man committed murder, I'd never stop working,' said Lou. 'I've no evidence to pin anything on Kerridge apart from bad jokes, but if you have, don't let me stop you.'

After he'd rung off, I stared at the receiver. I remembered Josephine saying 'we'll all cram in with Stanley' and Sybil saying that he didn't like his car being parked in town. He was the only driver amongst the cast.

I stared blindly across the office thinking of a long, black car, its wheels skimming through the night, the muffled slam of a door, a man staggering under the weight of a body.

'Pat,' I said, 'I'm just nipping out.'

I alighted from the bus, and pulled my straw hat further down over my ears, pressing hairpins painfully into my scalp. As I approached number twenty-three, I saw a white blur, which transformed into Bernhardt, lying on the warm paving stones at the bottom of the steps like a polar bear rug. If anyone came out, she was a perfect excuse for loitering – and I could say I was paying a visit to see if there was any news.

As I bent to scratch her ears, I crouched by a shining black mud-guard above a silver-spoked wheel. Stanley's car, a Talbot, had recently been cleaned. There was barely a speck of dust clinging to the gleaming paintwork.

The street was empty, and a glance behind me confirmed that nobody was watching from the upper windows of the boarding houses. I could hear the faint tinkle of the piano and assumed Sybil was practising again.

I hurried to the driver's door on the far side, and crouched slightly, trying the handle. I hadn't really expected it to open, but it swung smoothly outwards, almost catching my shin. Stanley clearly hadn't remembered to lock his pride and joy.

I wasn't entirely sure what I was looking for, but I leaned into the interior, which smelled of warm leather and cigarettes. There was nothing in the back seat but a green tartan travel blanket, neatly folded, and in the front, the glove compartment yielded only a rattling tin of ancient barley sugars and a pair of large, string-backed driving gloves.

I was about to extricate myself and check the boot when it occurred to me to search under the seats. I stretched my arm to its fullest extent and felt blindly under the front passenger seat, patting until my fingertips touched something cool and hard.

I drew it closer, straining with effort, as my hand closed around something that felt like a thick wire. With a final tug, the object slithered out and I realised I was holding the strap of a small, black leather handbag. I knew before I opened the clasp that it belonged to Ginny.

Inside was a scattering of old tickets, a small pot of Max Factor face powder and, as if there were any doubt remaining, her ID card and ration book. Heart pounding, I was about to open the boot when, inside number twenty-three, the piano music stopped and Daphne's voice called, 'shan't be long!'. I heard the front door open and close and sank to the dusty road, clutching the bag to my chest, hoping with all my heart that Lou would still be at the police station when I rang.

'He's just leaving,' said the switchboard girl, as I gabbled into the telephone. I was in the box on the corner of Grafton Street, Ginny's handbag clamped under my arm. 'Is it *ever* so urgent?'

'Yes!' I almost shrieked. 'Tell him it's Edie, and he needs to come to Grafton Street at once. Please,' I added as an afterthought.

'Keep your wig on,' she said. 'Hang on.'

I heard some muffled conversation and Lou's familiar irritated tone. I made out the words 'bubble and squeak' and 'exhausted', but eventually, she returned and announced, 'He says he's on his way. But he's got a face like a jar of wasps, so I'd watch out if I was you.'

Lou could be as furious as an entire suitcase of wasps, I thought, as long as he hurried. The wait felt like several hours, but according to my watch, it was only ten long minutes before his car pulled up alongside me.

'If you're not about to say, "Lou, I've cracked the entire case wide open and I know where Ginny is," you're in trouble,' he said by way of greeting.

'I don't know where Ginny is, but I think the rest of the sentence might be true,' I said shakily. I held up the bag. 'Lou, look, this is Ginny's. I found it under the passenger seat in Stanley's car.'

'Hop in,' he said, using a clean handkerchief to take it from me. 'I won't even ask what you were doing breaking into a car, or how I'm supposed to explain why your fingerprints are now all over it.'

'Sorry. I didn't know what it was.'

'How certain are you that this isn't a different handbag of hers?' Lou asked, drawing out Ginny's ID card. 'Perhaps she took her other one with her.'

'Without ID or rations? She left her money in her purse, up in her room,' I said. 'Besides, Josephine said Ginny travels lightly – and I remember her bringing this bag when we had supper before the show, it was hung over the back of her chair and I thought it was rather smart.'

'It's certainly not casting old Stan in a glowing light,' said Lou.

I blinked away the sting of tears. 'It really seems that she's come to harm now, doesn't it?'

He nodded, still gazing at the little bag. 'Yes, Edie,' he said, as sombre as I'd ever heard him. 'I'm very much afraid that it does.'

We fell silent.

'Look,' Lou said eventually, 'do you need to get home? If not, come back to mine – I need to eat and I hate to admit it, but I'd like Marie's opinion on all this.'

Despite everything, I felt a spark of excitement. I'd never been to Lou's house. In my mind, he lived in the various police stations of Manchester, forever smoking beneath the King's portrait – though I knew that in actual fact, he lived in Stretford and had a daily woman to clean and cook for him.

'I should be delighted,' I said.

. . .

Lou pulled up outside a sturdy, red-brick Victorian villa on a tree-lined road. There was a glossy laurel bush by the gatepost, and well-swept tiled steps leading to the blue front door. I could hear Marple's booming barks of excitement echoing from within.

'I'm coming, you fool,' shouted Lou, fishing for his key and jamming it into the lock. Marple exploded from the hallway, a blur of hair and ears, and launched himself at Lou who almost fell backwards down the steps.

Marie appeared in the doorway. 'Edie! What a lovely surprise!'

She had changed out of her silk costume and was wearing a simple lawn cotton blouse and a linen skirt. Somehow, she still looked like a fashion plate.

'I've made a discovery,' I told her.

'Since lunchtime? My dear, I need to hear everything, right away,' she said. 'Leave those two to their passionate reunion.'

Lou was now on the pocket-handkerchief lawn, playing with a besotted Marple, so I left the door ajar and followed Marie. Inside, the house felt pleasantly airy. 'Sorry about the draught,' said Marie. 'He will insist on having all the windows perpetually thrown open, it's like living in a barn. Please God I'm back in London by autumn or I may die of exposure.'

The hallway was plain, with an old Persian rug on the boards. A small, polished table held a letter rack and a glossy African violet, but as Marie ushered me into the living room, I was forced to suppress my exclamation of surprise.

I had somehow expected Lou to live in monastic discomfort, shuttling irritably between wooden desk and iron bed. Instead, bright, framed modern art decorated the walls, and a huge blue and red rug lay underfoot. There was a leather sofa with curved arms and a matching chair, and by the fireplace, a red velvet armchair with a stack of books beside it, which had, apparently, overflowed from the Victorian bookcase on the back wall.

Lou had a walnut radiogram and a polished gramophone beside a stack of records on the sideboard – I noticed *Geraldo and His Orchestra* and *Benny Goodman, King Porter Stomp* – no highbrow opera for Lou – and though there were few ornaments, bar a rather attractive Art Deco clock, there were comfortable cushions scattered across the seating and a wooden cocktail trolley holding a cluster of bottles and a silver shaker. A good quarter of the floor space was taken up with what at first resembled a collapsed Bedouin tent – a rippling pool of colourful, ragged blankets and chewed sticks.

'Don't mind Marple's nest,' said Marie, subsiding onto the couch and shoving aside a pile of fashion magazines. 'He likes to add a fresh blanket every few days, and Lou's given up trying to stop him.'

As she spoke, there was a clatter of claws on wood, and the front door slammed.

'Drink?' asked Lou.

Over whisky and sodas, Lou outlined the discovery of Ginny's handbag.

'And,' he concluded, 'the current chief suspect is now Stanley.'

'But Lou,' Marie said, 'why haven't you arrested Stanley yet?'

'Because,' he said, 'I need more information, or he can simply claim he gave her a lift and she must have forgotten her bag. I need to find out why her possessions appear to be scattered across Manchester – bracelets in dressing rooms and handbags in cars...'

'Perhaps her killer put them there,' I said.

'Perhaps he did,' agreed Lou. 'Or, perhaps Ginny wanted to frame the person she most disliked before she vanished.'

'I wonder still about Guy,' I said. 'Particularly if he and JoJo are somehow involved.'

Marie nodded. 'It does all seem very complicated between he and Rosemary, and he certainly has motive if Ginny was becoming troublesome.'

'What about Jack?' Lou asked. 'He's a quiet one, isn't he?'

Much to my horror, I felt my face flame as though I'd bent over a bonfire.

'Edie!' Marie said delightedly. 'Do I detect a little crush?'

'No!' I cried, taking a slug of my drink, which was far more whisky than soda, and spluttering as it burned my throat. 'But a few days ago, he...'

'He what?' Lou's eyes narrowed.

'He asked me if I'd like to have lunch with him, and I said not until we know what's happened to Ginny.'

'Assuming she isn't parcelled up in his steamer trunk,' Lou muttered. 'But once it's solved, you're off into the sunset with Webb, are you?'

'For God's sake, he asked me for lunch, and I haven't even said yes!'

'Well, given your history of saying "yes" to Nazi murderers, you can hardly blame me for being wary,' snapped Lou.

I took a deep breath – before I walked out of Lou's surprisingly comfortable house and never spoke to him again. 'Marie,' I said, 'perhaps you could point me towards the bathroom. I have a sudden urge to wash my hands.'

She shot Lou a look of such contempt, I was amazed he remained sitting rigidly in his chair rather than crumbling into ash, and directed me upstairs.

My breath was ragged, and my heart pounded with fury. *How dare he?* First Annie, now me – what gave Lou Brennan the right to judge and comment on our brief romantic histories? Did he think his engagement in Spain to Lorna, the beautiful and doomed war reporter, was so perfect he could afford to pass comment on everyone else's less pristine affairs?

'My God,' I wanted to shout at him, 'it's easy to be in love with a ghost. Try a real woman for a change!'

As I washed my hands in the neat, green-tiled bathroom, rather meanly using as much of Lou's Imperial Leather soap and pleasingly hot water as I could manage, my heart slowed to a more normal speed, and I determined to rise above his childish barbs. I had to solve this case, I longed to know what had really happened to Leonard, where Ginny had gone, who was so painfully angry with both of them they'd commit murder to get rid of them – and I couldn't do it without Lou. My dream of being a crime reporter remained out of reach, but the more I discovered, the better my eventual chances. I had to remain civil, and suppress my flaring temper. I also knew, on a deep and uncomfortable level, that Lou was right – I had been a love-struck fool over a handsome man. Why should Lou trust me – and why, in fact, should I trust myself?

I dried my hands on a hard white towel, and unlocked the door to find Marple spread-eagled over the threshold, looking worried.

'I'm all right,' I told him. 'But your master can be very silly.'

'Yes, he can,' Marie yelled from downstairs. 'And I've told him so in no uncertain terms.'

As I returned and sat down, avoiding Lou's eye, he said quickly, 'I'm sorry, Edie. What I said was unkind and unnecessary.'

'It was, rather,' I agreed. 'But I believe Marie may have pointed that out.'

He nodded. 'I'm getting too overwrought,' he said, staring into the remains of his drink. 'We're understaffed and over-worked. O'Carroll's gone to visit his aunt for a week, Beeston's frankly as much use as a cast-iron cabbage, and I can't help feeling it's down to me to solve everything – particularly this

ENSA mess. But that's no reason to say hurtful things to my friends.'

'You're right,' I said, as Marple huffed and laid his head on my lap, clearly slower to let Lou off the hook than I was. 'But you can make it up to me by listening to the idea I've just had.'

CHAPTER ELEVEN

'I think it's inspired,' said Marie.

'I think it's extremely dangerous and silly,' said Lou. 'Supposing he recognises her, then what? This is not how the City Police tackles crime, with a... a travelling fancy dress party.'

'I can do a different voice,' said Marie. She raised her usual cheerful tone to a breathy, high-pitched giggle. 'See? I'm just a brainless lady with no idea! Oh no, perhaps not,' she said. 'I'm not sure he'd believe I'm a reporter for *The Stage* if I sound that idiotic.'

'Try a bit of an accent,' I suggested. 'Can you perhaps be French? You might have come over here after the last war, and found a job in the theatre...'

'Ah, *mais oui!*' Marie cried. 'I speak fluent French, thanks to our French mother. When Walter and I honeymooned on the Riviera, the locals were convinced I was a native *Niçoise...*'

'This isn't a game!' Lou insisted. 'The man could be dangerous – supposing he gets wind of the deception, or bundles Marie into a cab and vanishes with her?'

'Well, that's why you'll be waiting outside,' said Marie patiently. 'When you see us coming out, if he tries to manhandle me into a taxi, you run up blowing your whistle, and—'

'This isn't *The Beano*, Marie,' interrupted Lou. 'I'm not some chubby PC plod, chasing a schoolboy who's stolen a pie off a windowsill. He might be a murderer.'

'He might, but he's got an awful lot to lose,' said Marie. 'And I suspect he's also terribly vain. I'll flatter him in my chosen accent, and get him drunk at my expense—'

'You needn't think that's going through the police coffers,' muttered Lou.

'—and I'll make him talk to me.'

'Why can't Edie do it?' asked Lou, rather insultingly. Apparently, chucking me into a murderer's lair was of less concern.

'Because I've already met him several times,' I said. 'And I'm dreadful at accents, and I'd panic. He's only spoken to Marie once, when he was distracted by Ginny anyway, and if she's disguised, he won't recognise her.'

He heaved a deep sigh. 'Don't say I didn't warn you,' he said. 'And if you get nothing out of him, I'm taking Stanley in for questioning. How are you going to approach him?'

Marie smiled at her brother. 'I shall write Guy a lovely note from a theatre reviewer tomorrow, inviting him to supper after the show,' she said. 'And I'm certain I'll find him waiting in his best suit, ready to dazzle me.'

'Just don't let him give you a gold cigarette case,' said Lou. 'There's a limit to the number of women one man can adore.'

Marie was to become Laurentine Cadieux, after her French grandmother. She would be a reviewer for *The Stage* newspaper, one who was highly impressed by Guy's career, and his appearance in Manchester. She had come over from France a few years ago, having worked for *Paris-soir,* because 'your British theatre is so *merveilleuse. J'adore* Shakespeare,' Marie had said, in a perfect French accent. I was far less worried than

Lou that Guy would see through her deception – my only concern was how much of a charm bombardment she'd be subjected to, and whether he would tell her anything useful in return for an expensive post-theatre supper.

'Where will you take him?' I asked.

'I think Les Frères de la Côte,' she said, 'Lou recommended it.'

'That's where Arnold is taking...' I began, then remembered Arnold's proposal plans were supposed to be a secret.

'Annie?' She smiled. 'I hope she says yes.'

We'd agreed that Lou would pick Marie up afterwards, leaving Guy to make his own way back to number twenty-three, and she would telephone me at work the following morning with a full debrief.

I wondered what would happen if Guy did confess, or even suggest, that he and Ginny had argued. It would only be Marie's word against his, and not remotely useful as evidence in court. But perhaps it would give Lou reason enough to take Guy in for questioning, alongside Stanley.

The following evening, Annie was working again, and Suki and Agnes had gone to a cello recital at Chetham's School of Music. I ate my tea of cheese and onion pie at the table in silence, as a bar of late sun slanted through the window. With Annie ready to marry Arnold, and my future accommodation so uncertain – I'd never afford Mrs Turner's on my own – I felt a creeping sense of melancholy. No more Suki just upstairs, no Annie to chat and laugh and share rations with, Clara off flying aeroplanes, Joan busy with her painting, Ethel perhaps married and moving to Edinburgh soon enough, and Marie back in London...

If self-pity hadn't been such anathema to me, I might have wept into my rubbery potato pastry at the thought of the long, lonely months that loomed ahead.

I slept badly that night, unable to stop my brain whirring like a clockwork toy, wondering what had happened with Marie and Guy, whether Leonard's death had been unnatural, whether Stanley had killed Ginny in a rage after being spurned... but if he had, where was her body? As three and four a.m. ticked by, I got up and moved aside the blackout curtain, watching a silvery dawn break over the flowering horse chestnut trees in the park. I gazed down at the empty street, thinking about Josephine and Rosemary, Ginny and Leonard. Was someone angry, or jealous? But who would be jealous of both the ageing Leonard Lessiter and of young, beautiful Ginny? Perhaps they had both discovered – or kept – a secret. Something that would destroy a career or a marriage... or a vast inheritance, if it ever came out. If Ginny was pregnant, and had confided in Leonard... whatever route my thoughts took, they always bypassed Stanley's involvement and returned, inexorably, to Guy.

I crawled back into bed and fell into an uneasy sleep at around five. I dreamed about Josephine. She opened a gold cigarette case and said, 'You must look, Edie, you can't ignore it,' and when I peered inside, I reeled back in horror because it contained a human heart. I woke myself with my loud gasp to discover it was only a quarter past six, but sleep was gone.

I washed, dressed and arrived at work so early the cleaners were still dusting the glass lampshades in the corridor. By eight, I was in such a ferment of worry and speculation, I put in a call to Newton Street to see if Lou had arrived.

'You're keen,' said Lou on a tiger-like yawn.

'Is Marie all right?' I demanded. 'What happened? I hardly slept, I decided at one in the morning that it was a terrible idea and that I was mad to put her in danger, and by two I was sure she was dead...'

Lou laughed. 'Marie scoffed a very pleasant dinner and several glasses of Nuits-St.-Georges at Les Frères de La Côte, and is currently sleeping it off at home, her wig at half mast,' he said. 'Edie, seriously, it was a good idea. Guy opened up like a pop-up book, he told her all kinds of things.'

'What things?'

'Hold on.' Lou put a hand over the receiver, and I heard him say, 'Nice trip?' followed by the unmistakable tones of Sergeant O'Carroll, who had once apprehended me, booming about his aunt's dogs.

'Edie,' Lou said quietly, back in my ear, 'I need to brief the sergeant on what's been happening in his absence – but I'll be going to the theatre shortly to search the dressing rooms of both Guy and Stanley before I go back to number twenty-three. Meet me there at nine thirty, and I'll explain everything Marie found out. There's news on Leonard, too.'

To my intense annoyance, he then rang off.

I drank two cups of strong tea from Violet's trolley, and turned to Pat.

'I've another interview to do for the Lessiter obit,' I said. 'Just going out for a bit.'

'You've done more research for that old turn than you have for everyone else dead put together,' said Pat. 'Handsome young man involved, is there?'

'Sort of,' I said. But not in quite the way Pat meant.

At the theatre, the doors were locked. A few people were looking at the posters for the *Victory Gang Parade* – Leonard was still depicted, as was Ginny – but I felt quite the old hand now, and made my way round to the stage door.

Lou lifted a hand in greeting. 'I'll explain as we look round – I want to get to Grafton Street before Guy decides he was far too indiscreet last night, and makes a run for it.'

He rang the hidden bell.

'Good morning, sir!'

Wallis Middleton popped out like the Wizard of Oz from his hatch. I wondered if he slept in his powder-blue uniform. 'How may I help you?'

'I'm afraid I need to make a search of the premises, in connection with the death of Leonard Lessiter and the disappearance of Virginia Sutton,' said Lou.

Middleton's expression was trapped somewhere between 'outraged' and 'baffled'.

'Do you have the permission of the authorities for this?' he demanded.

Lou held out his card. 'I am the authorities.'

I tucked that one away, to tease him about later.

'May I ask what it is that you're searching for, Officer?' Middleton attempted to save face, ushering us through. He nodded briefly at me in puzzled recognition.

'I'm afraid not,' said Lou. 'I think we know the way, no need to desert your post.'

The theatre was silent and, apparently, empty as we made our way backstage once again. The dimly lit corridors felt rather eerie, and I was glad Lou was striding ahead of me, dispersing ghosts with every determined footstep. He paused outside Stanley's dressing room. 'Stay here,' he said. 'I can't have you interfering with a potential crime scene.'

'I don't *interfere!*' I argued. 'You wouldn't even know about the handbag if it weren't for me.'

'Edie, I appreciate your profound nosiness, but you are not a serving police officer, so please – *I am the authorities,*' he added, mocking himself before I had the chance.

I smiled. 'Fine. But leave the door open, so I can see what you're doing.'

Lou turned the handle and entered, groping for the light switch. Illuminated, the room appeared perfectly ordinary, if rather untidy. Stanley's costumes were hung from a clothing rack on castors that had been wheeled into the corner, leaving space for a well-used armchair. A bentwood chair faced the mirror, and on the shelf beneath was a small box. Lou opened it and looked inside. 'Pancake and a styptic pencil.'

'A what?'

'Stops shaving cuts bleeding,' said Lou. On the little basin opposite lay a cut-throat razor and shaving soap, and a table held folded back-copies of *The Stage* and *The Racing Post*. I wondered whether Stanley liked a flutter on the horses – and if so, whether he was short of cash. I knew that dire financial straits could turn anyone to crime.

'Nothing of interest,' said Lou, shaking out the papers in case incriminating notes fell out of their pages. He turned and studied the basin, taking a torch from his jacket and training it closely on the tiles around it.

'If he did hurt Ginny, I don't think he did it here. There's no blood, no evidence of hasty washing or a struggle. Of course, he could have set everything back to normal afterwards, but...'

'But getting a body out of the theatre would be too risky,' I said.

Lou nodded. 'Right, there's nothing of significance here. Let's see what we can find in Mr Ferdinand's room.'

Guy's dressing room was round a corner, on an equally un-salubrious corridor. Lou tapped on the door, then pushed it open, turning on the light as he did so.

'Oh, I do apologise—' he began, as the dim bulb illuminated a figure reflected in the mirror. We both stepped into the room at the same time. Lou murmured, 'God almighty!' and I screamed. Guy Ferdinand was slumped in the bentwood chair, his blue eyes open and staring into a fathomless void. Buried in his back, just beneath his right shoulder-blade, was the same shining dagger he had held in his recital, 'The Green Eye of the Little Yellow God'.

'Edie, wait in the corridor,' barked Lou. He stood a distance away, studying the floor as I hovered in the doorway, my eyes averted from the small, dark stain on Guy's white shirt.

'They took him by surprise,' Lou said.

'How do you know?' I was shaking, I realised. I longed for a cup of tea with two sugars for shock, and a hug from Annie. Some hard-boiled crime reporter I was.

'Well, one doesn't tend to remain sitting when someone's obviously approaching with a dagger,' Lou said. 'But more importantly, there's no blood spatter – whoever did it waited till he was seated, then I assume, picked up the weapon and stabbed him instantly. No hesitation.'

He studied the mirror shelf in front of Guy. 'Nothing obviously significant,' he said, but he covered his hand with his white cotton handkerchief again and lifted an opened envelope, dropping it into his pocket.

'What's that?'

'No idea,' said Lou. 'Might be something or nothing, but I need to close off all entrances to the theatre and get the murder lot down here. Don't touch anything,' he added.

'I'm not—'

'We need to hurry, I don't want some poor bloody cleaner to find him,' he added. I thought of Norma and shuddered. We'd have to tell the cast – that was three of them gone now, I realised, cold with horror. Worse still, it occurred to me, whoever saw Guy last could be in the frame for murder – and as far as I knew, thanks to my ludicrous scheme, that person was asleep in Stretford, still wearing her shop-bought disguise.

Wallis Middleton was pale with shock.

'Will I be arrested, Officer?' he asked Lou, clutching the sides of his chair with whitened knuckles.

'Unlikely, if you answer my questions truthfully,' said Lou.

'Firstly, Mr Middleton, what time did Guy Ferdinand arrive at the theatre last night?'

Middleton pulled the ledger towards himself with a trembling finger and fumbled over the pages.

'Here,' he said eventually, 'it was ten to eleven, I wondered why he was back so late. Look, it says here he signed out at half nine, after the show. He told me he'd come to pick up a letter.'

'And did you wonder why he didn't reappear after he'd collected it?'

'No, sir,' Wallis said. 'We lock up at midnight, but I thought he must have gone out the front – you can open the main doors from inside, but not outside. And there's the fire exits, of course. To be frank, sir, over the years, I've become used to actors coming and going for all kinds of reasons. If I recognise them, I don't question it.'

'Was anyone with him?'

He shook his head. 'He was on his own.'

'Did anyone else enter the building, before or after Mr Ferdinand, once the show was over?'

'No, sir.' Poor Middleton looked wretched, perhaps afraid for his job.

'The cast all left, see, here.' He poked a finger at the page. 'All of 'em signed out by ten – nobody could have come in this way again without me knowing.'

'What happens after midnight, if someone wants to enter?'

I realised my legs were still shaking, and leaned against the wall.

'They can't, sir, they can only come out.'

'So you think whoever killed Mr Ferdinand was already in the theatre?'

'I'd say so, yes,' nodded Middleton, his peaked cap bobbing.

'Please be assured, I have to ask this question,' said Lou. 'Did you leave your post at any time after Guy arrived, before you left for the night?'

Middleton stared hard at the ink-stained blotter on his table.

'There was...' He glanced at me. 'Sorry, miss, but there was a call of nature, I'd say about a quarter past eleven. I drink a lot of tea, sitting here,' he added defensively. 'Passes the time.'

'So nobody was here for what – five minutes or so?'

He nodded again, silent with shame.

'But the door is locked, sir, I have to open it myself to visitors. Nobody can just wander in at will '

'How certain are you that you locked the door after Guy arrived?' Lou asked. 'And you must be honest, Mr Middleton, this tragedy is not your doing, and you mustn't be afraid to admit to some doubt.'

There was a long pause. Wallis placed a hand to his forehead.

'My memory,' he said eventually. He sounded on the verge of tears. 'It's not what it was, Detective.'

'All right,' said Lou. 'I understand.'

He borrowed the telephone to ring up the station, and I heard him issuing orders as I waited. Wallis was now crumpled in his chair like a deflated balloon.

'Could I make you a cup of tea?' I asked, and he nodded.

'That would be very kind, miss. The shock...'

I bustled about, largely to distract myself, and made us both a strong brew in the enamel mugs I found on the shelf.

Eventually, Lou put down the receiver. 'They're on their way,' he said. 'I hope you won't be offended, Mr Middleton, but I don't deem you at strong risk of absconding. Edie, can you wait with him while I go and brief the officers round by the front? Then I must go to Grafton Street.'

'Can I come?'

'No,' said Lou. 'I've asked for Beeston as backup – we need to interview the lot of them, and I'm bringing Kerridge in for questioning.'

'But I—'

'Edie, look, get yourself to my house, wake Marie from her innocent slumber, break the news and ask her to explain everything she discovered last night. I'll drop in this evening to tell you the latest.'

'Is she a suspect?'

'No,' said Lou, 'seeing as I saw her coming out of the restaurant with Guy and took her home. Having a DI younger brother as your alibi should be fairly solid, I hope – though she may need to give a formal statement.'

The hot tea was helping slightly.

'Are you quite all right?' I asked Wallis, who was drinking his with both shaking hands clasped round the mug.

He nodded convulsively. 'Just the shock,' he said again, 'he was a nice feller, miss. Always had time for a word with me, unlike some.'

'Who didn't have time?'

Wallis looked up at me. 'Kerridge. I happen to know he was dragged up in the Gorton slums, but to look at him swank, you'd think he'd hatched out of a golden egg. Never a word to me – not worth speaking to if I can't do him a favour, am I?'

It was a small thing, perhaps, but another black mark against Stanley, in what was fast becoming a forest of them.

CHAPTER TWELVE

Marie was awake when I arrived – and if she hadn't been, Marple's fusillade of barking would have woken King Arthur himself from centuries of slumber.

She opened the door now without the cheap wig, her dark hair sticking up in tufts. She was wearing a very expensive-looking cream satin dressing gown, and her feet were bare.

'Edie!' Marie cried, her voice cracked. 'I thought you'd be at work. Have you seen my brother yet? Has he told you everything? Honestly, I think I should get a job as a spy, it was terribly thrilling—'

'Marie,' I said, a sudden image of the dagger in Guy's back almost making me sick with the horror of it. 'May I come in? I have some upsetting news.'

'Oh God.' Her hand flew to her neck. 'Not the children?'

'Oh! No, no, nothing to do with them,' I said, cursing myself for my insensitivity. Not having any myself, I had forgotten that mothers immediately assume all potential bad news relates to their offspring.

'What is it, then? Oh Lord, have they found Ginny?'

She led me through to a small morning room painted in

primrose-yellow distemper, followed obediently by Marple, who in the master's absence seemed to have transferred his affections to his human aunt.

'No,' I said, 'you might want to sit down, though.' She slid into a wooden chair beside a plate of half-eaten toast and marmalade, her eyes fixed on me. I sat opposite, overlooking a pleasant little back garden, where chaffinches hopped on a bird table, and a magpie stabbed the lawn by the Anderson shelter with its razor-like beak.

'Marie, Guy's been killed.'

'What?' Her shout was so sudden, Marple jumped and banged his head on the table. I reached down to rub it for him.

'I – we – found him, barely an hour ago. In his dressing room. Oh Marie, it was awful.'

I shook my head to try and block out the image, but I suspected it would be forever fixed, like a photograph floating in a developing tray. Guy's strange posture, the gleam of the blade, the dark stain on his white shirt.

'How?' she asked, a hand over her mouth.

'Stabbed,' I told her, 'with the *Little Yellow God* dagger. I'd assumed it was just a prop, but it seems it was real.'

'Do they – does Lou know who...?'

'Not a clue,' I said. 'He's bringing Stanley Kerridge in for questioning. But I need to warn you, they may want you to give a statement. You were the last person to see him before he arrived at the theatre and Wallis Middleton let him in.'

Marie groaned. 'Laurentine Cadieux was the last person to see him. A bespectacled, French theatre reviewer with a blonde wig that cost two and nine from a fancy dress shop. I suppose I'll have to come clean with the police, and insist Lou didn't know a thing about it. Oh Edie, I feel such a fool.'

'It's entirely my fault,' I said. 'Look, you get dressed while I take Marple into the garden, and then I suggest you tell me what you discovered last night.'

Marie nodded, piled her breakfast things into the sink, and turned to go upstairs. 'The Daily, Mrs Carradine, will be round soon,' she said over her shoulder. 'I'd rather our chat was private, she knows the doings of every family within a seven mile radius. Shall we take a walk?'

Fifteen minutes later, Marie was dressed in a well-cut white frock and her hair was brushed to a gleam. We clipped Marple's lead onto his collar and set off for the nearby park. As we strolled past the greenhouses, where gardeners in shirt sleeves tended to neat rows of peas and beans rather than orchids and palms, Marie said sadly, 'It all seems so pointless now. I was terribly pleased with myself for deceiving Guy, thinking I was solving the mystery, but now none of it matters. Poor man. And my God, poor Rosemary. Gosh, I feel hateful now,' she muttered.

'It's not your fault, Marie,' I said. In the distance, the park café with its wooden outdoor tables shone like an oasis. 'Let's have a coffee, and try to make some sense of it all.'

Once installed, with what tasted suspiciously like Camp coffee essence and hot water steaming in front of us, she adjusted the brim of her straw hat to block the sun, and said, 'All right, then. Here's what happened.'

Marie had left a note for Guy at the box office, claiming to be a reporter for *The Stage*, and he had accepted her invitation to dinner, to 'discuss a possible interview' about his career.

They had met at Les Frères de la Côte, where Marie secured a discreet banquette table, and unleashed her impeccable French on the waiters.

'Guy turned up – I don't think he recognised me for a second, he was very polite and flourishing about taking my jacket,' she said. 'We talked about the ENSA plans for the Africa tour – I suppose that's all off now – then over the first course, which was really the most melting onion soup...' she broke off. 'How inappropriate to think about food, I'm so sorry... I asked about Leonard's death. Guy said it "seemed a bit rum" and claimed that he had been very fond of "old Lessiter", as he called him. He said, "Leonard never judged", which I took to mean he knew about Guy and Ginny. Of course, I plied him with wine, which meant I had to drink a fair amount, too, and then rush to the lavatory to make notes in case I got too drunk to remember what he'd said.'

'Impressive logic,' I murmured, and she nodded.

'I know. All wasted now, of course.'

A waitress was clearing nearby tables, banging and clanking, and Marie leaned closer in. 'Once he was getting a bit blotto, I asked him about Ginny. Of course, I had to pretend I didn't know they were an item, and behave as though she was just his colleague, but I said—' Marie adopted a passionate and breathy French accent. 'It must be so dreadful, to know she is missing – what do you think 'as 'appened?'

An elderly matron with a small lapdog, who was proving of great interest to Marple, heard Marie and mouthed '*collaborator*' to her equally disapproving friend. I almost laughed.

'Anyway, this is the interesting bit.' Marie took a sip of coffee, pulled a face, and tipped the rest into the grass. 'My mother would have the man who created that coffee arrested,' she muttered. I was beginning to realise that strong opinions ran in her family.

'Guy had sunk several glasses of Nuits-St.-Georges, and he told me he hadn't been sleeping with worry. Then he sort of leaned in, and he lowered his voice,' Marie looked around her, doing the same. The matron glared.

'And he said, "between you and me, Laurentine, I'm beginning to wonder if somebody's killed her." I looked as shocked as I could, and said, "But who would do such a thing?" – I might have added a "*mon dieu!*" for effect,' Marie added. 'Then he said, "Actually, I have an idea. It seems so terribly unlikely, but I'm afraid I'm right."'

'Did he say who?' I interrupted.

She shook her head. 'I expressed surprise, and I tried to persuade him to tell me the name of his suspect, off the record, but he absolutely refused,' she went on. 'But as we were having coffee afterwards – a far nicer version than this swill, I must admit,' she glanced at her empty cup, 'he said he was going to "talk to a policeman he knew," and show him something. In fact,' a cloud passed over her face, 'he said he was going to telephone him in the morning. But obviously, he didn't because... oh, Edie, you don't suppose someone at the restaurant overheard and followed him?'

'I think that's very unlikely,' I said. 'Far more likely that whoever he suspected got wind and took their chance to stop him going to the police. Did he say why he was going back to the theatre last night?'

She nodded. 'He was going to put me in a taxi, but I told him a friend was collecting me, and he said, "Well, you have my card – do get in touch with my agent about the interview if you'd like to go ahead." I said, "Are you going back to your digs now?" thinking he might mention Rosemary, and he said, "Yes, but I've been expecting a letter – I'll drop by the Gaiety first and see if it's arrived by the evening post, I didn't have time to check my pigeonhole earlier," and then he kissed me on both cheeks – perhaps because I was French, he assumed I'd like it – and we parted.'

'Marie,' I said. 'You really should be a reporter. Or a spy. Or a Detective Inspector. That was a masterpiece of interviewing.'

'Truly?' She looked delighted, then remembered. 'Oh, but it's all wasted now, because we'll never know who he suspected. Whoever it was has made sure of it.'

'Not necessarily,' I said. 'You said Guy was going to show Lou something. Perhaps that something was at Grafton Street, or on his person. Perhaps it was the letter he was waiting for. If so, it was on his table – Lou took it with him, to examine.'

Marie nodded. 'Of course. It could hold all the answers. Or we could be just as much in the dark as ever. I'm worried, though – whoever's doing this is going through the cast like a dose of salts. The sooner they sail for Africa, the better.'

'Unless,' I said, 'whoever did it is sailing with them.'

I left Marie and Marple strolling round the duck pond, and caught a tram back to work. It seemed a lifetime since I'd left my desk this morning, though it was only just after one when I returned.

'How was the Ritz?' Pat asked, licking her thumb and flicking through a sheaf of papers. 'Here, you'll need to fill in your expenses sheet – roast goose, wasn't it, and oh yes, look, it says here, "a two-pound jar of finest caviar".'

'Pat,' I said, 'I'm sorry I've been so long, but something happened.'

She looked up and saw my face. 'Crikey, whatever's up?'

'Guy Ferdinand's dead,' I said. 'Murdered.'

'No!' Pat's shriek was so penetrating, half the office span round.

'That actor's dead!' she yelled to a general hubbub of astonishment. 'Guy Ferdinand, the handsome one! Murdered!'

Almost immediately there was a huddle round her desk as if she were a Victorian newsboy in Whitechapel, bellowing news of the Ripper's latest crimes.

Mr Gorringe, returning from his brief and frugal lunch, looked over, irritation battling with confusion on his weary face.

'Sir, Edie's found a murder!' cried Gloria, and he paused, blinking.

'Miss York,' he said eventually. 'My office, please.' The huddle parted like the Red Sea and trickled back to work.

Once again in the leather chair, I tried to explain.

'One simply cannot fathom why you were there in the first place,' he said.

'I was interviewing the Gaiety's doorman in case I could add something to the Lessiter obituary before it goes to print.'

'A mine of poignant anecdotes, I assume?'

My face felt hot. 'A few,' I said quietly. 'But I met DI Brennan there, and I wanted to ask him about Ginny Sutton, so I followed him, and he... we found his body. Guy Ferdinand had been stabbed with the dagger from the performance.'

'Good Lord!' said Mr Gorringe. He paused, steepling his fingers. 'Miss York, we shall need to place this in the evening edition – can you manage three hundred words on what you saw, to run alongside the news piece from Des?'

Joy ballooned in my chest.

'Yes!' I cried. 'I can! I'll do it now!'

'Very good,' he said. 'Oh, and Miss York – are you quite all right? I imagine it must have been something of a shock for a young woman.'

'I am, thank you,' I said. I almost added 'never better', but that might have been deemed insensitive, even by a hardened newspaper editor.

The evening edition arrived in the office at around four o'clock, and I was standing by the door vibrating like a whippet with anticipation, when I heard the lift doors clang down the corridor. Basil trudged into view pushing an enormous wire trolley containing string-tied bundles of the latest *Chronicle*.

'Want one, Edie?' he asked, and in answer I almost ripped the paper in two, pulling at the string.

My piece, which had been cut to roughly half the length, I noted with disappointment, was on page two. The full page was headlined:

MURDER ON STAGE: NEW HORROR AT THE GAIETY

Des's write-up included the sub-heading:

Are Police Doing Enough?

My heart sank. Lou would be furious. Nevertheless, I had a byline, and my piece on Guy's murder was in the newspaper. It was a step forward, and I refused to let Lou, or anyone else, take my small triumph away from me.

I didn't feel quite so confident that evening, when Lou rang the doorbell. Fortunately, Mrs Turner was still away tending to her sister, so I ran downstairs to let him in.

'Where's Marple?' I asked, as he stood on the step, still in his work suit and hat.

'With Marie,' said Lou. 'He doesn't like shouting.'

'Look, it wasn't my fault, I don't write the headlines—'

'No, you just tell the world before I've had a chance to draw breath, and ensure it's splashed over the *Chronicle*, along with an ill-informed dig at the City Police,' he said tightly. 'If bloody Des had the slightest idea what solving serious crime actually involves, as opposed to sinking pints of milk stout and speculating in the Nag's Head... and as for you,' he added furiously, as I reluctantly led him into our rooms, '"*The true horror only became apparent as DI Brennan and I entered the dressing room*"?' he quoted. 'Do you really think I want my name all over the newspaper? I'm already fire-fighting thanks to this idiotic fancy-dress scheme of yours and Marie's, I've now got to explain what on earth a bloody female obituary writer was doing at the scene, and on top of that, it seems Lessiter's death wasn't natural causes after all...'

'What?'

'Yes, the new results came back from the Preston lab this afternoon.' Lou flung himself into his usual armchair and fished for his cigarettes. 'It seems that dear old Leonard's injuries weren't to blame for his death, despite Dr Willoughby's assurances. He was poisoned.'

'*Poisoned?*'

'Apparently. But as yet, we don't know what substance was used. Another fresh problem, to add to the stack already piled onto my desk like rotting fish.

'So... there's been two murders and a disappearance? Did you arrest Stanley?'

'Eventually. Given that he couldn't or wouldn't give us the slightest indication of why Ginny's handbag was in his car when we questioned him, and pleaded complete ignorance. Of course, they were all distraught about Guy, too. Josephine cried so much I thought she'd collapse. It was bloody horrible.'

I thought again of the gold cigarette case, and the good luck card. 'Where was Stanley last night?'

'Says he went straight back to number twenty-three and went to bed when the others did. But there's nothing to say he didn't get up again and drive back to town, kill Guy and sneak home once the others were asleep. I assume he had a front door key, as Daphne and Sybil seem to hand them out like tu'penny sweets.'

'So he's at the station?'

'In a cell, furious and insisting he's done nothing wrong. But that's hardly surprising.'

'Do you think he did it?'

'The evidence so far is completely circumstantial,' Lou admitted. 'The handbag's being fingerprinted – luckily, we can eliminate yours from last time you were questioned...' I sighed. 'But Kerridge could have touched it anytime, and we have no further evidence to link him to Guy's or Leonard's deaths. There aren't even fingerprints in the dressing room, so we can assume the killer wore gloves. We can't keep him for long if we don't find more reason to link him to Ginny's disappearance. I checked the car boot, by the way.'

'And?'

'Nothing. A well-thumbed Talbot manual from 1937 and a wheel nut wrench.'

'Which he could have used to kill Ginny.'

'Or he could have used it to mend his wheel. Forensics in Preston have got it anyway, so if he did use it as a weapon, it'll have blood traces on it.'

I shuddered.

'What about the others?' I asked. 'We know their movements when Ginny disappeared, but who could have poisoned Leonard?'

Lou sighed heavily and automatically reached down to scratch Marple's head, before remembering that the dog wasn't in his usual spot.

'We questioned them all,' he said. 'And of course, we've checked with the Kardomah what he ordered that night, as none of them could remember.'

'I think he had some sort of meat pie,' I said. 'I remember he and Guy both had it, so nobody could have poisoned it.'

'Perhaps his lunch, then,' said Lou. 'According to Daphne, she often leaves a big pan of soup on the Aga, and they can help themselves – she can't recall what flavour it was that day but says probably tomato or vegetable. But Jack and Ginny also ate the soup, apparently, so unless someone poisoned it knowing Leonard was about to eat some, that seems an unlikely culprit.'

'Hold on,' I said. 'Sometimes, people send chocolates to performers, don't they? They don't send flowers to men, so perhaps someone had sent him a box to say "good luck"?'

Lou looked up, halfway through lighting a Woodbine, his eyes narrowed against the smoke.

'I hadn't considered that,' he said rather grudgingly.

'Nobody's cleared out his dressing room yet. I'll get someone to go and search it, though anyone who can lay their hands on a decent box of chocs these days has my admiration.'

'And you've no idea who it was that Guy wanted to speak to you about?'

'I assume it was Stanley,' Lou said. 'But we searched his bedroom and Guy's and there was nothing of note.'

'What if it was Rosemary?' I said. 'She seemed very brittle about their arrangement, and she said that if any one of his "gold-diggers" found themselves pregnant and making a claim on the estate, Guy would be cut from the inheritance – I suppose she meant she'd divorce him.'

'Mm,' said Lou, blowing a thoughtful smoke ring. 'Say you're right – how would she have done it? And why kill Leonard?'

'I don't know – but she has a strong motive for Ginny and Guy at least, if she thought it wasn't just an affair but genuine love,' I said.

'Perhaps she thought Leonard was covering for them. I assumed she went home the other day as Guy was back at the digs, but perhaps she didn't. Or could she have offered Ginny money to go away?'

'But if so, why was her handbag in Stanley's car? Perhaps Guy and Rosemary had a row,' suggested Lou, 'about his feelings for Ginny – or as you say, perhaps Ginny was expecting a baby, and Rosemary found out. We'll need to have her in for questioning. Then there's Josephine, who may of course have been involved with Guy, too...'

He groaned. 'I've got more suspects than I know what to do with, and no evidence for any of them, bar a handbag in the wrong place. We'll press Stanley for a confession after his night in the cells, but unless we can come up with something better, we may have to release him, pending further enquiries.'

'What was the letter?' I asked suddenly.

'Letter? Oh, the letter to Guy?'

'No, the letter from Frances describing her favourite stuffed toy.'

'Don't take my niece's name in vain. We looked at it earlier – it was from Rosemary,' said Lou. 'It said...' He dug a notebook from his pocket, and flicked to the page where he'd copied it down. '*Dear Guy, as promised, I am writing to let you know I have returned safely to Foxwell. I am confirming your suggested meeting here on the 6th June, before you go to Africa, and I will then discuss your request. Rosemary.*'

'What request?'

'Quite. No idea. And why did he go to the theatre to pick the letter up? He must have known in advance that she'd write with a response to his "request" – it must have been important.'

'And for that matter, why does her letter sound like a formal summons? I'm not married, but I don't think that's generally how wives write to husbands,' I said. 'You'd expect a "fondest love", or "your loving wife", wouldn't you?'

Lou nodded. 'Or at the very least, a "chin up, old beetle".'

'Is that how you'd address your wife?' I laughed.

'Only if she was very fortunate,' Lou said. 'Right.' He stuffed his notebook back into his pocket. 'I'm off home to inform Marie that she's not likely to be arrested. This time,' he added darkly. 'And for goodness' sake, don't go blaring this all over the *Chronicle* – I've got the nationals breathing down my neck now, and I've had to put a man outside number twenty-three to see off all the reporters, thanks to you.'

'It would have come out, though...'

'At a time of my choosing, yes.' Lou sighed. 'Never mind. If you have any further flashes of inspiration, ring me up.'

He clattered downstairs, and the door slammed behind him. Two minutes later, as I was studying the sparse pantry shelves wondering what to cobble together for tea, the bell rang again.

'What have you forgotten?' I called, hurrying down and flinging the door open.

To my surprise, it wasn't Lou standing on the step, but a man I didn't recognise. In his forties, he was short and muscular, dressed in a striped suit that Annie would call "a bit spivvy". His trilby was perched on the back of his head, and he was good-looking in a rather louche way, with oiled black hair and a pencil moustache.

'Evening, sorry to bother you, miss,' he said. He had a strong Lancashire accent, and he seemed full of a coiled tension, as though he were anticipating something momentous.

'Good evening,' I said, 'Can I help you?'

'I hope you can,' he said. 'I'm looking for a Mrs Suki Sullivan – I've got some good news for her.'

'What good news?' I said, instead of saying 'Who?' as I should have done. I cursed myself inwardly.

'She doesn't live here,' I said quickly. 'I don't know where she is.'

'So you do know her, then?' He smiled raffishly. 'Nothing to worry about, sweetheart. She's won a few bob is all, and her friend asked me to give it to her. We all need a bit of extra cash these days, don't we?'

I felt lightheaded with horror. This surely was Frank Sullivan – and I'd been stupid enough to let him know he'd found the right place.

'I don't know her now,' I said. 'I haven't seen her for years.'

'Not what a chatty little bird told me. Come on, love, let me in, I'll drop off the money and get out of your hair.'

'I think you should go,' I said. My heart was battering against my ribcage, and I tried to shut the door, but the toe of his shining black boot was wedged into it.

'I can't do that, sweetheart,' he said. 'It's a personal matter, you see. Delicate. I'll find her myself.'

He used his foot as a lever and turned a pinstriped shoulder to nudge the door, hard. It flew open and Frank strode past me.

'Might want to practise your warm welcome,' he said, taking the stairs two at a time.

'Come back here!' I yelled, but it was too late. Frank was already on the second flight, and before I could warn her or shout for help, he was pounding an iron fist on Suki's door.

CHAPTER THIRTEEN

I flew up the stairs. As I hurtled along the first landing, I heard him roar, 'I bleeding knew it!' and Suki's scream of horror.

I made it up the second flight as Frank booted the door to slam it in my face. I shot out a hand just in time, badly hurting the base of my thumb, and almost fell into Suki's living room where she was now cowering, Frank's right hand around her throat, his left pinning her to the wall opposite the open window.

'Edie, go,' she choked, 'call the police!'

'Get off her!' I roared, pulling at his shoulder. He shoved his elbow back into my chest, knocking me to the floor and wrenching Suki sideways like a doll as he did so. Beside him, how small she looked, and how terrified. Her eyes semaphored pure, animal dread.

I picked myself up and kicked him hard in the back of the knee.

Frank roared in pain, buckling, and half turned to try and slap me away. I dodged and looked wildly about for something to hit him with – there was a thick pottery bowl of apples on the table, and I snatched it up, tipped the apples out, knocking over a chair, and swung it at him.

'Don't!' Suki screamed again – Frank ducked, and I missed. Enraged, he let go of Suki's shoulder and grabbed at my arm, pinning me to his iron-hard, muscular torso.

'Interfering cow!' he shouted, flecks of his spittle landing on my face. 'My wife – my *own wife* – this ungrateful little whore, who I fed and clothed and worked all hours to keep, so she could sit on her arse like Lady Muck – walks out on me,' he shook Suki like a dog worrying a cloth toy as she gazed at me, helpless, 'and I finally track her down, after weeks – *weeks* hiding away like the cowardly slut she is, and I'll bloody well deal with her as I see fit!'

His hand was like a steel ring around my arm – I remembered that his father had been a boxer. Frank suddenly dropped his hand from Suki's neck and pulled back his fist, about to slam it into her body. Both of us screamed, and a voice bellowed, 'Stop!'

I whipped round, wrenching my arm in Frank's grip, to find Lou and an ARP warden pelting into the room. In a blur of violent movement, I felt his hand fall loose and saw Suki crumple to the floor. I looked round to find Frank face down on the rug, cursing and thrashing, his arms pulled behind him as Lou knelt heavily on his thighs, binding his wrists with the striped tie he'd yanked from his own neck.

The warden, breathing hard, said, 'Are you two all right?'

'I am,' I said, ignoring the pain that was spreading across my chest, and the agony of fresh bruising on my upper arm. I sank down beside Suki and put my arm round her as she trembled against me, silent and shocked. 'Suki might need to go to hospital.'

'She needed a bloody lesson,' yelled Frank, his voice muffled by the rug.

'Shut up,' snapped Lou, flicking a hand against the back of

Frank's head. His hat had rolled away in the scuffle, and it was now clear that he was significantly balding, while traces of black hair-dye speckled his scalp.

'Give me a hand with this bastard,' Lou said to the warden, who obligingly knelt on Frank's bucking back. 'Edie, can you run to the telephone box and call the station? Ask them to send a car and two men.'

'Of course.' I got to my feet, with a sudden whooshing in my ears. 'Suki, can you walk?' I asked, holding out a hand. 'Come to ours and wait for me there.'

She nodded, limp as someone climbing from bed after a long illness, and I held her up as we left the room.

'Lock the door and make yourself a cup of tea,' I said, leading her gently into our flat. 'There's a bit of sugar in the tin, have two spoons, and I'll be back in a minute.'

She nodded. I shut her in and rushed downstairs to the telephone box, afraid that Frank would somehow shake off Lou and the warden and make a break for it.

When I returned, there were still muffled bangs and sporadic yelling coming from upstairs. 'Suki, it's me,' I called, 'let me in!'

I heard a scraping noise, followed by the key in the lock, and she peeped out.

'Quickly,' she whispered, pulling me inside. She slammed and locked the door behind me, and I saw that she'd pushed a chair up against the doorknob.

'It's all right now,' I said. 'They've got him, there's a police car on the way.'

'Yes, but they can't imprison him just for threatening me,' whispered Suki. She was white as marble. 'They'll have to let him go, and he'll come back and next time, he won't stop until I'm dead. Wherever I go, he'll find me, I know he will.'

I felt cold all over, both with shock and the realisation that she was right. Past beatings would come down to Suki's word against his, and judges tended to look unfavourably on 'domestic violence' cases, as I knew from my years on the newspaper. *The lady in question remained with her husband, so it can't have been that bad*, was the general assumption.

'We'll cross that bridge when we come to it,' I said, I put my arms round her. 'You're safe at the moment.'

As we huddled on the sofa, a car pulled up outside and we could hear doors slamming, a heavy tread on the stairs. A moment later, swearing broke out again, as Sullivan was manhandled downstairs and into the police car, which roared off, bells clanging in the quiet summer evening.

I heard Lou talking to the warden, the click of the front door, and then he came back upstairs, and tapped on the door.

'He's gone,' he called. 'May I come in?'

'I can't thank you enough,' Suki said to Lou, who was in his usual armchair. 'Both of you.' Her teeth were chattering. I rubbed her bony back, and fed her sips of sweetened tea. I felt I could rather do with a mug myself, ideally containing a large slug of brandy. After finding Guy this morning, the day had taken on the surreal quality of a feverish nightmare. I flinched as the clock struck eight with a ringing chime.

'How did you know?' I asked Lou. 'You'd already left.'

'I was sitting in my car, with the window open,' he said. 'It was pure luck, I wanted to scribble down a couple of the things we'd discussed, before I forgot. I was about to set off when I heard shouting from the upstairs flat.'

'Thank God your windows were open,' I said to Suki.

She nodded. 'Agnes hates a fug.'

'What a nasty little man he is,' Lou said to Suki. 'I'm very sorry that he somehow tracked you down.'

'He knows where I am now,' said Suki. There was a red mark around her slim neck.

'I'm so very sorry he got in,' I said. 'He took me by surprise, and—'

'It's not your fault,' she said. 'I brought that beast to your door. But Edie, I'm going to have to move, perhaps far away. And even then...'

Silent tears slid down her face.

'I don't want to get your hopes up,' said Lou gently, 'but Sullivan's been at the edge of our sights for a while, he's a known associate of George Chivers, whose gang runs the black market operations up round Shudehill. He's not a big cheese, so until now, we've not gone hard after him – but things change, don't they?'

He raised an eyebrow.

'Do you really think he could go to prison?' I asked Lou.

'I'll do my very best to put him there,' said Lou. 'The useless little toerag.'

Suki spluttered a laugh, and I joined her. 'I think Agnes has some brandy left,' said Suki. 'Shall I...?'

'I'll go,' said Lou. 'And Edie will find some suitable receptacles, and we'll all drink a toast to the long-term incarceration of Frank bloody Sullivan.'

By Saturday, I was greatly relieved to have a morning off. Reassured by Lou that Frank would remain in custody until at least Monday, Suki explained, 'I can't go back to work till I know what becomes of Frank.'

'I suppose that's how he found you?' I asked. 'Someone in the salon let it slip?'

'It was Madame Faye,' said Suki. 'She didn't realise – he went in on my afternoon off, and said he was my cousin home on leave and asked for my new address. She'll be so upset that she told him.'

Agnes was at home all day, and I felt Suki would be

comforted by her motherly presence. I was aware, too, that tonight was the night Arnold would ask Annie to marry him – and for reasons I didn't want to examine too closely, I felt the need for distraction. I would return once again to Grafton Street, I decided, to offer the remaining cast my condolences over Guy and research his obituary. Most importantly, perhaps I would finally find some evidence to incriminate Stanley Kerridge for three murders.

A light rain was falling as I rang the bell of number twenty-three, and the temperature had dropped. There would be nobody sitting in the garden today, and I felt nervous as to what sort of state they'd all be in. It also seemed impossible to fathom that one of them could be a killer who might shortly be chatting with me, expressing his or her grief. I profoundly hoped that Lou had the right man. The previous evening's *Chronicle* had reported on Kerridge 'helping police with enquiries', but despite the thrill of my byline, I felt haunted by what I'd seen – Guy's blank blue eyes in the mirror, the shining dagger buried in his back.

'Edie!' This time it was Sybil who answered the door. 'Come in, dear,' she said. 'I'm not sure anyone can tell you very much, we're all in a state of shock. Everyone's in the kitchen, drinking tea – well, I say everyone – there's barely anyone left.'

'Oh, I'm not just here for the *Chronicle*,' I assured her. 'I came to see how you all were – and after finding him, I suppose I wanted to talk to the people who knew him.'

Sybil turned halfway down the hall, her red hair transformed to a blazing halo by the morning sun. '*You* found him?'

'I'm afraid so, yes. I was with DI Brennan; we were trying to find out more about Ginny's disappearance. We went to the theatre to look, and well...'

'How dreadful,' she murmured. 'The shock... and did you find anything to suggest where our little bird has flown?'

I shook my head. 'Nothing, I'm afraid.'

'Let us sincerely hope she's simply run away,' said Sybil. She ushered me into the kitchen, where Jack, Josephine and Florence were seated at the table. Jack stood to greet me, and the others smiled wanly in my direction. Josephine's eyes were swollen from crying.

Daphne was by the Aga – she seemed to live there – and the room was pleasantly scented with steam from the soup she was stirring.

'Pea and mint,' she said. 'Do stay for a bowl, won't you, Edie? We've an absolute glut of peas this year.'

'It's Sybil's magic touch,' said Jack. He turned to the land-lady. 'If you hadn't been an actress, you'd have been a marvel-lous market gardener.'

'Needs must.' Sybil shrugged. 'It gets one out of the house, and it does help to feed the five thousand.'

'What made you stop acting?' I asked her, as she took her usual seat at the head of the table. Her smile dropped away.

'Personal reasons,' she said quietly. 'Family matters. I ran number twenty-three by myself for a long time, then Daph joined me when she was widowed. But all of our guests have brought such joy, and kept me so happily immersed in the world of theatre – well, until this terrible week,' she added. 'I never imagined... as the bard of Avon said, "*When I waked, I cried to dream again.*"'

'We all did,' said Florence heavily. She sighed, stirring honey into her tea. 'Leonard brought us this as a gift,' she indi-cated the pot. 'Cedric keeps bees... oh Lord, the waste of it all.'

'Florence,' I said, 'now that Guy is gone, if you won't tell me, please tell Lou exactly what Ginny said during her tarot read-ing. It will be confidential, and you never know what might help.' I thought of my beloved detective novels. 'Sometimes, it's the most unlikely bit of information that provides the key to the crime.'

Florence raised her dark eyes to meet mine.

'All right,' she said. 'I had truly hoped she'd only run away and it wouldn't matter, but now her handbag's been found, and Guy's been killed... I'll tell you, Edie, rather than the detective, but it must be in private.'

My heart leapt 'Thank you,' I said. 'Thank you so very much.'

Jack gazed around the table. He looked wretched. 'Look,' he said, 'do we really all think it was Stan? I know he can be an absolute oaf, but I never thought... I never could have believed it of him.'

'Oh, I don't know,' said Sybil, sipping tea. 'I've known him for a long time, and he's terribly arrogant. If he was jealous, or thwarted...'

'But why kill Guy?' persisted Jack.

'Perhaps he thought Guy had some evidence that would reveal him as Ginny's killer,' said Josephine unexpectedly. 'At that point, he didn't know you'd got the handbag, Edie. He may have panicked that he was about to be found out.'

Jack nodded. 'Yes – but how did he know Guy would go back to the theatre?'

We all looked at one another.

'He didn't,' said Josephine. 'He couldn't have done.'

'What about Rosemary?' I ventured. 'Do you think her jealousy...?'

I wasn't sure how much the cast knew about the arrangement she and Guy had, but perhaps they suspected. They certainly all knew about Guy and Ginny.

Florence nodded. 'I read for her once. In London. She thought it was rather a joke, but it was before the war, at a cast party, and I offered.'

'What did the cards say?' I asked, trying not to imagine Lou's disgusted expression if he could hear me.

'They told me that her marriage wouldn't last,' said

Florence. 'The hanged man – sacrifice. The three of swords – pain and loss. The four of staves – gossip and betrayal.'

'Do you really remember?' I asked, astonished by her recall.

'Actors remember entire scenes, dear,' she said. 'I can certainly remember one of my readings that gave me pause.'

'Did you tell her?'

Florence shook her head. 'She wouldn't have listened. But based on that reading, I don't think it was Rosemary who killed him.'

Sybil put her cup down. 'Edie, if you'd like to chat to the others separately, do use the front parlour. I'm off outside. Gardening always makes me feel better, somehow, no matter what's happened.'

'I need to dust upstairs,' Daphne said. She turned to me. 'We did have a housekeeper, Mabel, but she left to work in the aircraft factory at Trafford Park. I do miss her.'

'May I speak to you all separately, then?' I asked. 'Not for the newspaper, I promise – just in case there's a tiny chance it may help us to find Ginny?'

'Of course,' said Jack. 'We're going nowhere today. Tonight's show is cancelled, as I didn't think any of us could face it. Leonard, Ginny, now Guy... It's hard to believe.'

I nodded. 'Will you try and get other actors?'

He shrugged. 'I suppose we'll have to, but they're thin on the ground. We had the cream of the crop, and now... I may have to cancel Africa, too, if we can't find any replacements in time. It really does seem that we're cursed.'

In the parlour, Josephine sat opposite me. Instead of her usual smart dress, she was wearing creased slacks and a thick Fair Isle cardigan buttoned over her blouse. Her hair was tied back with a black ribbon, and she looked much younger than usual.

Without make-up, her face was pale and exhausted, and, in her hand, she clutched a balled hanky.

'I didn't sleep,' she said. 'Not a wink. I feel as if I'm in a nightmare, and I'll wake up and they'll all be back here – laughing and joking and telling stories. How can this have happened?'

Her voice wavered, and I reached over to touch her hand.

'I'm so very sorry,' I said. 'Anything you can remember – anything at all – might help, and I promise it's all off the record.'

She sniffed hard, and leaned back against the flowered cushions. 'I think Rosemary must be on her way here. The police will have telephoned her with the news.'

'They might need to question her,' I said. 'Because of Ginny...'

Josephine nodded. 'I suppose so.'

A tear rolled down her cheek.

'Oh, JoJo,' I said. 'Did you love him, too?'

At my words, she buried her face in her hands and sobbed – a wrenching, tearing sound that was almost unbearable to hear. Bernhardt shot from under the piano and streaked into the hall-way, and as Josephine's sobs subsided, I moved to sit next to her on the raspberry-pink brocade couch.

'I'm so sorry,' I said. 'It must hurt horribly.' She nodded jerk-ily, still gasping in the aftermath of her storm of tears.

'It's been awful,' she whispered, her voice shaking. 'Just awful.'

'Can you tell me what happened?'

She nodded. 'It'll be a relief to get it off my chest at last,' she said with a shaky half-laugh. 'I'll try not to cry again. Oh, God, what a mess. It began just over two years ago, before the war.'

She fixed her eyes on a framed Victorian playbill above the piano, which praised Miss Sybil Charnwood as '*the most charming little Alice in Wonderland this critic has ever witnessed.*' 'I was in a production of *The Misanthrope* –

Molière, do you know it?' I shook my head. French had not been my strong suit at school.

'Well, Guy was playing Alceste, the leading man, and I was cast as Célimène, the high-society love interest... we had several scenes together and it was the loveliest spring. We used to climb up onto the roof of the theatre and rehearse together, looking out over London. I knew he was married, but when you're in a play, it's as though the outside world fades away. It's just you and the cast and crew, in a bubble of rehearsals and props and parties – it's your whole world for those few weeks or months, and you're all working together to make it as good as it can possibly be, sleeping and breathing the words and the movements around the stage... Oh, it's so hard to describe it properly,' she broke off. 'Nothing I say justifies it, really, does it?'

'I'm not going to judge you,' I said. 'Go on.'

'Well, I'm sure you can guess.' She took a shuddering breath. 'One night we all went for a drink at the Astor Club, where actors often go after a performance, and gradually, the others left. It was awfully late. The club was closing, they were putting chairs up on the tables, but Guy and I wanted to carry on talking, and he invited me back to his rooms near Cheyne Walk. We walked all the way back down the embankment, and as dawn was breaking, he... well, he kissed me, and that was it. I'd already fallen in love with him, but after that... I had never felt like that about anyone,' she went on. 'Some silly fumblings with boys my age, and a couple of older actors. But meeting Guy was like a bolt of lightning right through me. He was intelligent and kind and talented, and so desperately handsome...' She paused.

'And married,' I said sadly.

'Yes. And married. He made it perfectly clear at the start of our affair that he wouldn't leave Rosemary,' she said. 'Not just because of the money, he claimed, but because they "understood one another". I didn't know then that he meant she'd turn a blind eye to all his liaisons, but now I do.'

Josephine pressed the hanky to her eyes. 'Sorry. It still hurts so. Being with Guy was like walking out into spring sunlight after you've been inside a cold, dark house all winter – everything was illuminated just by being together, knowing he'd chosen me. I knew I shouldn't, but I began to hope he might feel the same way, and leave Rosemary for me. Little fool that I was.'

I sympathised – Guy may have been married, but I had been no less foolish over Charles Emerson, an infinitely worse individual than an unfaithful actor.

'We carried on until the end of the run, in June,' she said. 'Then he had to return to Foxwell, Rosemary's estate, where they live when he's not working, and I was off on a summer rep tour to Margate and Broadstairs. I felt my heart would shatter.'

'Did he make you a promise?' I asked. 'That you'd be together?'

She shook her head. 'He hadn't said anything about what would happen when we parted, and I was too afraid to ask. On our last night, it was the end-of-run cast party, before we all went our separate ways, and I kept thinking that afterwards, Guy would take me home with him to Cheyne Walk, so we could at least – I'm sorry to be crude – spend a final night together. But as everyone was leaving, he beckoned me aside, and he said he had a present for me.'

She pulled her legs up onto the sofa, making herself as small as possible. 'Now, of course, I see how deluded I was, but, for a moment, I thought it was an engagement ring, and perhaps he was going to ask me to marry him when he and Rosemary were divorced. But he... well, he handed it to me, and I realised straight away that it was just a cigarette case. He'd had it engraved on the inside, and it said: "*As full of spirit as the month of May – Henry VI, part 1. With thanks for an unforgettable spring, Your adoring G.*"'

'So for him...' I began.

'It was just a dalliance,' said Josephine bitterly. 'I was a pleasant distraction while he was in London. He was signing me off like an expenses sheet, before he returned to his aristo-cratic wife. I suppose he thought he'd never see me again. I ran out to the street and hailed a cab and went home by myself.'

'How utterly horrible for you,' I said.

She nodded. 'Then I met Ginny. She was on the summer rep tour with me, and we got on so well. We were the only two young women in the cast, and we did everything together. We've been great friends ever since – so when I heard she was booked for the ENSA shows, too, I was thrilled and so was she.'

'But you didn't know Guy would be on them as well?'

'Not till the first day of rehearsals, when I heard his voice as I took off my coat,' said Josephine bleakly. 'And I didn't know that he and Ginny would fall in love.'

'How did you bear it?'

'Because I had to. I couldn't leave Jack and the troops in the lurch once I'd signed up, and Leonard knew, and was terribly kind to me. He'd always ask me for lunch or morning coffee so I didn't have to watch them gazing at each other between rehearsals, and I kept myself to myself and hoped it would blow over between them, but it didn't. It blew up, if anything. Guy was never like that with me. And of course, Ginny confided in me all the time, she was so excited and thrilled and worried about Rosemary. It was like listening to myself, but this time, you see, it was all reciprocated. I thought there was a very good chance he would leave Rosemary and marry Ginny, and the idea...' She pressed her hand into her stomach. 'It was a physical agony.'

'Oh Josephine,' I said. 'Why didn't you tell Ginny?'

'What difference would it have made? I couldn't keep them apart. Ginny only ever knew I'd had an affair that ended badly before the rep tour. She's a darling, and I didn't want her to feel any worse on top of her guilt about his being married.'

'So you had to act with him every night, and watch their love blossom, and hear her tiptoeing down to his bedroom past your door. Had your feelings faded at all?'

Josephine shook her head. 'Not a bit. Just the same as ever, despite the way he treated me. And now he's gone and Ginny's nowhere to be found. What a waste it's all been.'

'Is that why you still used the cigarette case? To remind him?'

'You noticed that?' She half smiled. 'Pathetic, isn't it? It was all I had of him. All I'll ever have, now.'

After a moment's silence, she stood, brushed down her slacks, and said, 'I'll get Jack, shall I?'

'Does he know?' I asked her. 'About you and Guy?'

She nodded. 'I think he guessed. But Leonard was the only one I ever spoke to about it. He understood about forbidden love, you see.'

CHAPTER FOURTEEN

Josephine left the room, still blotting at her face, and shortly afterwards Jack tapped on the door, and entered.

'Flo hasn't forgotten,' he said, 'she's just upstairs doing whatever mystical gypsies do in their spare time. Reading the *Picture Post* with her feet up, I expect.'

I laughed. Jack's presence was a salty sea breeze after Josephine's desperate, confessional grief, and I warmed to him.

'Isn't it an absolute show?' he said, throwing himself into the mustard velvet button-back armchair. 'And not the entertaining sort. I'm afraid I still can't quite believe it.'

I noted how many of the cast had used that phrase to me, and wondered what one could reply to that, beyond, 'Well, it's true.'

'Can you think of anything that might help us to find the person who killed Guy?' I asked. 'Do you think it was Stanley?'

Jack puffed his cheeks out. 'It's hard to imagine. Why would he? Because Ginny rebuffed him, but not Guy? She's surely not the first woman to do so, Stanley's hardly a silver screen matinée idol, is he?'

'He is not,' I agreed. 'But if he was in love with Ginny, perhaps...'

'Oh surely not,' demurred Jack. 'I can't see Stanley being in love with anything except his Talbot and his bank balance.'

I smiled. 'You don't think much of him.'

'I tolerate him,' said Jack. 'He brings in the punters, and we need that these days. But no, he's very much not my sort of chap. And now it seems he may have harmed Ginny and Guy, too... look, do you mind if I smoke?'

I shook my head, and he lit a Player's Weights, offering me one and lighting it for me.

'Helps me think,' he said.

'Me too,' I admitted.

'Filthy habit, but I won't tell if you don't,' Jack said with a wink, and I wondered, puzzled, if he was flirting with me again.

'To be frank, Edie, I don't think I can tell you anything new,' he went on. 'We all came back from the theatre that night around the same time. Guy said he was meeting a *Stage* reporter for supper and walked the other way... look here, has anyone tracked her down? I believe she was French.'

'She's already been interviewed by the police,' I said quickly. 'She's not a suspect.'

'Ah, good. Well, I came back here and went up to my room, read my book for a bit and fell asleep. As far as I know, the others did, too. Dull, I know.'

'Did you see anyone when you came in?'

'Only Sybil, giving Bernhardt her late-night supper. Daph was in bed.'

'No noises that might have been Stanley wandering about, going out again?'

He shook his head. 'I'm a horribly deep sleeper. Takes two alarm clocks and a cockerel on the bedpost to rouse me once I'm gone.'

I nodded. 'I'm sorry to ask this, but I feel I have to – were you ever romantically involved with Ginny, or Josephine?'

Jack looked startled, and took a long drag on his cigarette. 'Never. I told you, I never get too close to the actresses I work with. It causes all sorts of bother, I've seen it happen too often, and decent plays have been ruined by less.'

'Yes, you did tell me,' I admitted. 'Are you with anyone else, then – a wife, or...'

He laughed. 'No, I'm not. Solo as a shilling. Wartime makes it rather difficult to get to know anybody, they're always being carried away on the breeze. Unless they're in a reserved occupation, of course. Like a newspaper reporter, for instance.'

He held my gaze, and I felt a sudden warmth in my face.

'Sorry,' he said quickly. 'Hardly appropriate amid all this tragedy. I just wondered... I like you, Edie, you're straightforward and clever, and I notice how kind you've been to us all... and well, I wondered if you might like to join me for supper later. Nothing more,' he added hastily. 'Just a chat, over something decent to eat. I think I'll be off back to London next week, I need to see the ENSA committee about the rest of the tour. So I don't expect anything more from you than your company, I swear... dear God, I'm making a dreadful botch of this. Ignore me.'

I laughed. Jack could be a murderer of course, though it seemed unlikely – there was nothing linking him to any of the crimes, and unless he too was secretly in love with Ginny, no motive. He was also handsome, good company and, I remembered afresh, tonight was the evening when Annie's life would change for good – and mine with it. I envisaged myself standing by the window in evening shadow, waiting for my newly engaged friend, exclaiming over her sparkling ring, creeping off to my single bed like a spinster aunt... or I could permit a good-looking man with no expectations to take me for supper.

'Why not?' I said. 'If it's just dinner for two people at a loose end, then that would be lovely.'

After Jack had left, Florence tapped on the door.

'It's Miss Buchanan,' she said loftily.

'No need to knock,' I said, 'please, come and sit down. I'm so grateful to you for speaking to me.'

'You're like Hercule Poirot,' she said, though not admiringly. 'Asking us all to the library. It was the butler wot did it,' she said in a Cockney accent.

'I'm sorry if I seem intrusive,' I said. 'I know how upset you must all be. But I want to help DI Brennan find out what's happened to your friends.'

'Not to get a story in the paper?' She regarded me beadily with her black eyes. 'I saw your byline. "I found the body." You strike me as an ambitious young woman, Miss York.'

I felt wrong-footed. 'I'm... well, I take my job seriously,' I said eventually. 'But I'm an obituary writer, not a reporter.'

'Much as you'd like to be,' she said, holding my gaze, and I wondered how she knew.

Bernhardt returned, leapt onto the couch, and began to knead Florence's skirt as if she were making bread, purring violently with each new push. 'What a good girl,' said Florence, crooning at the cat. 'My little puss-puss. I do miss my cat in London, Miss York. He's called Banquo because he slips in and out like a ghost. And he's a terrific mouser.'

'Who's looking after him?'

'I don't know,' she said. 'My house was bombed in the Blitz. Luckily, I was on my way home at the time. The cards tell me that Banquo is alive, but beyond that...'

'I'm so sorry,' I said, startled. Something occurred to me. 'Have you done a tarot reading to see if... well...'

'If Ginny is alive?'

I nodded.

'Yes, I'm afraid I have.' Florence paused. 'I saw nothing. Only darkness. That's all I can say.'

I swallowed. I hoped her esoteric gifts were only in her mind. I didn't believe in psychic powers, but Florence had a way of making me question my long-held certainties.

'Can you tell me,' I asked, 'what Ginny said that night?'

Florence stopped rhythmically stroking Bernhardt and gripped my wrist tightly.

'I will do so,' she said, 'if you tell DI Brennan and nobody else. That means none of the cast, none of your colleagues, not your friends... because if you do, I will know, and I will curse you. A Romany taught me how to do it, many years ago, and I promise you, Miss York, it works.'

Despite Lou muttering '*abject nonsense*' in my head, I felt a chill spread through my veins like frost over a windowpane.

'I promise.'

She glanced at the door and lowered her voice.

'All right. Though this is the first time I have ever divulged a confidence from a client – and friend. And I hope it shall be the last.'

I nodded, as she seemed to expect some acknowledgement.

'Ginny came to see me after the show that night,' she said, 'because she had something on her mind. She was in love.'

'With Guy,' I supplied.

'Yes, with Guy. I thought she wanted advice on what to do, whether to leave and find somebody unencumbered, so that was the reading I began. And then halfway through, she asked me to stop.'

Florence paused. 'I do wish I'd helped her, Miss York. I had every intention of doing so, but Leonard's death... and then she was gone.'

'It wasn't your fault.'

'Well.' Florence heaved a sigh. 'She told me that she didn't need to know about the love affair – they would be together, she said, that had already been decided. He was going to leave Rosemary.'

'Really?'

'Yes,' said Florence. 'Her money and title were no match for Ginny's youth and beauty, in the end. They were going to marry once his divorce came through. Anyway,' she continued, 'she wanted to ask about something else altogether.'

Florence dropped her voice to a whisper. 'I shuffled the cards for her again, and asked her what she needed to know. And she told me...'

I held my breath.

'She told me that she was sure she was expecting,' she said, 'and that the baby was Guy's. And she wanted to know what she should do.'

'My God,' I said.

'Yes.' Florence nodded. 'A dilemma for any young, unmarried woman – but one with a glittering career such as Ginny's...'

'She wouldn't have tried to do anything illegal? Harm herself?'

'No, no. Nothing like that. But she wanted to know if she should tell Guy straight away. She was frightened and shocked and said she couldn't think straight.'

'And what happened?'

'I read the cards,' said Florence implacably. 'And I told her that she should tell him. He was the father, he needed to know. And of course, Rosemary would need to know too if Ginny was going to run off with Guy and have a child.'

I thought of Marie saying, '*It was not to be. Besides, Rosemary's so busy with her charities and good works, where would she have fitted them in?*'

So it was not Guy who had struggled to provide an heir. No wonder Rosemary's caveat had always been that her husband could not allow any of his mistresses to become pregnant.

'And did she?' I asked quietly. 'Tell Guy, I mean?'

'I don't know,' said Florence. 'I didn't ask, and then it was too late. But, given what's happened since... well, I imagine she did, yes.'

I thought of Guy's shock, the realisation that his fortune and good name were lost, and of Ginny's fear, and her desperate hope that Guy would be pleased, despite everything. Of Rosemary and of how a woman who couldn't conceive children to inherit her vast estate would feel, knowing that her husband had fallen desperately in love with a beautiful young actress.

Jack met me at the bus stop that evening. He had offered to pick me up in a cab, but I wasn't sure I wanted to be trapped at close quarters with him – just in case.

'You look glorious,' he said, pecking me on the cheek. Suki's offer to alter a couple of Agnes's old dresses to fit Annie and me had been genuine, and she'd done a wonderful job. Annie's was powder-blue silk, while mine was a cap-sleeved navy crepe with scarlet buttons. For once, I felt what Pat would call 'quite the thing'.

Jack, too, looked far smarter than I'd previously seen him, in a dark suit and hat.

'I took the liberty of booking a table for two at Les Frères de la Côte,' he said, then stopped as he saw my face.

'Is it no good?' he asked. 'I can cancel...'

'It's not that,' I said. 'But I think my best friend is getting engaged tonight, and that's where they're going.'

'Good heavens!' He laughed. 'So you don't want her to think you're spying on the proposal?'

'Yes, something like that.'

'How about if I ask for a very discreet table, around the side of the main restaurant?' he suggested. 'If you don't want to risk it, that's entirely fine of course, but I've heard marvellous things about the food.'

'As long as she doesn't see me,' I said. 'The last thing she needs is me turning up mid-proposal.'

As he'd promised, Jack had a quiet word with the maître d' as we arrived, and we were swiftly ushered to a small banquette table in the short L-shape of the main restaurant. Nobody could see into the booth, and as I was facing Jack, who was against the wall, I judged us fairly safe.

I leaned against the padded crimson velvet, feeling profoundly grateful for a night off from worrying.

Jack ordered for both of us, which was a relief as the menu was in French.

'What should I not order?' he asked.

'I like everything really,' I said. 'Oh, well, perhaps not sweet-breads. Or lamb kidneys. In fact, if we could avoid offal...'

'Done,' said Jack.

He ordered our drinks and food, then sat back.

'Thank you for joining me,' he said. 'I imagine this is all terribly strange for you. One moment you're at the theatre, the next you're investigating a string of deaths and disappearances.'

'Well, yes,' I said. 'It is strange. And worrying.'

He nodded. 'I know we must all be under a cloud of suspicion, but I can only assume that Stanley killed Guy and – well, I don't want to think it, but perhaps Ginny, too.'

'It's rare for any woman to run off without her handbag, jacket or any money,' I agreed. Even Suki had packed before escaping.

I wondered whether to mention my suspicions about Rosemary, but realised I couldn't break Florence's confidence. Telling Annie didn't count, I reasoned – and I'd telephone Lou tomorrow. I hadn't done so earlier, because I'd thought he might ask what I was doing later, and for some reason I hadn't wanted to tell him.

Jack was excellent company. Just solicitous enough – 'food all right?' he asked, when our fragrant *soles meunieres* arrived – and although full of stories about the theatre, he also made sure to ask me about my life and work.

'It's so interesting,' he said, as I described Mr Gorringe's morning conferences and how much I longed to join them. 'One never thinks about how the newspaper is put together. It just seems to appear.'

'Just like a play,' I said. 'Will you go to Africa, do you think?'

He sighed, as the stiff-backed sommelier silently refilled our glasses with whatever wine Jack had chosen. It was white and delicious, and I reminded myself to drink water, so I didn't keel over – or fall into his arms.

'I had so many plans,' he said quietly. 'I feel a fool for being so enthusiastic. Now it's up to the top brass I suppose, but it's not looking too likely with five of us gone, counting Avril.'

'If Stanley is released...'

'Yes, but if he's released pending enquiries, he can't leave the country,' Jack said. 'It all seems rather futile, we can't possibly find enough cast members in time, and get them rehearsed. Besides, it feels more like a funeral march than a gang show. Oh, do listen to me,' he said, rolling his eyes. 'A lovely restaurant on a summer's evening with a beautiful woman and I can't even be cheerful.'

I was about to snort at his compliment, when a woman's high-pitched voice pierced the low rumble of chatter.

'Yes!' she cried. 'I will!'

It was Annie, I realised – and she had just agreed to marry Arnold.

There was a brief ripple of laughter from the surrounding tables, and somebody called 'Congratulations!', swiftly followed by the comedic pop of a champagne cork. Arnold was pushing the boat out tonight.

I almost stood up. I longed to rush over and congratulate

them both, see Annie's thrilled, flushed face and Arnold's proud delight – but it would surely seem as though I had been spying on them, a lonely spectre at the feast.

'That's my friend,' I said, smiling to cover my sudden pang of loss. 'I believe she's just got engaged, as planned!'

'How marvellous!' Jack glanced about, looking for a waiter. 'We must send them champagne! Don't you want to go and exclaim over the ring and all that jazz? I shan't mind a bit.'

'No, no,' I said. 'As I said, it's their occasion. I shouldn't be here at all.'

'Some sense at last,' said a familiar voice, and I peered round the curved edge of the banquette to find Lou Brennan standing behind me, wearing an expression last seen on a Victorian land-lord throwing a weeping orphan into the snow.

'Edie York,' he said. 'A word, if I may.'

CHAPTER FIFTEEN

'What on earth are you doing here?'

'I might ask you the same question,' he said furiously. 'Excuse me, Mr Webb, I have some business with Edie that I must—'

'You do not!' I hissed. 'It's a Saturday night and I'm having dinner with a friend. Annie and Arnold are just round the corner, and if you've turned up to spoil their engagement, I shall...'

'Nothing of the kind,' said Lou coldly. 'Though I may be about to spoil your dinner. Come with me.'

'I shall not!'

A waiter glanced over, as Jack murmured, 'Now look here—'

'Don't "look here" me,' said Lou. 'I'm the Detective Inspector on this case, three people have probably been murdered, and the whole lot of you are suspects. Edie, if you think *going for dinner* – he said the words as he might have said *fan-dancing on the table* – 'with one of my suspects, particularly after what happened last time, is an acceptable way to—'

'I had no idea I was "one of your suspects",' said Jack coldly, as I snapped, 'Oh, will you *shut up* about bloody Charles Emerson!'

The waiter hurried over, damp with panic.

'Mademoiselle, Messieurs, I must ask that you do not disrupt! Les Frères is not the place for a disagreement!'

'I'm so sorry,' I began, mortified, as Lou barked, 'I apologise,' and Jack shook his head.

'It's Edie to whom you should be apologising,' he said.

'I'll take instruction from a pantomime planner when I'm no longer trying to find the person who murdered your colleagues,' said Lou.

'Oh for God's sake.' I threw my napkin down and stood up. 'I'm so sorry, Jack, I'll be two minutes.'

As Lou stalked through the crowded, candlelit tables ahead of me, rage pounded through my blood. *How dare he?* I almost tripped over a foot, apologised, and then realised it belonged to someone wearing a powder-blue silk dress.

'Edie!' Annie's gasp was almost louder than her previous shriek, and several people turned to look.

'What on earth are you doing here – hold on, was that *Lou?* Are you...?'

'Gosh! A couple at last!' said Arnold, who was smarter than I had ever seen him, in a suit and silk tie with his hair slicked back.

'I've no time to explain,' I whispered, as Lou vanished through the revolving oak doors and onto the pavement.

'But I can't congratulate you both enough,' I added. 'I'm thrilled for you!'

'How do you know...' Annie began, but I couldn't leave Jack fuming and puzzled round the corner. I would give Lou one minute of my evening, and send him off with a flea in his ear.

. . .

Lou stood on the crowded street beside a heap of grubby sandbags. It was still daylight outside, and buses and taxis thundered past. After the soft glow and hushed murmur of Les Frères, I felt as though cold water had been dashed into my face.

'Please explain,' I said tightly.

'You're having dinner with a murder suspect,' he said. 'Have you entirely lost your mind?'

'Why is he a suspect? There's not a shred of evidence to say it was Jack!'

'And there's not a shred to say it wasn't, you button-headed idiot!'

'But Stanley's in the cells! And I found out today that Ginny was pregnant, so Rosemary could have done it!'

Lou stilled, a cigarette halfway to his lips. 'What did you just say?'

'I was going to tell you tomorrow.'

'After you'd leafed through fashion magazines all afternoon, and had dinner with a potential murderer? I was a damned lunatic ever to have trusted you on police business. I shan't make that mistake again.'

'Except you didn't know about Ginny!' I said, my face aflame with fury. 'It was me who found that out, me who discovered her handbag, me who...'

'You who compromised the entire case by blurting your involvement all over the newspaper and then seducing a suspect!'

'Seducing?' I cried. 'We're having dinner! I'm hardly doing the dance of the seven veils...'

Several people were now gathering to watch our little scene, and a man in a cap turned to his companion and said, 'Better than the pictures, in't it?'

'Go home at once, Edie,' barked Lou, 'you can telephone me tomorrow morning to explain whatever you know about Ginny, and after that, consider yourself back to interviewing vicars or whatever it is you do when you're not inserting yourself into the middle of serious police business.'

He turned and strode down the street, scattering gawping pedestrians like pigeons.

'Blimey, he's a charmer,' said the man in the cap. 'You all right, love?'

'Fine, thank you,' I said stiffly, though my voice shook with fury and embarrassment.

The doorman silently held the door open for me, and I slinked back into the restaurant where Jack was still waiting, presumably wondering why on earth he'd ever invited me for dinner.

The evening petered out shortly afterwards. Jack tried. 'I can see why he was worried,' he said kindly. 'He obviously feels responsible, Edie, and doesn't want to see you in danger.'

'There are other ways of doing it,' I said, still hot with the horror of it all. I had hoped that Jack and I would have an evening free of worry, perhaps get along well and enjoy ourselves. Lou had stamped his size eight boots all over that pleasant prospect.

There was no sign of Annie and Arnold, and a waiter was sweeping crumbs from their table with a little silver dustpan and brush as we passed.

'Would you like to go on somewhere else to dance?' Jack asked after he'd paid the bill without the awful sort of flourishing flamboyance that some men went in for.

'Would you mind horribly if we called it a night? I think DI Brennan has rather spoiled my enjoyment,' I said.

'Of course not,' Jack said. 'But you mustn't feel guilty on my account. I've never been a murder suspect before, it'd be quite exciting if it weren't all so awful.'

I smiled at him.

'You must let me drop you off in a cab,' he said. 'No funny business, I assure you.'

I might have thought twice, but Lou had so enraged me I would have swum down the Irwell if it would have further irritated him at that point. 'Thank you,' I said, and as we climbed in, Jack sat beside me. I found his presence reassuring rather than intimidating – he seemed as troubled as I was by the recent deaths and disappearances. Under other circum stances, perhaps we could have become something more than friends.

We drew up at Mrs Turner's, and Jack leapt out to open the door for me.

'Thank you for a lovely evening,' I said. 'I'm very sorry about Lou.'

'You were wonderful company,' Jack said. 'Perhaps when all this is over, we can do it again.'

'I'd like that.'

He leaned down to kiss my cheek as I turned my head to say something, and our lips brushed.

'Please take good care of yourself,' he said, climbing back into the cab. 'I really couldn't bear it if something happened to you as well.'

I stood by the gate, watching the cab's dipped tail lights vanish up the road, then let myself in and ran upstairs, aware that I was smiling rather foolishly.

'You're back!' Annie cried. She was in her dressing gown, sitting on the sofa with a cup of tea, and I was so surprised to see her, I shrieked.

'*You're* back!' I said. 'I thought you'd be twirling through silvery stardust with your fiancé till dawn!'

'Well, I might have been,' said Annie. 'If... well, you go first.

What in blazes was Lou doing striding out of the restaurant? I've never seen him look so hatchet-faced!'

I told her, and she gasped. 'You had a row *in the street*?'

'It was more of a brief exchange of views,' I said. 'But it was horrible and embarrassing, and he was completely unreasonable.'

'I suppose he's right in that Jack *is* still a suspect, officially speaking,' said Annie carefully. 'And after last time...'

'Oh, don't you start! It's hardly a love affair, Jack's leaving soon. It was just a pleasant dinner. Well, it was supposed to be.' I picked up her teacup and swigged, but it was cold.

Annie sighed. 'D'you know, Edie, you and Lou should probably just get married. It'd save an awful lot of bother.'

'Come off it.' I felt my face flush.

'Seriously – you're made for each other. Most men are frightened of you, but he's not.'

'Most men aren't jumped-up, bossy, ridiculous, self-important...'

'People who care about you,' Annie finished. 'I know he shouldn't have barged in like that, but...'

'I've no idea why you're making excuses for him,' I muttered. 'Anyway, never mind Lou. You're engaged! Tell me everything!'

'Well, I think you heard most of it.' Annie gave a small smile and waggled her left hand at me. On her finger was a slim gold ring with a little square-cut diamond winking in the lamplight.

'Oh, it's beautiful,' I said. 'Did you know he'd ask tonight?'

She shrugged. 'I hoped he might. We don't normally frequent that kind of restaurant.'

'But why are you back so early? Shouldn't you be out, kissing under a full moon?' I crooned a couple of lines of 'They Can't Black Out the Moon', a song that was currently popular.

'Oh shush,' said Annie. 'What happened was, Arnold got onto one knee and said, "Annie Hemmings, will you do me the great honour of becoming my wife?" I was taken aback, because our puddings had just arrived and I was so excited about the raspberry mousse, I wasn't really paying attention... but of course I said yes, and nothing would make me happier and that sort of thing, and it was all wonderful.'

She fell silent.

'So what's wrong?'

'Nothing really, it's just... well, we began to talk about the wedding, when and where, and all of that, and then Arnold said, "and of course, you'll come to live at Whiting's."'

'The funeral parlour?'

'Well, not bunked down among the coffins, but the flat above, where he and his mother live.'

I began to grasp the problem.

'Two bedrooms, and his mother's in the other one?'

She nodded dolefully. 'I know beggars can't be choosers, and of course I'd like to be married to Arnold, but she's hard going. Enormously religious, nitpicking, house-proud and never thinks anyone's good enough for her boy.' Annie said, 'And those are just the bits Arnold admits to. Can you imagine the things he isn't saying out of loyalty to her? He was assuming I'd stop nursing and just stay at home with his mother all day, polishing her statuettes of the Virgin Mary while he embalms dead bodies downstairs.'

I suppressed a snort of laughter. 'When you put it like that... well, I can see why you're doubtful.'

'It's more than doubtful,' Annie said. 'I love him dearly, he's the kindest, sweetest man in the world, but I don't want to move into a funeral parlour with him and his mother.'

'And you told him so?'

'Yes. I asked why we couldn't get our own little place, and he told me she wouldn't hear of it, and as she was a grieving widow and his brother's away fighting, he couldn't leave her on her own.'

'His father died years ago!'

'Well, you and I know that,' said Annie, 'but his mother seems to carry on as though it were yesterday. Arnold's "all she's got", apparently, and without him she'll waste away. She's the shape of an overstuffed kitbag, so I doubt it,' she added bitterly.

'I wish he'd told you all this before he asked you to marry him,' I said.

'He sort of did, I suppose,' Annie said. 'But I didn't exactly listen, because I so wanted to be engaged to him. I hoped it would all work out.'

I nodded. Annie's commitment to romance had long trumped all other considerations.

'So... we didn't have an argument, exactly,' she said, 'but I said she could come and live with us in a little house if she must, and he said she'd never go along with it because she wouldn't leave the home where she'd been so happy with his father...'

'In a funeral parlour?'

'I know. And he said besides, we've no savings and we can't afford a decent house yet, and he'd just assumed I'd be happy to move in...'

'Oh, Annie.'

'Yes. So in the end, we left the restaurant and he said he was thrilled I'd agreed to marry him, and perhaps I could sleep on it and let him know my decision. Then he brought me home in the mortuary van and here I am.'

We looked at each other.

'And will you sleep on it?' I asked.

'I don't need to! I know I can't move in with his mother in a flat the size of a pocket watch. I like nursing,' she added mournfully. 'I didn't at first, but I feel useful, and Matron says I've really come on. I can't give up my war work to pray with Mrs Whiting.'

'Will you marry him?'

'Yes,' said Annie. 'But I've made up my mind. We won't

wed until we've saved up enough for a little house of our own. It'll be at least a year, and we'll have to scrimp horribly, but that's the way it is. And he'll just have to tell his mother that she's either moving in with us, God forbid, or staying put with the bodies.'

Despite my disappointment for Annie, my heart lifted.

'You'll be staying here then?'

She nodded. 'For the foreseeable. If that's all right with you.'

'Annie,' I said, 'I think long engagements are a wonderful thing.'

On Monday, there was no word from Lou, and I was in no rush to speak to him. But as I sat at my desk, leafing through the weekend's correspondence, I was horribly aware that, by the day's end, both Frank Sullivan and Stanley Kerridge could be back on the streets.

Suki had expressed her own fears. 'I keep dreaming about him,' she'd admitted. 'He's letting himself into the house and coming up the stairs, and I know he's going to murder me. The thing is, he easily could. I don't want to move, Edie, and go on the run.' Her face had crumpled. 'I love it here, I love living with Agnes and having you downstairs, and my own little dress-making business is just beginning... Oh, why can't he just drop dead?'

I agreed with her – it seemed desperately unfair that all over Europe, good, kind people were being bombed to kingdom come, and evil-doers like Sullivan and Guy's murderer were running free. Now, with Pat beside me pondering over the crossword ('Primary-coloured child's toy for washday, five, four?' – 'Dolly blue,' I said automatically, and she gasped with satisfaction), I was seized with the urge to at least try and resolve the terrible chaos of the theatre murders, even if my friendship with Lou was over.

The thought of that made my chest ache with a loss I couldn't name, but I slammed a lid on my unruly emotions, and picked up the receiver to telephone Marie.

At lunchtime, I said 'I'm just popping out – do you need anything?'

Pat usually had her sandwich in 'the luncheon room', which was such a grand title for a side-office overlooking a back alley that we usually said it in an aristocratic accent.

'I do, as a matter of fact,' Pat said. 'Black Sylko thread in number six, a small packet of powdered gelatine and ten Player's for Monica, she's coming round later, and can you pop to Boots, and change my book for the new Christianna Brand, *Death in High Heels*, please? The librarian promised she'd put it aside for me.'

I suppressed my inward sigh, knowing I'd be late back, but I slid her book into my bag, and set off at a fast clip for the Gaiety.

This time, Wallis greeted me like an old friend.

'Your pal's waiting in the foyer,' he said, signing me in. 'Detective Brennan on his way, is he?' I guessed that Marie had told a white lie to get us in.

'I believe so,' I said, and he wafted his hand.

'Go on, then,' he said. 'You know your way.'

I found Marie waiting by the potted ferns. 'I thought about wearing a disguise again,' she said, 'but it seemed unnecessary, more's the pity. I quite enjoyed that wig.'

We made our way backstage, down the dim corridors, and to Leonard's dressing room.

'I asked Lou, and he said the sergeant was coming to search later today,' said Marie, 'but best we have a quick look first. I don't know what time they can keep Stanley until.'

I nodded. 'Clean gloves on,' I said, and we both extracted fresh white summer gloves from our bags and slipped them on, before turning the handle. Inside, Leonard's dressing room was dark, the blackout blind still drawn over the little window. It smelled faintly of cough drops and greasepaint, a medicinal tang that wasn't unpleasant.

Marie clicked the light on, and the bulb fizzed and flickered before coming to life with a disconcerting pop. 'I'm surprised they haven't all died of electrocution,' she said. 'This theatre really is on its last gasp, isn't it?'

'It's a shame,' I said. 'It could be restored so beautifully, if anyone had the money.'

'Gas lamps and gilded boxes, and Hansom cabs drawn up outside,' she said wistfully. 'I suspect those days are long gone, along with the likes of Leonard.'

Leonard's shelf was tidy, a thin layer of dust coating his box of stage make-up, a pair of wigs lined up on disembodied plaster heads. His rack of costumes had a white dust sheet thrown over it, and good luck cards were tucked around the mirror. I thought again of Josephine's card that quoted Byron. If Guy hadn't sent it, who had?

Underneath the table was a wicker wastepaper bin, and as Marie donned her reading glasses and peered at the cards, I crouched to look through it.

There was a crumpled copy of *The Times*, bought on the day Leonard died, a shower of pencil shavings – perhaps he also liked to do the crossword – some scrap notes, a square of brown paper and red ribbon, and an empty tube of Max Factor Flexible Greasepaint. But the item that made my heart race was near the top. A discarded pink box of Almond Roca chocolates. I lifted it out and opened the lid to reveal an empty cardboard tray.

'Marie,' I whispered, 'he ate them all.'

She looked at me. 'Search for a note.'

Amongst the scattered reminders – *jacket fitting, 1.30 p.m., Montgomery's*, and *buy whisky for Jack* – I found it.

'I hope you break a leg,' the note read in black-inked capitals. 'Kind regards from an admirer.'

'Break a leg?' I repeated, confused.

'It's what they say in the theatre, instead of "good luck", which they think is bad luck,' Marie explained. 'You know what they're like. Superstitious.'

I wrapped the box and note in a tissue from Leonard's shelf, and handed it to Marie. 'Might you give this to Lou?' I asked. 'I would, but...'

'But you're not speaking again. I know,' sighed Marie. 'Of course I will. Do you really think they were poisoned?'

'I think it's likely,' I said. 'Sometimes, my passion for crime novels is useful – I know there aren't many deadly poisons so slow-acting that you could dose somebody at lunchtime and not see them falling ill until the evening. Mushrooms, perhaps, but it's not mushroom season, and I think the symptoms would begin to show by...' I broke off.

'Almonds,' I said.

'Sorry? What's wrong with almonds?'

'Marie, there's a poison that somebody could put into almond chocolates that they wouldn't notice because it already tastes of bitter almonds,' I said. 'Agatha Christie used it, in *And Then There Were None*. It's fast-acting and it's derived from the prunus family, which includes almonds... one dose can cause death within minutes.'

'Cyanide,' she said. 'I read it, too – I belong to the Collins Crime Club, it's marvellous for gripping new books.'

I stood up, still holding the note. 'But who among the cast would be able to get their hands on cyanide?'

A cursory further search revealed nothing of note, and the cards were all seemingly innocent, mostly from the rest of the cast and one from Cedric – *All my love and hopes for a good run, dearest boy* – which made me feel sad for him and his lost dreams of a Knutsford antique emporium with Leonard.

'Shall we look in the other dressing rooms again?' asked Marie, her hand on the door.

'I don't think there's much need,' I said. 'The police have already looked at Guy's, and we searched Stanley's.'

'Josephine's?' she suggested. 'Though admittedly, it feels rather a betrayal of a friend.'

'A quick glance,' I said. 'Just to be absolutely certain. She did, after all, have more reason than most to hate Guy and Ginny.'

'But not Leonard.'

'No,' I said. 'Not Leonard.'

We crept into Josephine's dressing room, feeling rather disgusted with ourselves. Little had changed since our first visit, though here, the wastepaper basket had been recently emptied. I rifled briefly through the costumes on her rack.

'Hold on,' I said. 'That's odd.'

I lifted out the hanger holding Josephine's Marlene Dietrich dress, artificial pearls and fur wrap.

'Marie, look,' I said.

'What?' She looked puzzled. 'That's the outfit she sings in with Ginny – well, she did.'

'Yes,' I said, 'but there's something missing. She had on white silk evening gloves when she wore it onstage, do you remember?'

I looked over the room. 'The thing is, there's no sign of them.'

'Perhaps she sent them out for laundering.'

'Perhaps,' I said, but their absence in the wake of Guy's murder made me wonder if Josephine was worthy of further investigation. That was the worst thing, I thought. Nobody was above suspicion – and every last one of them knew exactly how to act the innocent.

. . .

As we hurried down the back stairs, Marie said, 'I'll take this chocolate box straight to Newton Street, and see if I can find out what's happening with Frank Sullivan and Kerridge.'

'They're probably the best of pals by now,' I said gloomily.

She smiled. 'All we have to do is somehow tie those chocolates to Stanley and we've got our man.'

'Did he hate Leonard?'

'Who knows? I don't suppose he'd have much time for his sort,' she said, raising an eyebrow.

Wallis proffered his signing-out book, and I asked, 'Mr Middleton, do you remember anyone delivering chocolates for Mr Lessiter on the day he died?'

'Well now,' he said. 'We get a lot of admirers wanting me to hand things to the cast, flowers and gifts and such like. Less so since this war began, mind you. Let's have a think...'

We waited, tense as whippets as he flicked back through the ledger.

'There was nobody but the cast came in to see him,' he said, 'but I do recall, just before the performance, someone left a little parcel with me to pass on – could that be it?'

'Who?' Marie and I asked simultaneously.

'Tall, had a hat and sunglasses on,' he said. 'Can't remember the rest of the outfit, I'm afraid.'

'What did he sound like?'

'He?' Wallis shook his head. 'This was a lady, Miss York. A well-spoken, very pleasant-seeming lady.'

CHAPTER SIXTEEN

Hurrying back towards Market Street, trying to remember Pat's peculiar shopping list – had she said Sylko number five or six? How much gelatine? – I almost crashed into a tall figure heading the other way.

'Edie!' Jack bent to kiss my cheek. 'Fancy seeing you here!'

'I'm just rushing to Lewis's in my lunch hour,' I said, thinking it prudent not to mention where I'd been. 'Have you had any news?'

He shook his head. 'Nothing – but Stanley's not back, so it's beginning to look as if he really may be the culprit, I'm afraid. It's quite unbelievable.'

I wondered whether news of the tall, presumably disguised, woman would change everything. I hoped Marie would get the information, and the tissue-wrapped box, to Lou as soon as possible.

'Look,' he went on, 'I'm so sorry Saturday night wasn't as we'd hoped. I was going to telephone you at work later, but as fate has stepped in... it looks as though tonight could be the second to last night of the show. Without Stanley, there's barely anyone left to perform,' he added. 'I'm going to step in for a couple of his sketches, and Josephine will sing while Florence does her monologues. It's a poor effort really, but we're expecting a full house of troops from Lancashire barracks tonight and tomorrow – they're about to set sail for Egypt. It's the least we can do to see them off.'

'I wish I could sing, and help you out,' I said. 'But I'm afraid I can't carry a tune in a bucket.'

He laughed. 'I wouldn't expect you to try,' he said. 'But I did wonder if you'd like to watch from the wings and perhaps join me for supper again afterwards. I'll take the remaining cast out after the final show tomorrow, so this might be my last chance to see you.'

'I'd love to,' I said. Even as the words left my mouth, I wondered whether I might be able to engineer a chat with Josephine about what exactly had happened to her evening gloves. Surely she had been wearing them for more recent performances?

I spent fifteen minutes in Lewis's looking for Pat's shopping, and arrived back at the office hot and sticky, and rather late.

'Warm out, is it?' she said, fossicking in her purse for the money to pay me back.

'I think it's going to thunder,' I said. There was an oppressive weight to the air, a sense of being muffled beneath a damp blanket. The windows were open, but there was no breeze ruffling the papers on our desks.

'Our Monica'll have one of her headaches,' said Pat. 'Always does when it thunders.'

I remembered Daphne's headaches and wondered if she, too, was lying down with a cold flannel on her head. I would miss the cast and their landladies when they left in a few days, I realised. Despite everything, they had brought exotic colour and fun to the city, and without my visits to the Gaiety and number twenty-three, things would be rather dull – particularly if Lou was no longer to be a fixture in my life.

. . .

After work, I caught the bus home to change before the theatre. There had been no real air raids for weeks, and the atmosphere of slightly manic jollity on board reminded me of the 'phoney war', that early period before the bombs began to drop. The air remained thick, warm as blood, and I couldn't shake a sense of impending doom.

Florence and all her nonsense bothering you?' asked Lou in my head. *'The only impending doom is your own idiocy, York.'*

'Oh, shut up,' I murmured out loud, and received a puzzled glance from the clippie.

Distant thunder grumbled as I walked down our street and a flash of lightning illuminated the park, but still no rain fell as I let myself in.

'Horrible weather – so close,' said Annie, emerging from the bathroom with her hair in a towel. 'I'm meeting Arnold at the Kardomah to tell him my decision. Pray for me.'

'He'll understand,' I said. 'I'm certain he will. He loves you.'

'I love him,' she said, disappearing into her bedroom, 'but I'm not sure that's got anything to do with savings and difficult mothers.'

I changed into my yellow cotton dress – it was too humid for the navy crepe – and put on the white, cork-soled sandals that Annie's cousin Helen had sent us. They were too high to be comfortable, but I hoped they might compensate for the ordinariness of my frock.

I ate a swift tea of ham salad and pickled onions – remembering too late that Jack might try to kiss me later – collected my gas mask, shouted 'good luck!' to Annie, and set off back to the bus stop, where I waited as the thunderclouds continued to gather and roll a few miles away. After twenty minutes, a car drew up.

'No point waiting there,' called the driver, a cocky-looking fellow in uniform. 'They've found an unexploded incendiary up on Princess Road and all the traffic's been stopped. There's a policeman up by the junction, says it could be another hour or so.'

With a groan of frustration, I set off on foot, but I had gone no more than two streets when the first drop of rain the size of a shilling splashed onto the hot, dusty pavement, swiftly followed by a biblical deluge that turned the roads to rushing streams and set clouds of steam billowing from the paving stones. Thunder crashed overhead and sheet lightning turned the air around me a brilliant white. My feet were quickly soaked as I tottered on the unfamiliar cork wedges, my cotton skirt clinging heavily to my legs.

If I was late, I'd have to wait till the interval in my soaking clothes – on time, I had a chance of borrowing something dry. I ran on, water pouring from my hair, my ankle aching where I'd twisted it a few weeks earlier, finally understanding what 'soaked to the skin' meant. As I plunged onwards to Oxford Road, a passing delivery van shot through a vast puddle and an arc of filthy water crashed over my legs.

'Nice pins!' called a newspaper boy who couldn't have been more than fourteen. I didn't have the breath to tell him off.

By the time I arrived at the Gaiety, I felt I was part-mermaid. My dress was a sodden rag, and water had soaked through my summer straw hat, shrinking it to a tight, painful band around my head, while my hair hung in damp strings. If I'd hoped to make a good impression on Jack this time, my intentions had been entirely thwarted.

I dripped my way into the foyer, apologising as I brushed past bone-dry people who'd had the sense to take umbrellas out with them. The soldiers massing round the confectionery stall turned to look at me and mutter ribald comments to one another as I passed. I dearly wished I'd told Jack I was staying in to wash my hair.

'There you are!' he said, as I finally made my way to the stairs through the press of steaming bodies. 'Oh good Lord,' he added, taking me in. 'Did you fall into a pond?'

'I couldn't be any more soaked if I had,' I said. 'I don't suppose Josephine has any spare clothes?'

'She might have,' he said, 'but she's bigger than you – why don't you borrow something of Ginny's? She's more your size.'

I pulled a face. 'That seems a bit intrusive, somehow.'

'She wouldn't mind, I promise you,' said Jack. 'Needs must.'

We slipped through the backstage door to the grimy stairs, and I followed him to her dressing room. I felt very uneasy about taking Ginny's things in her absence, but Jack was right – I was wringing wet and didn't have a great deal of choice.

'I'll leave you to it,' he said. 'I'll wait outside while you change.'

The little room was as I remembered, neat and free of dust – Norma must have been in. I crossed to the rack of clothes, where the blue cotton frock Ginny had worn to sing 'Over the Rainbow' was hanging, and used the scratchy towel on the back of the door to blot myself at least partially dry before putting it on. It fitted well. I left my own dress and hat hanging up at the end of the rail, and dried my shoes a little before putting them back on, though the leather retained an unpleasant clamminess. I used the comb from my bag to neaten my hair, standing bent over the mirror – it felt wrong to sit down, as though I was invading Ginny's private space – and I returned to the corridor to find Jack.

'You do look nice,' he said admiringly. 'I thought you might choose the floor-length evening gown.'

'A bit much, perhaps,' I said. I was about to ask if he knew what had happened to Josephine's gloves, but remembered, once again, that Jack was still technically a suspect, and I shouldn't be alerting him to anything I'd noticed.

'*Finally, some sense,*' said Lou in my head.

I followed him down the corridors, past old ladders and ropes dangling from rafters, piles of cardboard 'flats' propped against the narrow walls and several fire buckets. A young lad ran past shouting 'Beginners, please!' which, it occurred to me, meant all two of the remaining cast, and we emerged at the side of the stage.

'I must change into uniform,' said Jack. 'Will you be all right here?'

I nodded. Standing here, once the curtain rose, I'd be able to see half the audience, with them unable to see me. I felt a little of the excitement the performers must feel, transforming themselves before stepping onto the lit stage, creating worlds with only their movements and voices. I had never wanted to be onstage myself – I preferred to lurk in the background, asking questions – but I did admire those who possessed the ability to entertain. I knew that many of the audience would have come thanks only to the show's notoriety – 'The ENSA murders' as the newspapers had taken to calling them, and Stanley's arrest, which had made the front page of the *Chronicle*. I wondered, in fact, what sort of a show they could cobble together with just three of them – one of whom wasn't, in fact, an actor at all.

'Break a leg,' I murmured as Josephine and Florence hurried past me, and Jack appeared.

'Kiss for luck?' he asked, and I pecked his cheek. They assembled on stage, the curtain rose with a great swish, and they burst into song. Jack, I was relieved to hear, had a decent baritone, and the audience seemed happy to sing along. I revelled in the novelty of being in the wings, so close to the performers yet safe from prying eyes.

It wasn't until Josephine was alone, singing 'Lili Marlene', that I noticed she was wearing white evening gloves. Had she borrowed Ginny's? I tried to remember what I'd seen in the dressing room earlier – and it struck me with the clarity of a film scene that after I had combed my hair, bending to peer into the mirror, I had glanced at the shelf in front of me, with its china dish – and Ginny's charm bracelet was no longer lying in it.

I barely noticed the rest of the show before the brief interval. Norma had said she would leave the bracelet where it was. Guy had left it as a talisman to draw Ginny back, and Josephine had sworn it was there... Why would somebody have moved it?

'Florence,' I said, as she hurried past me, dressed in her 'charlady' outfit, 'have you time for a quick word?'

'It'll have to be brief, I've got to get changed for the next song,' she said, switching halfway from wasp-chewing Cockney to her own well-modulated tones.

'It's just that Ginny's charm bracelet isn't in the dressing room, and I wondered if you'd seen it.'

In the dim light of the wings, she looked older and exhausted, even with stage make-up. 'What do you mean it isn't there? We all agreed we'd leave it where it was.'

'Yes,' I nodded. 'I know – the cleaner, Norma, said she wouldn't move it.'

Florence frowned. 'I'll ask JoJo, though I can't see why she'd have taken it.'

'Thank you,' I said. 'I'm sure it'll turn up.'

I wasn't at all sure, however, and at the end of the show, waves of applause rising from the audience and breaking over the performers, I caught Jack's arm as he came offstage. He was perspiring heavily in the formal khaki uniform. 'Need a cig,' he said, his voice cracking. 'That was tough.'

'You were wonderful,' I said, though in truth, I hadn't paid a great deal of attention. I had perched on a milking-stool prop in the shadows and thought about murder.

'Thanks,' he said. 'Let me get out of these things, and we'll get supper.'

'Jack, I just need to...'

'Could it wait a mo?' he asked. 'This outfit weighs a ton, and I need some water.'

I followed him back down the corridors, and waited outside while he washed and changed in his own dressing room. I realised that nobody had recited 'The Green Eye of the Little Yellow God', and suspected that they never would again.

'I am restored.' Jack smiled, opening the door. He was wearing a white shirt and blue trousers, he had cleaned his face, and used water to tame his hair. He was young and handsome, and I looked forward to our late supper.

'Jack,' I said, 'before we go, I must ask... have you seen Ginny's charm bracelet?' I repeated what I'd told Florence.

'How peculiar.' His wrinkled his forehead in thought. 'No – Guy particularly asked that we leave it in the dish for her, in case she came back.'

'Could Rosemary have taken it?'

'I can't see why she would. Even if she crept in and killed Guy, why would she stop for the bracelet – and how would she know it was there?'

A door closed down the corridor, and Josephine appeared in her outdoor clothes, carrying an umbrella.

'Well done, Jack,' she called. '"And then there were none", indeed. Good show, stepping in like that.'

'You were superb as ever,' he said. 'JoJo, look, Edie's just discovered that Ginny's bracelet is missing – did you move it?'

She looked genuinely surprised. 'No – we agreed to leave it there. Do you think the murderer took it?'

'Perhaps. A grisly sort of souvenir? Unless Rosemary...' I remembered that Josephine didn't know about Ginny's pregnancy and broke off.

'We could have a quick look for it,' Jack suggested, 'just in case it's been dropped or knocked off the shelf. Then if there's no sign, Edie, you could tell DI Brennan.'

'If he were speaking to me.'

'Oh dear.' Jack looked horrified. 'I feel entirely responsible. Perhaps I should apologise...'

'You'll do no such thing. I need to collect my wet clothes from Ginny's room,' I added. 'Why don't you two come with me, and we'll all look?'

'Oh, you've reminded me, Josephine turned back to her own dressing room. 'I need to put her evening gloves back – mine seem to have disappeared.'

'Do you remember when you lost them?'

'Well, I had them the night Guy was killed,' she said. 'I left them in my dressing room after the show as usual, and then I couldn't find them anywhere. I thought Flo must have needed them, but she said not. So I borrowed Ginny's.'

'I think,' I said, 'that perhaps we should check every dressing room. Just to be certain that the killer didn't steal your gloves to avoid getting prints on the dagger.'

Josephine looked horrified. 'Wouldn't they wear their own?'

'Perhaps not,' I said, 'if they were afraid of getting blood on them.'

'But my gloves would never fit a man!' Josephine said. 'The silk would split!'

'Maybe it did.'

We looked at each other.

'Shall we fetch Florence?' asked Jack.

'No,' said Josephine. 'I'm not sure I can bear much more of her psychic muttering. Sorry, but I'll be relieved when tomorrow night's over and we can all go our separate ways.'

'Africa...' he began.

'We won't be going anywhere until the killer's found, Jack,' she said, 'and unless we can replace Ginny...'

'I suppose it's too much to hope she might yet return,' he said.

Josephine caught my eye.

'Yes,' she said quietly. 'I'm very much afraid that it is.'

In Ginny's dressing room, I crossed immediately to the little shelf – and just as I'd remembered, the white china dish was empty.

Everything else appeared to be as I'd left it; my clothes, now just damp, still hanging on the rack. Josephine took Ginny's evening gloves from her handbag and draped them back over the hanger holding the dress and fur wrap.

When I glanced at her, she had tears in her eyes.

'Sorry,' she said. She took a shuddering breath. 'I just miss her so. The idea of something terrible happening to her...'

'Sybil and Daphne call her their "little bird", don't they?' I asked.

She half smiled. 'Yes. Ginny loved talking to them about the old days of theatre – all the greats, and what they were like. Sybil knew simply everybody.'

'It's not in her make-up box, or on the floor, and there's nothing in the bin,' said Jack.

'Norma must have been in,' I said.

'Well, perhaps she took it.' Josephine raised her eyebrows.

'I don't think so. I spoke to her, and she truly didn't seem the type.'

'Edie, you've got tiny hands,' said Jack. He was standing by the empty fireplace, swept out for the summer. 'Can you reach into the chimney? I fear my great plates of ham might get stuck.'

I crouched down, peering upwards into the darkness.

'I hardly think anyone would put the bracelet up there,' said Josephine. 'Why on earth would they?'

I crouched and reached my hand into the sooty void, dreading my fingertips encountering a dead bat or pigeon, scraping my wrist against the old bricks, and shrieked as I touched something soft.

'What is it?' Jack said, worried.

'I don't know...' I caught a tiny piece between my fingers, and pulled gently to free it, relinquishing the item and shrinking back in case a bird's blackened corpse crashed down.

A balled piece of cloth, heavily stained with soot, fell into the hearth, and I released the breath I'd been holding.

'My God, whatever's that?' asked Josephine. To my relief, Jack stepped forward and gingerly lifted it to examine. As he did so, the ball unravelled to reveal a pair of long, once-white evening gloves. He held them up, shock frozen on his face. The gloves were Josephine's, and on the side of the right hand was unmistakably a small, dark bloodstain.

'You can't think it was me!' she said, as we both looked at her. 'I'd never use my own gloves, if I were a murderess,' she added, echoing my own earlier thoughts. 'And as if I'd harm Guy. You both know how I... well, I needn't spell it out.'

'I don't think you did harm him,' I said.

I hadn't told them about Mr Middleton's recollection of the 'tall woman' – Josephine was of average height, only slightly taller than me – but I now felt convinced that this mysterious femme fatale had not only killed Leonard but stabbed Guy.

Rosemary, I thought. Who else? Florence was tall, admittedly, but it was impossible to imagine her on a murderous spree. Nevertheless, I would have to take all of this to Lou.

'Should we call the police in?' asked Jack, voicing my thoughts.

'I shouldn't think there's much point at this time of night,' I said. 'If you let me have the gloves, I'll hand them over to Lou first thing in the morning.'

Jack used the tips of his fingers to wrap them in his clean handkerchief and placed them carefully into my handbag.

'Though having them so close to me feels very unpleasant,' I added.

'I'm surprised the police didn't find the gloves,' said Josephine.

'Too high up for blokes' hands,' Jack said. 'Which suggests...'

'That it was a woman who wore them, and who put them there.' I felt sure of it. The small gloves were stained, but not ripped. If the wearer had been a man, the buttons would surely have pinged off and the delicate fabric torn.

'For God's sake.' Josephine shuddered. 'Why did it have to be mine?'

'And the handbag in Stanley's car,' I said slowly. 'And the disappearing bracelet. It's as if the killer wants to cast suspicion on everyone in the cast. Look, I'm beginning to think it was none of you, but somebody else altogether. Perhaps somebody who's now far away, down South.'

'Rosemary?' Josephine said. 'But why?'

I couldn't tell her about Ginny's pregnancy. I didn't believe in Florence's curse, exactly – but I had made her a promise.

'Jealousy,' I said. 'Guy really loved Ginny, I think.'

'Hold on, though,' Jack interrupted. 'What could Rosemary possibly have against Leonard?'

'That's the bit I can't fathom,' I said. 'Unless she disapproved of his... well, the way he lived.'

'Can't see it,' said Jack. 'Half the upper classes are bent as ninepence.'

'Jack!' Josephine cried.

'I've nothing against it!' he said. 'Half the theatre is, too. Frankly, I don't imagine Rosemary disapproves of much, unless it threatens her inheritance of Foxwell. I imagine she lives in dread of a secret male heir being discovered.'

I wondered if he suspected how close he might be to the truth.

'We should check the other dressing rooms, in case anyone's

hidden the bracelet,' I said. 'I'll do Stanley and Jack's. Josephine, you take Florence and Guy, and Jack, you have a look round in Josephine's.'

'It's rather an intrusion...' he began.

'I don't mind,' she said briskly. 'Better to know if someone's tried to frame one of us again.'

After ten minutes, we conceded defeat.

'It's just not here,' I said. 'I'm sorry for wasting your time.'

'You didn't,' Jack said. 'But I'm afraid it's too late for supper – I know they take the last orders for food at ten, and it's long past the hour. I'm so sorry.'

'It's all right,' I said, although I was starving.

'I've an idea,' said Josephine. 'Not quite so romantic, I know, but why don't you come back to number twenty-three, Edie? Sybil does a splendid late supper of fried potatoes, tomatoes and onions that she grows in the garden – she calls them her midnight feasts.'

The idea of fried potatoes made me feel faint with longing.

'I'd love to,' I said, 'if you're quite sure she won't mind.'

'Sybil? Mind a chance to chat about the theatre?' Jack laughed. 'Hardly.'

Outside, the dark air was cooler, though the rain had stopped.

I had stuffed my dress and cotton jacket into a crumpled paper bag provided by Josephine, and hoped to dry them off on the Aga rail before going home.

Jack hailed a cab with an impressive whistle, and we rattled off to Grafton Street. The Gods of romance seemed to be ranged against me and Jack – although I liked him, and it appeared to be mutual, circumstances would not allow anything further to develop. By Wednesday, he'd be back in bomb-ravaged London, meeting the ENSA 'brass' to decide his future. Perhaps he would simply be sent to fight, given the abject disaster of the *Victory Gang Parade*, though I felt certain that none of it was his fault.

Meanwhile, I was due for a reckoning with Lou Brennan first thing in the morning – and oh, how I was dreading it.

By the time Jack let us in with his key, I was too hungry to think about Lou. Florence was sitting in the little wallpapered parlour chatting with Sybil and Daphne over cups of tea.

'Hullo there!' she said, as we clattered in. 'What took such ages?'

'It's a long and tiresome story,' said Jack, clearly unwilling to share our discovery with Florence. 'Sybil, dear, I don't suppose there's any chance of a fry-up? We missed supper,' he continued hopefully, and she smiled at him.

'Midnight feast? Don't see why not. The first crop of tomatoes is just about ripe, so you're in luck.'

'You're an angel,' Jack told her.

Daphne smiled. 'I made some fresh biscuits earlier, too. They're a bit dense, I'm afraid – I threw in some seeds and may have overdone it.'

Josephine subsided onto the little couch and kicked off her sandals. 'Put a record on, would you, Syb?' she said. 'I need something to take my mind off all the horror.'

Sybil reached across and placed a disc on the ancient gramophone. The needle crackled, and a smooth, strong voice recorded long ago filled the room.

'Bessie Smith,' said Sybil. '"Down Hearted Blues". *Gee, but it's hard to love someone... when someone don't love you,*' she sang along. 'Takes me back.'

'Did you love someone who didn't love you?' Jack asked teasingly, but stopped when he saw Sybil's face change.

'I did, as a matter of fact,' she said. 'I never really got over it.'

She blinked away tears, and pressed the heels of her hands to her eye sockets.

'Sorry,' she said. 'It's just, all these latest losses...'

Daphne frowned at her. 'Buck up, old girl,' she said. 'I'll start chopping, if you make another pot of tea.'

As Sybil stood to fill the kettle, there was a sudden rattle at the front door, followed by the sound of a key turning in the lock. Josephine leapt to her feet.

'Ginny?' she called out, in a voice that trembled with hope. 'Ginny, is that you?'

CHAPTER SEVENTEEN

The five of us stood like effigies staring at the door, waiting for the footsteps to reach the parlour.

'Have I interrupted something?' Stanley Kerridge hauled himself over to the couch and subsided into Sybil's recently vacated spot. 'Stick the kettle on, there's a good girl. I'm parched as a bloody salamander on bonfire night.'

'Well,' said Florence eventually. The record had finished, but nobody moved to take it off, and the needle scraped and clicked in the silence. 'I take it they've decided you're not a murderer?'

'For now,' he said heavily. 'I'm "released pending further enquiries". I tell you what, the only enquiries I want to make concern what they put in their porridge in the clink. I could have grouted a wall with it.'

Josephine had turned away, not wanting the rest of us to witness her acute disappointment. 'Now,' she said, 'but what about the handbag?'

'Not you as well,' groaned Stanley, lighting a filthy-smelling cigarette. 'Got these from a bloke in the next cell. Irish name. Decent feller. Having a bit of bother of the female kind.'

Frank, I realised. Of course Stanley would think him marvellous.

'I'll tell you what I told the police, Miss Josephine Gardner,' he went on. 'Someone's trying to frame me. I don't know how Miss Sutton's handbag got into my car, I never gave her a lift, she never sat in it, so I assume someone was playing silly buggers, excuse my French, and had it in for old Stanley here.'

'They tried to *frame* you?' Florence repeated, as though she were describing a portrait session.

'Well, can you think of another reason? Besides which, if I had done her in...' Josephine winced '... I'm hardly likely to leave the evidence in my own bloody pride and joy, am I? May as well write a note – *it's a fair cop, it was me all along, officer* – and stick it to the windscreen.'

It was a less elegant version of what Josephine had said earlier.

'How's that tea coming on, Daph?' he asked. 'I'm dead on me feet. Nothing but water when you're at His Majesty's Pleasure. Not my pleasure, I can tell you that.'

He gazed about, waiting for us to laugh, but nobody did.

Sybil was now chopping busily, lard sizzling in the cast-iron pan, and Daphne lifted the whistling kettle from the stove.

'Did you have a headache earlier, Daphne?' I asked.

'Headache?'

'Because of the storm.'

'Oh, I see. No, not too bad, thanks. It's more when my nerves get up, you know. When I'm worried.'

'Daphne is a slave to her nerves,' said Sybil dryly, and Daphne shot her a look of irritation.

I wondered what it would be like to have a sister – whether we'd have got along well or annoyed each other. Probably both, I thought sadly. Sybil and Daphne clearly loved one another, and Sybil had taken Daphne in when she was widowed. It would be wonderful, I thought, to know there was somebody in the world who would give you a home, no matter what. I'd been granted a reprieve by Annie, but not forever.

We gathered around the table for the midnight feast, served with doorstop slices of Daphne's wholemeal loaf, and for a few moments, nobody spoke – it was too delicious.

'Far better than a fancy post-theatre supper,' said Jack, smiling at me.

'Sybil, you must be the best vegetable grower in Manchester,' I said.

She laughed. 'Well, it's a calling of sorts, I suppose.'

'Shame there's no bacon,' grumbled Stanley. 'Tell you what, it was all I could think about in me cell. A bacon butty, lovely and crisp, bit of HP sauce. Fried eggs, done in dripping. Ooh, I feel shivery just talking about it.'

Sybil looked put out.

'One does one's best, given the circumstances,' she said coldly.

'I bet you had some post-theatre suppers in your time, eh, Syb?' he went on. 'Fancy dinners at the Ritz, cocktails at the Savoy – the toast of London, she was.'

'Yes, all right,' said Daphne. 'It was all a long time ago, I'm sure Sybil would rather not—'

'Stage-door Johnnies, lining up to kiss her hand...'

'Stop it, Stanley!' Sybil snapped. 'If you had the first idea why I left the theatre – the slightest clue about what happened to me – perhaps you wouldn't find it quite so droll.'

'All right!' Stanley gaped at her, a fried potato speared on his fork. 'Pardon me, I was only joking.'

'It's only a joke if it's funny,' Josephine murmured.

Florence said, 'There's a great deal of bad feeling here at the moment. Like a dark cloud over us all. I shall be glad to get back to London – the cards tell me I'm about to be offered the role of a lifetime.'

'In the pictures, do you think?' asked Jack conversationally.

He evidently disliked confrontation as much as I did – a great relief after Lou's permanent state of combat.

'Perhaps,' said Florence. 'Or a return to the stage. Though of course, the bomb damage along Shaftesbury Avenue... it's unbearable to think of it, those venerable, ancient ladies of the theatre, crumbling and cast into darkness.'

'That'd be you, would it?' Stanley chortled, and Florence darted him a look so bitterly quelling, even he subsided.

'I see nobody's got a sense of humour any more,' he muttered.

'Stan,' Jack said quietly. 'It looks as though three people have died. All probably murdered. Is it any wonder we're not laughing?'

'Well, it wasn't bloody me who killed them,' said Stanley, rising to his feet. 'I'm going for a smoke in the garden before I turn in. Anyone want to join me?'

We shook our heads, and he huffed out, a thin stream of foul-smelling smoke curling back into the kitchen.

'Roll on London,' murmured Josephine, standing to help clear the plates.

'I should go,' I said. It was past midnight, and I was suddenly exhausted.

'Do you want to change in Ginny's room?' Josephine asked. 'You could just leave the dress there, and I'll return it to the theatre tomorrow. Or I suppose you could keep it. It's not as if...' She trailed off.

'No, no,' I said. 'Of course I'll leave it with her other things. I'll run up there now, if that's all right.'

Sybil nodded, and I collected my paper bag from the hall and hurried upstairs to the attic rooms, as desultory chatter resumed in the kitchen. There was no sign of Bernhardt – perhaps she was in the garden, stalking prey in the moonlight.

Ginny's room was just as I'd last seen it – the bed made, the clothes neatly tidied away and the stale glass of water and book on Africa still on the bedside table, awaiting her return. The blackout curtain was drawn, and I flicked on the lamp, feeling like an intruder. I took off the blue dress, leaving it on the bed for Josephine, and I changed back into my own damp dress, ramming the shrunken straw hat onto my head. My feet throbbed in the high cork wedges, and I dearly wished I could swap them for a pair of Ginny's flat sandals. I wondered which shoes she had been wearing when she disappeared – and why she had taken off the bracelet, if not to leave a message for Guy.

Before leaving, I crossed briefly to the mirror on her chest of drawers, to reapply my lipstick. I was about to reach into my bag for it, when I realised the surface was no longer clear. By the mirror, a small heap of silver glittered in the lamplight.

My breath catching in my throat, I lifted it and the tangle resolved itself into a thin, shining linked bracelet, from which charms dangled like Christmas baubles. A minuscule bible with real pages. A four-leafed clover. A silver boat. A tiny key. And a little enamel black cat.

I dropped it back onto the chest of drawers as though it had stung me.

How had Ginny's bracelet got here – who had brought it back from the theatre, and why? I had convinced myself that none of the remaining cast could be guilty – that Rosemary was the culprit – but if that were true, when had she visited Grafton Street, and who had let her in?

I left the bracelet where I'd found it, turned the lamp off and descended to the first landing. I was about to run downstairs to the hall, when I heard a distant squeaking coming from behind one of the closed doors. I paused and listened, and the little noise came again. It seemed to be coming from Guy's bedroom, as I still thought of it. Gently, I turned the handle, and Bernhardt shot out between my ankles and downstairs. Someone must have shut her in by accident, though thankfully, she didn't seem to have caused any mess during her incarceration – the room still smelled faintly of French tobacco and sandalwood.

I could still hear the rumble of conversation from downstairs, and I judged it safe to have one more look around Guy's room, just in case Rosemary had been in and left something incriminating. I almost laughed at myself – what would she have left? I wondered, A parchment scroll reading *The Inheritance Shall Be Mine*? I told myself off for being melodramatic, but all the same, this was the last chance I'd ever have to poke through Guy's things.

I slipped into the room, clicking the overhead light on. If anyone came up, I'd say Bernhardt had been trapped and I was checking for her calling cards – which was at least partly true. The room, like Ginny's, was tidy, and I felt a weight of sadness settle in my chest as I studied Guy's small pile of bedside books – a slim copy of *Hamlet*, its pages spiked with pencil notes, *The Man From Tibet* by Clive B Cason, and a well-thumbed volume of Du Maurier's *Rebecca*. Perhaps I should have liked him more than I'd thought, based on his reading tastes – though it occurred to me that one or two, at least, were Ginny's books, including *Rebecca*, the film of which I'd seen with the unspeakable Charles Emerson. It was about a much younger second wife, forever haunted by the mocking ghost of the first. I put it back and looked about for anything out of place, but the room was as calm as a cruise ship's cabin, unwilling to reveal anything further regarding the life of its recent occupants.

Rather despising myself, I slid open a drawer of the bureau, finding nothing but tidily folded silk socks and braces, and the second proved equally blameless, full of crisply laundered white shirts. I tried the small wardrobe – there was nothing in the pockets of the hanging jacket and raincoat, and I was about to give up when I saw the suitcase on top, shoved to the back so it was barely visible. I fetched the room's only chair, which had a sagging wicker seat and barely looked as though it would hold Bernhardt, kicked off my sandals and balanced precariously. If anyone came in now, my excuse would look somewhat thin.

I grasped the edges of the suitcase and slid it towards me, almost crashing to the floor as it slithered from the top of the wardrobe straight into my neck. I caught it just in time, wobbling violently on the fragile chair, and realised that the brown leather case was far heavier than I had thought. For a terrible moment I imagined a woman's small body curled inside, wisps of pale blonde hair trapped in the catch, but I closed my eyes against the vision and flung the case onto the bed, then stepped down to the floor, my heart pounding. I suppressed a wave of nauseous dread as I clicked the latches, and almost laughed in relief at my own foolishness when the lid flew up and revealed nothing more than a box of collar studs and a sliding heap of dog-eared scripts.

Jack's shout floated upstairs. 'Are you all right, Edie?'

I crept to the landing. 'Fine!' I called. 'I'm just sorting out my face.'

'No great rush!' he called back. 'I'll borrow Stanley's car when you're ready and run you home.'

'Thanks!' I said, wondering how on earth I'd heft the suitcase back onto the wardrobe – I might have to empty it out and replace the contents script by script. I could explain to Jack, perhaps – but I wasn't sure how Josephine would feel about me crashing through the personal belongings of her lost love.

Swiftly, I rifled through the scripts on top, shaking them out just in case, but they all seemed to be things that playwrights had sent to him on spec. Occasional typewritten notes drifted out – *Wondered if you'd take a look at this, old chap, Morty has you in mind to play Conrad–* and it was clear that Guy had hoped to find the time to look through them during the Manchester run.

I gave the last script at the bottom a final shake, and as I did so, a piece of folded writing paper dropped out. Expecting another *Bertram's backing the new Rattigan production and I was wondering...*, I glanced briefly at it, horribly aware of seconds ticking by and the imminence of bedtime, even for the night owls downstairs. A couple of words caught my eye, the flourishing stalks of the letters – it was Guy's own handwriting, and I unfolded it properly.

It was headed *Where is Ginny?* and it was clearly a set of notes that Guy had scribbled down to help him think.

Possible reasons: Upset about Leonard? Upset about the current 'Situation'? Rosemary??

Last seen: Me, just before lunch. Stanley, in the morning, 11 o'clock? JoJo, morning...

I scanned his list, turning the page over.

Last to see Ginny alive, Sybil and Daphne. ASK THEM AGAIN.

'Again' was underlined three times, and that was where his notes ended. If he had written more, he had taken it elsewhere with him, or destroyed the pages.

Sybil and Daphne. Like the name of a double act, I thought – or a sister act, the kind so popular in the old music halls. Loyal, devoted sisters, singing in harmony, who would stand by one another no matter what. Would they do so even if one of them had committed murder?

I stood irresolute, the paper clutched in my hand, as another questioning 'Edie...?' floated up the stairs.

I tucked the paper into my handbag, closed the lid of the suitcase, hauled it to the floor, kicked it under the bed, and let myself onto the landing, silently closing the door behind me.

'Coming!' I called, as Bernhardt reappeared at the top of the stairs, gazing balefully at me as though she knew exactly where I'd been, and what I had found there.

I said nothing about either of my discoveries to Jack as he drove me home. I was so tired I was seeing double, and in the black-out, as clouds passed over the moon, trees seemed to shiver and bend and the empty streets warped before my eyes like oil in water.

'I'm done in,' I said on a yawn. 'I'm sorry tonight didn't work out as we'd hoped.'

'Ah well,' said Jack. 'What sort of idiot begins a romance when he's both a murder suspect and about to sail to Africa?'

I laughed. 'Do you think you'll go, after all this? Will you have time to find new actors?'

Jack sighed. 'I don't know. I don't think their hearts are in it as they once were, and nobody seems able to bear much of Stanley. He's dreadful, I know, but the troops love him.'

'Because they're men,' I murmured, and Jack nodded.

'You know, Edie, I've been thinking – I know it wasn't me who killed the others, I tend to believe Stanley's insistence that it wasn't him – and that really only leaves female suspects.'

'Yes.'

'Rosemary?'

'Perhaps,' I said. 'The letter that Guy had just read when he died was from her, about a meeting he'd requested before he went to Africa. It sounded important.'

'Odd that she'd write him a letter, then turn up later the same night and stab him.'

'It is, isn't it?'

I thought about how keen Guy had sounded to get back to the theatre and pick it up – so he must have known it was coming. If Rosemary was furious about Ginny, would she have told him to expect a letter about divorce? That suggested they had spoken on the telephone, perhaps earlier that day, and she hadn't wanted the letter intercepted by her rival. That must have been why she'd sent it to the theatre, not Grafton Street.

I felt certain I was missing something blindingly obvious, but I was almost asleep in the comfortable leather seat of Stanley's Talbot and couldn't think beyond the idea of climbing into my own bed and drawing the covers over my head. When Jack pulled the car up outside Mrs Turner's, it was the very dead of night, and we both felt the need to whisper.

'May I telephone you tomorrow?' asked Jack. 'As it's our last night in Manchester?'

'Of course,' I said. 'I'll be at work.'

He leaned over and gave me a tentative brush of a kiss. I allowed him to linger for a moment, but this was not the time for romance. I suspected sadly that it never would be with Jack Webb.

On the bus to work the following morning, I felt I'd been crushed by a steamroller. Exhaustion lay on me like a dead weight – Annie had taken a good look at me and asked, 'Are you sure you don't want to have the day off? I can ring up and say you're poorly.' I'd shaken my head. I needed to see Lou, much as I dreaded it. Then, perhaps, I could hand the entire problem over to him and get back to my normal life, such as it was.

I walked up to Newton Street from the bus stop, part of me hoping that Lou would be out on urgent business, but though I lingered at the fire service ponds, and peered at the allotments – someone's runner beans were doing beautifully – eventually I had to turn down Newton Street, past the bomb-damaged shops and sewing businesses, and trudge up the steps of the familiar police station.

I explained myself to the desk sergeant, and after a few

moments, Lou appeared, looking granite-faced and very tired. He appeared to be on his way out and his hat was on backwards, but I wasn't going to tell him.

'York!' He looked startled. 'What brings you here?'

It was the first time we'd spoken since our row on Saturday evening, and neither of us quite knew where to look.

'I have some information,' I said stiffly. 'May I see you in your office?'

Lou threw his hat back onto the coat stand and sat behind his desk.

'Right,' he said. 'I've a meeting with the pathologist shortly to discuss the Lessiter results, so make it as fast as you can, please.'

No apology, no 'thank you for coming'. Apparently, I was now an underling on a par with a tweeny maid, suitable only for the investigative equivalent of black-leading the grate.

'I've discovered quite a lot,' I told him.

'Yes,' he said impatiently. 'Marie told me all about the little private investigation that the two of you cooked up. That's all I need, frankly – Laurel and Hardy blundering into police business.'

I stood up, shaking with fury. 'I shan't tell you, then. As I'm of so little use to you, why would you care what I've found? I'll take it to Mr Gorringe and I'm quite sure he'll be interested enough to publish a piece on why it took a female *Chronicle* reporter to move on a triple murder case, while the City Police ignored vital evidence that was plain as day before their eyes.'

Lou was about to interrupt, but I couldn't stop.

'Not only that, but the DI storming into a restaurant where I was having a perfectly nice supper with a friend and ruining it, humiliating me by shouting in the street, dismissing my ideas until they turn out to be right and suddenly it suits you to pretend they were your own, and frankly, if you're too pig-headed to let anyone help you solve the brutal deaths of three innocent people, then bloody good luck to you,' I finished. I opened my handbag and flung Josephine's tissue-wrapped gloves onto his desk, followed by the note in Guy's handwriting.

'The gloves were up the chimney in Ginny's dressing room,' I hissed, 'and the note was in a suitcase in Guy's bedroom. You should also know that Ginny's charm bracelet was back on the bureau in her bedroom, though God knows who put it there or why. Presumably, if you can be bothered to go and look, you'll find it's still there. Though why would you? It's only ten full days since Ginny disappeared. I'm sure she's fine.'

I wrenched open the door and stormed down the corridor to the exit and out into the clear, bright day, where last night's puddles shone silver in the cobbled road.

I'd had enough of Lou Brennan. I had done all I could, I decided, and it was no longer anything to do with me. From now on, I would simply concentrate on writing pleasant obituaries – as soon as I'd shared what I knew with my editor.

'Morning,' Pat greeted me. 'You're late. Pea under the mattress keep you awake all night, did it?'

She offered me an Anzac biscuit. 'Our Monica made them for her dad's birthday,' she said. 'Go on, there's a full two ounces of marge in them, she saved up her whole ration.'

I took one, grateful for the sugar – I felt quite shaken after my outburst.

Slightly restored, I was sorting through post and looking forward to the arrival of Violet's tea trolley, when my desk telephone rang. I snatched up the receiver, hoping it would be Jack.

'A Mrs Archibald for you,' said Olive on the switchboard. 'Putting her through.'

'Edie?'

'Marie!' I said. 'I know you're married to the Admiral, but I can't reconcile you with a Mrs Archibald. How very grown up that sounds.'

'I do prefer "Marie",' she admitted. 'Mrs Archibald sounds like a sixty-five-year-old landowner with a pack of gun dogs and a nightly gin habit.'

I laughed. 'How may I help this formidable woman?'

'I need to see you,' she said. 'Number one, I've had Lou on the telephone having utter Tom kittens – apparently, you've just had the most spectacular falling-out?'

I sighed. 'I'm afraid so.'

'Secondly, he told me the latest on Lessiter's post-mortem and he's gone straight back to number twenty-three to interview them all again, based on that and what you discovered.'

'The bracelet? Or the gloves, or the note?'

'All of them,' she said. 'Look, I must go, Suki's coming round to measure me up in a moment – truly, what a godsend she promises to be, I can't thank you enough – but can we meet? The Kardomah again, one o'clock?'

'Yes,' I said, 'of course. As long as this isn't some cunning scheme to make Lou and I resolve our differences over a ham sandwich. I'm far too cross.'

'Edie, dear, I wouldn't even try that with Clive and Frances,' said Marie. 'I'm not a complete idiot, you know, even if my brother is.'

I laughed.

'And Edie, of course I can't stop you, but Lou has begged me to ask that you don't tell your editor anything just yet. He's afraid it might compromise an arrest, apparently.'

'Fine,' I sighed, another dream of a byline crushed. 'I'll wait.'

CHAPTER EIGHTEEN

She was at a central table this time, conducting the light jazz trio on the little stage with a waving hand. I rather hoped they hadn't noticed.

'My dear, I hardly know where to begin,' said Marie, as I sat opposite her. 'But first, Suki – oh, what a gem! She understands everything about the peplum jacket. My London dressmaker has been struggling with the concept for ten years, and we're still no closer.'

'I'm so glad I could introduce you,' I said.

'She has such a delicate touch as well,' Marie went on. 'The number of times I've had a dressmaking pin shoved into my thigh... I almost wonder if the girls at Madame Modiste's used to do it on purpose. But Suki...'

I felt we should get onto the more pressing topic of murder. 'What did Lou say?' I asked, after the waitress had taken our orders.

'Dear me.' She studied my face. 'Are you very upset? He told me he'd behaved quite dreadfully towards you. He sounded very regretful indeed.'

'I was upset, yes,' I admitted. 'In fact, Marie, I wonder if he really likes me at all. He's been quite unpleasant to me lately – storming into the restaurant the other night, and dismissing all my suggestions. I know he can be a bit arrogant...'

'Can't he just!' Marie said fervently.

'But we usually get on very well. I'm so fond of him, and we've solved crimes together, and I – well, I suppose I feel rather hurt by it all.'

Marie reached a gloved hand across the white tablecloth and clasped mine.

'My dear,' she said, 'of course you do.' She shook her head. 'I adore my little brother, but he is a man of great passions, and when he's under pressure, well... his very worst side emerges. I wish he could see himself as others do, because that might bring him up rather sharply.'

'I suppose that's why he loves his dog so much,' I said. 'No expectations. Where is Marple, by the way?'

'Ah,' said Marie. 'With his best friend, the spaniel next door. Such a lovely woman, the owner – a young, attractive widow, I can't imagine why Lou doesn't get to know her better.'

I felt rather irritated. 'Perhaps because he's under so much pressure,' I said.

'Yes, of course, you're right. Anyway, look, I've told him in no uncertain terms to apologise to you,' she went on. 'I've no idea if it might arrive in the form of a call, a letter or an RAF fly-past, but it's entirely up to you whether you accept his apology. I promise it shan't affect our own friendship, either way – at least I do hope not.'

'Of course it won't,' I said. I felt that was enough talk of feelings. As the waitress delivered our specials – cock-a-leekie soup, and a 'corned beef roast', whatever that was – I said, 'Can you tell me what Lou said about the murders?'

'Of course.' Marie laid her napkin carefully across her lap, like a hanging judge laying the black cap on his wig.

'It's quite astonishing,' she said, her voice lowered. 'The lab results have come back, and it seems that Leonard really was poisoned with cyanide.'

'No!' My gasp made the couple on the next table turn round, and I smiled blandly at them until they turned back to their conversation.

'Where on earth would one get cyanide?' I wondered. 'I don't think the chemist sells it. In Agatha Christie, it's generally procured from evil pharmacists, but....'

'I know,' she agreed. 'Not something you'd easily come by in the theatre. Lou says the chocolates were poisoned. There were traces on the box. It's a fairly quick death, and Leonard must have eaten them between scenes.'

'He could have offered them to other people, though,' I said, 'a child, even. It's utterly wicked.'

'Yes.' Marie nodded. 'I think this person is very wicked – or quite mad. Though where one ends and the other begins, I couldn't tell you.'

'Do you think Ginny was poisoned, too?'

Marie shuddered. 'I don't know. But if she was, where is she? It's hard to move a body very far, and people might see something – the risk would be enormous, even in the blackout.'

I sighed. 'We just seem to go round in circles,' I said, pushing my soup-bowl away.

'Ah.' Marie smiled. 'Not for much longer, perhaps. They've taken Rosemary in for questioning, apparently, searched her car, and they're looking into how long she really stayed in Manchester. Meanwhile, Lou is back at number twenty-three, interviewing the cast once again. Perhaps this time he'll... What's the matter? Are you choking?'

I had sat bolt upright and clutched the edges of the table. A wave of adrenaline passed through me, one so powerful I thought I might collapse.

'Edie? Can you hear me?'

'Yes – sorry,' I said. 'Marie, I think I know what's happened.

It struck me then, when you said... I can't believe I hadn't thought of it before. I'm an idiot. And it would all make sense... if I'm right...'

'For goodness' sake!' Marie said. 'What? Tell me!'

I glanced at my watch. 'I can't,' I said. 'I must get back. But listen, Marie, this is important. I need you to make sure everyone is out of number twenty-three this evening.'

'Well, they will be, they'll be performing at the theatre, it's the last night...' she began.

'No,' I said. 'Everyone. Daphne and Sybil too. And we'll need Lou and a couple of constables.'

'I've never even met Daphne and Sybil!'

'Doesn't matter,' I said. 'Tell JoJo you'd like to treat them, after all they've been through. She'll ask them for you. Oh, and tell Lou it's very important that he brings Marple with him.'

'Anything else, DC York?'

'I know it sounds ludicrous,' I said, putting my jacket back on, 'perhaps it is – but it's the only explanation that makes any sense at all. Tell Lou I'll meet them there at seven, when the show starts, and we'll need a key to the house – can you manage to steal one from one of the cast, and leave it under the plant pot on the step?'

'Steal one? Good Lord, Edie, I'm not the Artful Dodger, how on earth am I supposed to...'

'I know you'll manage it,' I said.

'And what about returning later? Am I supposed to chaperone them all home again? Surely Jack will take them all for a "last night" supper afterwards – it could be two o'clock in the morning.'

'By then,' I said, 'If I'm right, Lou will be making an arrest.'

Marie gazed at me. 'I have never, in all my sophisticated London life, met anyone quite like you, Miss York,' she said. 'Luckily, I'm all the better for it.'

She pecked me on the cheek. 'I'll do my utmost,' she added. 'But can you really not say?'

'I may be wrong,' I said. 'I know we're currently not speaking, but I trust Lou to know whether my theory's likely. If it's not, I'm going to feel idiotic, and I'd rather only feel it once.'

'Oh, all right then,' said Marie. 'I was going to visit the Picturehouse matinée and see that new Merle Oberon film, *Affectionately Yours* – it looks fun. But I suppose Merle will simply have to wait.'

The afternoon passed like a dripping tap, the minutes trickling by. At five, I gathered my things and was covering my typewriter, just as the desk telephone rang.

'It's me,' said Marie. 'Operation Grafton Street is on – at least as far as getting everyone out goes. I asked Josephine to invite Daphne and Sybil to come to the theatre as my guests to see the cast off, and they were delighted, apparently. I'm collecting them in a cab, so I'll try and do my Fagin's gang business with the key when I arrive.'

'Oh, well done. I can't thank you enough,' I breathed. 'What about Lou?'

'Don't know,' Marie said. 'He was still out, presumably at twenty-three, so I left a message with the switchboard girl telling him to come when you said and bring Marple.'

My heart sank – I may have achieved part of the plan, but without Lou, I was stuck. I would have to hope, I decided. Currently, that was all I had.

After a rushed tea of mince rissoles and lettuce, which I had to force down thanks to the nerves crackling through me, I changed into slacks and an old jumper.

'Have you signed up as a land girl?' Annie asked when she came in.

'I'll explain later, I promise,' I said. I didn't want any of Annie's usual warnings about rushing in, and 'courting danger' – she was officially my best friend, but she also did an excellent job as a substitute loving mother, big sister and strict headmistress.

'If you're digging for victory, all I know is that it takes an age to grow anything and then it goes mouldy within ten minutes,' she said. 'My friend Bea at work tried, and her carrots all emerged like wizened dolls-house vegetables. She says now she just flirts with the greengrocer instead.'

I thought of Sybil and her blooming garden, and the midnight feast we'd enjoyed.

'Some people have green fingers. Some have greengrocers,' I said, deliberately cheerfully. 'I might be late back, but don't worry.'

'I always worry when you say "don't worry",' said Annie suspiciously. 'Lucky I'm having an evening off and putting my feet up with *The Light Programme*. If you need me, I'll be here.'

'Thanks,' I said, blowing her a kiss. 'I'll be fine, I promise.'

I caught a bus to Grafton Street and arrived ten minutes early. I lurked round the corner near the closed newsagent's shop until I saw Marie's taxi draw up. She looked exquisite in scarlet heels and a pale blue spotted dress I hadn't seen before. Marie ran up the steps, and re-emerged shortly afterwards followed by Sybil, her rangy form draped in coloured scarves and flowing silks, and Daphne, who was wearing a yellow-striped summer frock and a straw hat, and rather reminded me of the jolly farmer's wife in a children's book. They climbed into the taxi, and it drove away. My heart sank, but just as the car reached the corner, the driver performed a violent reverse manoeuvre – I saw Daphne clutch her hat – and returned to number twenty-three.

'So sorry!' Marie called, leaping out. 'I shan't be a sec!'

She had evidently borrowed a key – she ran in, and came out again holding a silk scarf. On the step, she dropped her handbag, which flew open scattering tissues, coins and cosmetics. Marie bent to gather them, and I saw her tuck something beneath the plant pot.

'Coming!' she called, and as she climbed into the cab, I heard her say, 'Oh, bother, I've idiotically left your key on the hall table, Daphne – I'm so sorry, can Sybil let you in later...?'

Daphne nodded, and the cab once again pulled away. I finally breathed out. 'Well done, Marie,' I whispered, as I checked the street for passers-by and hurried to the door.

The key was under the pot, and I swiftly let myself in and went into the front parlour, to watch the street for any sign of Lou. Bernhardt issued a questioning mew at my presence, then returned to washing her hind leg with great care, snow-white toes splayed like a starfish. As the clock ticked on, I began to suspect I'd made a mistake. The street outside was quiet, and I wondered how long to give him before I returned the key to the hall table and slipped away, humiliated.

'What do you think, Bernhardt?' I asked, and as she lifted her head, tongue still poking out, I heard an engine. I peered out, knocking my head on the poker-work sign. Lou emerged from his familiar black car, and opened the passenger door for Marple. My relief was tempered by the realisation that he had brought nobody else with him – it was going to be just the two of us and our bad tempers for the evening.

'Edie,' he said, as I opened the door, 'I want to apologise, again. Marie gave me a thorough dressing down and it was very much like being six again.'

I smiled grudgingly.

'I haven't been kind or particularly reasonable of late,' he said. 'So I'm truly sorry. I hope we can be friends.'

Marple had scented Bernhardt and was now sniffing frantically at the closed parlour door.

'Let's go into the kitchen,' I said. 'And I'll explain.'

'Do you forgive me?'

'Yes,' I said. 'Partly because I've no choice if we want to solve these murders, and partly because I love Marple.'

'Is that it?'

'I'd take what's on offer if I were you,' I said. We sat at the kitchen table as Marple thudded miserably to the floor, thwarted in his cat-chasing.

'I've been here most of the day interviewing them all.' Lou sighed. 'I can't think what you've come up with that I haven't already squeezed out of them. Bloody actors,' he added. 'So dramatic. Can't just tell you what happened, it has to be the Shakespearean version of how they ate soup, or what the postman said.'

'What did you find out?'

I longed for a cup of tea, but felt putting the kettle on might be poor etiquette during a break-in.

'Not much we didn't already know. Nobody admitted to a clue about the cyanide. Apparently, the general consensus was that the chocolates were sent to Leonard by a lunatic admirer who felt thwarted in some way – the mysterious "tall woman". As for the bracelet, nobody confessed to moving it – some suggested that perhaps Guy had brought it back here before he died, to wait for Ginny's return.'

'But Josephine said...'

'Witnesses are appallingly unreliable,' he said. 'Particularly when they're emotionally involved in a case. Florence finally admitted that Ginny was pregnant, so that gives credence to the theory that Rosemary had her done away with, then finished Guy off, but it doesn't explain Leonard's death. I considered the possibility that there were two killers, a random stranger who'd taken against Leonard, then the Ginny-and-Guy killer – that would in some ways make more sense, but the coincidence of all three within a week is a stretch, admittedly.'

'Did you question everyone?'

'Yes, of course.'

'Sybil and Daphne, too?'

'Yes. They told me where they'd been at the relevant times – mostly playing the piano and in bed with various headaches, by the sound of it. Possibly caused by the piano playing. There was some talk of Florence and Sybil having lunch together on one day, too, I gather they've been friends for decades.'

'And Jack?'

'Yes, and I apologised to him and was extremely polite. More than I was to Stanley, the odious little cretin.'

I suddenly remembered.

'Frank Sullivan...' I began.

'Ah,' said Lou. 'Yes. While you were raging, I was speaking to a couple of prisoners I know at Strangeways, and obtaining some useful information. The upshot is, he's in court soon for illegal possession of a firearm, regularly fencing stolen goods, and – if we can finally pin it on him – aiding and abetting the killing of what I believe the criminal fraternity call "a snitch" a couple of years ago. He's not getting bail.'

'So Suki's safe?'

'For the foreseeable,' said Lou. 'I can't say how long he'll get, but it should be enough time for Suki to get on with her life and meet somebody far better than that evil little toerag.'

'Thank God,' I said. 'And thank you, Lou. She'll be so glad to hear this.'

'Now,' he said, 'tell me your theory. I've not had time to eat anything, so it had better be worth it.'

I took a deep breath.

'It was Marie who made me realise,' I said. 'When I saw her

earlier, we were talking about Ginny again, and Marie said, "It's hard to move a body very far, and people might see something".'

'Right...'

'Don't you see?' I asked. 'She's quite right. We've been assuming all along that if she's dead, Ginny was killed somewhere else and moved in a car, but there was no trace of her in Stanley's Talbot, you said so yourself. Nobody could kill her at the theatre and get the body out safely – there's always people passing, day and night, and Mr Middleton never leaves his post while it's open. If she had been kidnapped, say, on her way to the Gaiety that day – why did nobody see? Who would have picked her up in a car? I suppose Rosemary could have done it, and Ginny might have got in, but that leads to the same problem – where's the body? Not in Rosemary's car boot. A strange man offering Ginny a lift, then killing her? Perhaps, but then why kill Guy, or Leonard too?'

'Much as I'm enjoying the rational byways of your mind, are you going to get to the point at some stage of the evening?' Lou asked.

'I am getting to it,' I said. 'Tell me, what's the smallest distance someone would have to carry a body during the blackout to conceal it?'

'I don't...'

'I'll tell you.' I pointed at the back door, its wooden pegs hung with drying-up cloths and Daphne's clean apron.

'Straight out of there, and into the garden,' I said. 'That's where I think she's buried.'

Lou looked steadily at me. 'By whom?'

'By the person who knows exactly where to dig,' I said. 'Sybil.'

We sat in silence, as the grandfather clock in the hall chimed the half-hour. Lou leaned down to scratch Marple's head, a sure sign that he was thinking hard.

'Why?' he asked eventually. 'Why would an ageing landlady who loves the theatre and adores actors kill three of her residents? It doesn't make sense.'

'It does,' I said, 'if she had reason to be desperately jealous. Sybil won't talk about why she left the theatre – nobody knows, not even Florence. She was enormously successful, then suddenly, it was all over and she never appeared on stage again. People don't just give up their great passion for no reason. Clearly, she still longs for it – the whole house is crammed with posters and playbills from her heyday, and she loves talking about it.'

'But Ginny was never a rival, she's too young.'

'Yes, but I think her career mirrors Sybil's,' I said. 'Sybil starred in *Hedda Gabler* and so did Ginny, with glowing reviews. Sybil starred in *Hamlet* as Ophelia and Ginny was about to...'

'Lots of actresses have played Ophelia,' said Lou. 'Surely that's not enough to turn a woman into a killer. And besides, there's Guy, and Leonard...'

'Hear me out,' I said. 'I agree, that alone is not enough. But supposing Sybil once met someone like Guy – a married man – and found herself expecting? He lets her down, her career is ruined... and then almost forty years later, the same situation is played out in her own home, but this time, it's set to have a happy ending. Guy leaves Rosemary, they marry and Ginny continues her glittering career. It's a scandal, yes, but not of the sort it would have been in Sybil's day.'

'Which married man?' Lou asked, squinting at me through his smoke.

'It's a guess,' I said, 'but I think it might have been Leonard.'

'Leonard!' Lou spluttered a laugh. 'How may I break this news to you? He's not exactly the marrying kind.'

'Allow me to break some news to *you*,' I said. 'Leonard was married in 1894, to a Miss Elizabeth Spink, from a very wealthy American family. She died in 1906 from typhoid fever, on a trip back to New York. Leonard didn't go, he was starring in *Hedda Gabler* at the Prince of Wales theatre, which also starred the young Sybil Charnwood. Sometime after that, but presumably long before the last war, he embraced another path, as you say.'

Lou was staring at me. 'How do you know all that?'

'The *Chronicle* has contacts at Somerset House,' I said. 'I rang them up this afternoon and said I was researching Leonard's obituary and they unearthed it all for me.'

'I didn't realise they kept details of ancient theatre productions amongst the country's legal records.'

'No, that was Mrs Borrowdale in our cuttings library. And I had to hear about her painful corns for twenty minutes before she'd look in the files for me.'

'Right. So your theory is, Sybil killed Leonard because he had dropped her once she was pregnant, seeing Ginny brought up all her old rage about losing her career, she murdered Ginny through jealousy, and what – killed Guy because he was too handsome?'

'No,' I said patiently. 'She killed Guy because he suspected her. Didn't you read the note he'd written? Ask Sybil and Daphne AGAIN, underlined. I think he was getting close, and she knew it. Perhaps he'd left some other notes out, and she saw them.'

'My God,' said Lou. 'I suppose it all has a peculiar sort of Gothic logic to it.'

'I think it's the only possible explanation,' I said.

'What about the baby, though, if you're right and Sybil was *pregnant out of wedlock?*' Lou adopted the booming tone of a judgemental Scottish vicar.

'Adopted, I expect,' I said. 'Or perhaps she lost it – infant mortality was still very high back then.'

'That would indeed make her feel very bitter, I imagine,' said Lou. 'But Edie, it's still a great stretch of the imagination. We have no idea that any of this ever happened at all.'

'I know,' I conceded. 'And there's nothing to explain why, if she lost the baby, she didn't return to the stage afterwards. Or why she remained friends with Leonard.'

'Unless she hoped he might return to her.'

'Forlorn romantic hope isn't unheard of.'

'No,' Lou nodded. 'You're right there. By the way,' he said, 'why did you request extra constables, as if I'm the Grand Old Duke of York with ten thousand men? You know how short-staffed I am at the moment.'

'I just hoped,' I said, 'because otherwise, it's going to be you and me doing the digging.'

Lou made me drink a tot of the brandy on the drinks trolley. I swigged it straight from the bottle, and almost choked, my eyes streaming as it hit my throat. 'That should do it,' he said. 'Dutch courage can be very useful. I wish I'd known this theory of yours earlier,' he added. 'I'd definitely have dragged in a couple of men to help. Let's just hope that lot don't come back early from the theatre, thanks to a headache.'

'Lou,' I said, 'I don't think Daphne does have headaches. I think she knows the truth – but she's too loyal to her sister to say anything.'

'What makes you think that?'

'Because Sybil is a talker,' I said. 'I can't imagine her keeping such a terrible secret. I think she would have found it too much, and told Daphne what she'd done.'

'Surely nobody would keep that secret!' Lou said, outraged. 'It's a major crime, she'd be an accessory to murder.'

'But what Sybil has done – if she has – means the death penalty,' I said. 'Daphne says that Sybil took her in when her husband died. They adore each other. Daphne would never let her sister go to the gallows, no matter what she's done.'

Lou paused. 'Say you're right,' he said eventually. 'We did check the garden, but that was when we were looking for traces of Ginny alive. The air raid shelter was empty, nothing seemed disturbed. I hate to ask, but to save us attempting to dig up the entire garden, where would you bury a body?'

'They would only have had about seven hours at most, before anyone came back that night,' I said. 'Sybil looks strong, but I don't think Daphne would cope with hard exercise for very long. Somewhere that was already dug over, ready for planting.'

'The Manchester soil is acidic clay loam,' Lou said. 'Tough to dig, but it was a dry evening after a warm week. If they didn't bury her too deeply, I'd say four hours or so between them. Then in go the seedlings on top.'

'But it wouldn't have been dark,' I suddenly realised. 'Dusk doesn't fall until about nine o'clock. That wouldn't give them long enough.'

'Somewhere that isn't overlooked, then,' said Lou.

He unlocked the back door, and clicked his fingers to Marple.

'Let's go and find a likely spot.'

On the little terrace, the wicker furniture was still convivially arranged, striped by the evening sunlight, and the magnolia was in bloom. An early swallow darted across the sky, its brief shadow crossing the long lawn.

I felt suddenly lightheaded and grabbed the back of a garden chair.

'Are you all right?'

I swallowed. 'Lou, if she is here...'

'I don't expect you to help me get her body out,' Lou said gently. 'If we find anything, I'll call the nearest station and get some of the lads down. Edie, look, you don't have to be here at all – Marple and I can search.'

'No,' I said. 'I feel I ought to stay, for Ginny's sake – let's at least find out if I'm right.'

Although, even as I said the words, I desperately hoped that I was not.

CHAPTER NINETEEN

We paced the garden, Marple sniffing and trotting alongside us. It was a bucolic dream of bean rows and cold frames – Sybil's flowerbeds were entirely given over to the war effort. Inside the Anderson shelter, a neat structure of corrugated iron, were stacked several wooden crates holding new potatoes, and an old Peek Freans biscuit tin containing packets of seed. The Ministry of Food would have been proud.

Lou surveyed the neighbouring houses, studying the upper windows.

'The garden's mostly overlooked,' he said. 'The only areas that nobody could see are down at the far end, behind the bean rows. I'd say there's about eight feet or so behind the air raid shelter where next door's trees overhang the wall, and the currant bushes block the sightline.'

'Let's start at the back then, by the shed.' I put my hand on Marple's fur-ruffed neck for strength, and followed Lou down the lawn.

'Was it a full moon that night?' he wondered. 'That would have helped them.'

'No, it's tonight,' I said. 'It would have been... is it waxing or waning? I can never remember.'

'Waxing,' said Lou, studying the ground before us. Shielded from view by bean rows and clusters of hard, green tomatoes the size of marbles, the wide bed at the far end of the garden was planted with lettuces.

'They look as if they've been growing for a while,' I observed. 'Would they grow that fast in ten days?'

'What I know about gardening could be inscribed on the head of a pin,' said Lou. 'But I agree they look somewhat bushy for less than a fortnight's growth.'

'I know a bit,' I said. 'Pat's always giving me tips about slugs and pinching off – it's never occurred to her that I don't have a garden.'

There was a spade propped by the tiny wooden shed, and Lou picked it up.

'Did you check inside the shed?' I asked.

'Of course,' Lou said. 'Just gardening stuff, according to O'Carroll.' He peered through the little window. 'It's very tidy. No spiders in there,' he added. 'They probably got tired of listening to theatrical anecdotes from 1890 and scuttled off.'

I laughed, then remembered our bleak purpose.

'I suppose you'd better...' I said.

Lou handed me his jacket and rolled up his shirt sleeves.

'Right,' he said. 'If you're wrong, we're going to have to buy Sybil some new lettuces.'

I felt sick as Lou began to dig, creating a neat pile of soil behind him.

'Come on, Marple,' he said, 'for once, you're allowed to dig. In fact, I'm asking you to do so.'

Marple glanced nervously at him. At Lou's encouraging

nod, he plunged into the bed and began a powerful scrabble, sending showers of earth and lettuce leaves flying behind him.

'I do hope they don't come back early,' I murmured.

After twenty minutes, Lou bent over, holding his lower back. 'That's set off a lifetime of chronic lumbago, I imagine,' he said. 'No wonder Sybil's fit as a flea if she does this all day.'

'Let me have a go,' I said. 'I can do a bit, then you can try again.'

'No,' said Lou. 'I'm not letting a small, sensitive woman dig up a body, thank you.'

'I'm not sensitive!' I said, outraged.

'Be told. I don't think there's anything here,' he added, as Marple plunged on happily. There was now a craterous hole in the lettuce bed and, judging by the rocks and old bits of broken willow-pattern china down there, it didn't seem to have been disturbed since Victorian times or before.

'Shall we try the other bed, behind the shelter?'

Lou nodded. 'May as well, before it gets dark. Though I'm beginning to wonder if this theory of yours is right. Maybe Rosemary hated Leonard for supporting Ginny and Guy, or for letting Elizabeth Spink go to New York and catch typhoid. All these ancient families know each other, don't they? She probably went to boarding school with a Spink, who never got over her mother's death and saw her chance to avenge the—'

'Come off it,' I said. 'Rosemary surely had a governess.'

'Probably. Come on, Marple, more digging.'

This time, as we contemplated the carrot seedlings so neatly planted in regular rows, I felt less certain of myself. Perhaps I'd dragged Lou away from his tea and ruined Sybil's garden for nothing, while the murderer – some stranger we'd never heard of, with an inexplicable grudge against ENSA – went free.

Lou wearily began to dig, while Marple attempted his journey to Australia once more, destroying most of the seedlings with one urgent scrabble of his enormous paws.

Ten minutes passed, as Lou dug deeper, panting.

'As if the bloody grave digger in *Hamlet* would have time to be contemplating skulls,' he said bitterly. 'I'm surprised he could still stand upright.'

I looked across the garden. The shadows had lengthened in the fading light, and somewhere in the distance, a child was being called inside. I suddenly felt terribly lonely.

'Can you see anything?' I asked.

'Only mud. I'll probably be seeing mud forever,' he said, striking on relentlessly with the spade. I had been wrong after all, I thought – my precious theory, so obvious and neat, was nonsense, and I'd broken into the home of people who had trusted me and fed me, caused unforgivable damage to their garden, and given Lou another reason to be furious...

Marple barked.

Lou set the spade aside.

'What is it, pal?' he asked. 'Found an ancient dog bone?'

Marple was standing over the hole he'd dug, front legs splayed, now barking frenziedly. If the neighbours had been unaware of our presence, they could surely not remain that way. I thought of the explanations, the apologies I'd have to issue – could I lose my job?

'What's that you've discovered?' Lou bent down to examine the bottom of the hole that Marple had made. He glanced up at me, his face pale in the dusk.

'Edie, don't look,' he said.

Of course I looked. I couldn't make it out at first, it appeared to be a muddy food wrapper or an old piece of green garden netting. But Lou moved aside, and the odd scrap resolved itself into a piece of emerald-coloured silk, soaked through with dirt and damp.

'Oh God,' I whispered. 'I think... the... that's the green wrap Ginny was wearing when... whe—... she dis—... —ppeared.' It was as though my jaw had locked. I was finding it very difficult to speak.

Lou stood up.

'Good boy, Marple,' he said. 'No more digging. Inside.'

In the kitchen, I clung to the residual heat from the Aga rail. I couldn't get warm, the outdoor temperature had dropped as evening fell, and my bones felt rigid with cold.

'You're trembling,' said Lou. 'Edie, I'm going to run to the phone box – Marple will stay here with you. Drink this,' he added, slugging more brandy into an empty mug, and I did, its china rim banging violently against my teeth.

'Now sit down, put your head between your knees, and don't move until I get back,' said Lou. For once, I did as I was told.

It felt as though hours had passed, but the clock showed it was only ten minutes until Lou returned. I was now sitting up, holding onto Marple's reassuringly tufty right ear like a pilot gripping a joystick. If I only thought about his ears, and not the small body buried beneath the earth just outside...

'Right,' Lou said. 'A team are on their way, my men will be dragged from pleasant evenings with the wireless and their betting slips, and I suspect the cast will need to find other accommodation tonight, because this house is now a crime scene.'

'What about Sybil and Daphne?' I asked.

'What indeed,' said Lou grimly. 'I'm about to drive straight to the Gaiety and arrest them.'

'Can I come and watch?'

'Edie.' Lou looked aghast. 'It's not a charabanc outing! Your idea was excellent and correct – but without a confession from Sybil, it's going to be very tricky to prove it was her. Besides which, we still have nothing to link them to the deaths of Guy or Leonard.'

I stood up, releasing Marple. 'Wait!' I said. 'I need to check something...'

I hurried to the back door, snatched a key from its peg, and ran out into the garden again.

'What? Edie, they'll be here any minute, you can't just '

I averted my eyes from the bed behind the air raid shelter, though I felt every inch of its malign presence behind me. I couldn't think about the fact that it was really Ginny, that she wasn't ever coming back, that all our hopes had proved vain. I slotted the key into the lock, and the door creaked open.

It was dim inside the shed, and smelled of sun-warmed wood and creosote. Under other circumstances, it would have been pleasant. Sybil's gardening tools were tidily hung on nails hammered into the wall, and on a shelf above the little work-bench, where seedling trays lay ready, was a line of repurposed glass bottles that had once held lemonade or dandelion and burdock, their old labels covered over with glued paper. *Blended tomato food, liquid soap.* One brown glass bottle was turned to the wall, and I gently span it towards me, squinting to read the label. When I did, I almost dropped it in my shock.

'Lou!' I shouted, running outside still clutching its neck. 'Lou!'

'And there we have it,' he said, placing the little bottle on the kitchen table, where it glowed amber in the last of the evening sunlight. 'How did you know?'

'Pat,' I said. 'I suddenly remembered what she'd said. I was telling her last year about the Agatha Christie I was reading, and she said, "funny they use cyanide – I've used it in the garden since just after the war started, you can't get pest-killer anywhere." It's one of the few chemicals provided to keen gardeners now.'

'How O'Carroll missed this...' Lou sighed. 'Useless shower. Thank God for your Pat.'

The doorbell drilled, and Lou went to let the policemen in. The kitchen filled with large, serious men in dark suits and hats, and as he briefed them, I slipped out to put Marple in the car so Bernhardt could escape the parlour. Outside it was night, the moon now full, illuminating the city like a stage-light and making a mockery of the blackout.

The front door clicked behind Lou, and he descended the steps for the last time. 'Come on,' he said, opening the car door for me. 'I'll run you home first, a few minutes won't make any difference.'

'Please don't,' I said. 'You can't expect me to have come this far, then shuffle off home while you do the exciting bit.'

'Edie,' Lou sounded pained. '"The exciting bit", as you put it, is my job. I'm very grateful for all you've done, of course I am, but I can see no benefit in you tagging along to watch the humiliating public arrest of two ageing women.'

He pulled away from the kerb, and accelerated towards the main road.

As he did so, an eerie, horribly familiar sound cut through the air, and in the distance, the thin beam of a searchlight strafed the sky.

'Oh, bloody hell,' Lou said. 'That's all we need. Where's the nearest shelter?'

'I don't know!' I said. 'Perhaps towards town?'

Lou glanced at me sideways, driving on as the siren's piercing wail undulated through the quiet streets.

'I'm taking you home, it's quicker,' he insisted. 'And go

straight to Mrs Turner's Anderson shelter, no messing about. Where's your gas mask?'

'At home,' I muttered.

'Edie! For God's sake.'

He swerved to avoid a mother and two children who were running down the middle of the street hand in hand, and pulled up.

'Want a lift to the shelter? I'm a policeman.'

'It's all right, thanks!' called the woman over her shoulder. 'We're going to Nanna's at number eleven, she's room for us there.'

'A sensible woman,' said Lou pointedly.

As we turned the corner, we heard a long, high whistle followed by a pause and distant boom.

'That's Oxford Road,' he said. 'We'll have to go the other way.'

'Lou, there's not time!' I peered upward from the car window, and saw aeroplanes like dark, glittering insects in the moonlight, droning overhead in close formation.

'It could be a big one,' I said. 'Let's just get to the nearest shelter.'

He gunned the engine and we roared up Upper Brook Street, now deserted but for hurrying ARP wardens and one dishevelled young man, weaving hastily from the pub towards the public shelter.

'I'll drop you off there,' Lou said, pointing at the arrowed sign.

'You can't think you're driving about in this?'

As I spoke, another, closer explosion shook the street.

'Lou!' I shouted. 'Park here and come with me!'

Sirens howled around us. The skyline was alive with white, flashing heat, plumes of dust and debris billowing upward.

'We need to bring Marple—' I began, but my words were

drowned by an explosion so vast that my teeth rattled in my head, and my eyes could see only rings of vivid colour.

'Christ!' Lou said. 'I think that was the Gaiety. Get out, I'm driving on – if Marie...'

'No,' I said, 'I'm coming with you. It's my fault she's there.'

'Edie, I mean it...'

'Drive!' I shouted as another crash and detonation came far too close behind us.

Lou drove.

As we shot down Whitworth Street, we had a clearer view of the Oxford Road air raid. Fire wardens were already running in great boots and helmets from their trucks, and ARP workers, grim, dusty faces lit by orange flames, were crouching over unmoving casualties on the pavement, waiting for the ambulances to get through from the Infirmary. Windows were blown inwards, jagged black holes where panes should have been, and once again, splintered wood and dusty brick that moments ago had been shops and houses formed blackened slag heaps. Still the sirens wailed.

Annie was not at work, I reminded myself with relief, and would be in Mrs Turner's shelter. I thought of Suki, Arnold, Ethel, Joan, Clara and her parents – where were my friends tonight and would they all be safe? Marie... I could not think yet about Marie.

As we approached the junction, a young constable stepped from the pavement, waving his arms.

'Stop,' he bellowed. 'You need to get to a shelter now, sir!'

Lou opened the window, letting acrid smoke billow into the car. 'It's me, Constable Bainbridge,' he said. 'DI Brennan, I have to get through to the Gaiety Theatre.'

The man looked anguished. 'You can't, sir,' he said. 'I'm sorry, the theatre took a direct hit a few minutes ago. Road's

closed, there's rubble everywhere and the raid's ongoing.
They've just started pulling people out. I'd advise you to divert
up past the library and—'

'Lou,' I interrupted frantically. 'Leave the car here.'

He slewed the vehicle to the side of the road, wrenched the
brake on and let Marple out, clipping the lead to his collar in a
single movement. 'Run,' he said.

We hurtled down towards Deansgate, leaping over bricks
and shattered glass, ears ringing as further bombs exploded
across the city. The sky was black and red, a spinning magic
lantern of chaos, and the oily smoke curling through the streets
was so dense it was hard to breathe.

An ARP warden yelled, 'Oi!' as we pelted by, and Lou
called 'I'm the DI!', though it was unlikely the words reached
him above the noise.

I was now wheezing through the smoke, slowing as we ran
on, and Lou reached behind and grabbed my hand, pulling me.

'Not far,' he shouted, 'keep going.' The pressure of his
warm, dry hand in mine gave me an anchor in the turmoil, and
kept me running alongside him.

At the corner of Peter Street, its sign barely visible through
the smoke and flames, a warden stood guard. 'Turn back!' he
shouted as we sprinted towards him.

'I'm DI Brennan,' shouted Lou, 'Let me through.'

'All right, sir, but the young lady...'

Lou gave my hand a tug and pulled me after him, the
warden gesticulating furiously in our wake.

The familiar theatre lay in ruins. The shops and businesses on
either side had also been hit – the furrier's sign and the tobac-
conist's neat window displays were blown apart, and several
prone figures lay on the other side of the street. Policemen and a
couple of auxiliary policewomen were running towards the

collapsed building, and a phalanx of fire engines, their clanging bells barely audible over the sirens and distant explosions, were pulling into the street, helmeted firemen already leaping out and dashing towards the burning remains.

'Marie!' Lou bellowed, and Marple unleashed a volley of barking at his master's evident distress. 'Marie!'

'Lou, she won't hear,' I shouted. 'Let's get as close as we can and help.'

He looked back at me, his eyes wild with fear. 'How will I tell them... Clive and Frances...'

'She may be all right!' I said desperately. 'Look, some people are being rescued.'

Through the plumes of smoke and dust, a thin line of people was silhouetted, led by a policeman – they were climbing from the part of the building that was still intact, though the steps had vanished, and they were forced to leap several feet onto rubble from the gaping door frame.

Jack, I thought. Josephine... Florence... now we knew they were innocent, my heart clenched in pain to think of them gone. I hoped it hadn't hurt, and they hadn't known. And clever, vivacious, kind Marie – who was only here because she had done as I asked, and trusted me. I closed my eyes against the agonising thought.

We made our way past collapsed joists and burst seats – impossible to imagine that, minutes ago, they had all been part of a normal evening for hundreds of people, sitting in tidy rows. Now, I saw the plant pot from the foyer flung into the window of the shop opposite, and flames devouring the stage door where I'd first met Wallis. Had he been there? It seemed likely – an old soldier who never left his post. There was no time to think of him. I followed Lou to the only exit, where people were still struggling out like Jonah emerging from the whale.

'Are there others alive?' Lou called to one man whose hair was sticking upright, his face and suit grey with caked dust.

'Yes, I think so,' he said, on a burst of coughing. 'Lots were moving, we just escaped and found the door. But some dead,' he added. 'I saw bodies, I'm afraid.'

Lou nodded. 'Thank you. The ambulances are coming,' he said, as the first swung into the street, its red cross glowing in the light of the fires. A few uniformed soldiers had emerged and were helping to lift people down from the gap and carry others to the opposite pavement. Lou pulled on my hand again.

'Come on,' he said, 'we must find her. Marple, Marie! Find Marie! He loves her,' he said, over his shoulder. 'He'll find her if anyone can.'

I withheld my sense of futility – they were all dead, surely, for who could survive this satanic inferno – and followed him over the rubble, where we hauled ourselves onto the ledge by the blown-out door. A policeman was guiding the trickle of walking wounded to the ambulances, a couple of escapees were seated on the edge of the kerb, their heads in their hands, jackets and dresses stained with blood and soot, and other wardens and APs were comforting them as we slipped inside.

'This way,' Lou shouted to me, and we edged our way down the little corridor of the collapsed foyer, directing the remaining straggle of shell-shocked theatregoers who passed us to the exit.

The ground was strewn with plaster, brass stair rods, broken wood – I stepped over the confectionery stall sign, and, to my horror, the limp body of an usherette, face down – perhaps the one I had spoken to the first time I came here – it was hard to make sense of the hellish scene.

'Lou,' I called, but he looked at her, and shook his head. 'Too late.'

Eventually, squeezing under fallen joists and choking through drifts of smoke, we found ourselves in the stalls of the auditorium, where a handful of people were moaning or shouting, and struggling upright between the broken seat rows.

'Marie!' Lou yelled. 'Marie Archibald!' He turned to me. 'If she was in the circle, she's gone.'

I looked up. The staircase had vanished, and the entire dress circle had been ripped away, chunks of gilded plaster and seating littering the back of the stalls.

Marple stiffened, and nosed the acrid air. He leapt over a pile of mangled seats, pulling the lead from Lou's hand, and pelted over the rubble-strewn auditorium to pause a couple of rows from the front of the splintered stage, where part of the vast theatre curtain had fallen, covering seats in its velvet folds like a still-life arrangement. Marple made his way down the row, then stood over something we couldn't see, barking.

'Oh dear God,' said Lou. 'Is she...?' We scrambled after the dog, whacking our ankles on metal rods where seats had stood, guided by the light of the flames coming through the holes in the ceiling. I was afraid it might collapse at any moment. *Annie can have my crime books*, I thought, *and Suki the cork sandals*, and I clambered on.

As we reached Marple, a further chunk of the ceiling dropped onto the stalls closer to us, and I screamed in shock. 'We'll get out in a minute,' Lou said, bending to the heap of clothes that Marple guarded.

'Marie,' he said. 'It's me, Lou. Can you hear me?'

The prone form didn't move. 'Please, Marie, love,' he said, more urgently. 'Wake up!'

I looked away, biting back tears, though whether they were for Lou, Marie or myself, I didn't know.

For a long time, there was nothing. And then, her gloved hand fluttered, like a bird's wing.

'Marie!'

The heap of clothes stirred, grey and stiff with plaster dust. 'Can you hear me?' Lou asked. 'It's me, and Edie.'

'Lou?'

Her voice was a croak, as though she hadn't spoken for many years.

'Can you move your legs?'

A red shoe lifted gingerly, and the other joined it in the air. I was suddenly reminded of the ruby slippers poking from under the chimney in the *Wizard of Oz*.

'My God,' said Marie, her voice stronger. 'Have I died?'

I laughed hysterically with relief.

'You're still here, I'm afraid,' I told her, and Lou whispered, 'Thank God.' He reached for her hand and clasped it.

'Ow,' she murmured. 'I might need my fingers.'

She sat up, leaning against the back of her twisted seat. 'I think I fainted,' she said. 'But nothing hurts.'

'Did anything hit your head?'

'No. But the people next to me... Sybil!' she remembered. 'And Daphne! Where are they?'

Lou and I exchanged a look. 'Edie, help Marie outside,' he said. 'Marple and I will look for the others.'

She leaned on me as we picked our way out. Among the rows, people had fallen and lay there still. I stopped at each, to check for a pulse, but those who remained unmoving had all gone. Some were sitting up, calling out for help, and I shouted, 'The ambulances are here. If you can move, follow us!' I would think about the horror later, I told myself. Now, it was simply about saving all the lives we could.

Marie was dazed but coherent. 'I must be a curse,' she said, as we bent low to duck under the fallen beams, my arm around her waist. 'Two theatre bombings in a month. And three murders... Edie, did you find out what you wanted to know? Do you know who killed them?'

'Let's get you looked at first,' I said, but as we climbed from the doorway and a dusty young soldier grabbed Marie and swung her down, I forgot all about the need for medical attention.

Jack was sitting opposite us, an ambulance worker bent over him, and I dashed across the debris-strewn road to his side.

'Edie!' He seemed to be in shock, a gash across his forehead and his leg propped on a hastily assembled pile of bricks. His face was white and his eyes hollow in the cold beam of the arc lights, which now shone onto the broken building.

'Jack!' I dropped to my knees next to him and took his freezing hand.

'Careful, miss,' said the ambulance worker. 'He's just come out, I need to check his vitals.'

I moved away, and sat beside Marie who was now slumped on the edge of the kerb, gazing blankly at the smouldering ruin of the theatre.

After a few moments, I heard the man say, 'All right, sir, you'll live,' and he moved on to the next casualty, leaving Jack with a pad of bloodstained gauze pressed to his forehead. 'What happened?' I asked him, sitting beside him. 'Do you know if...'

'If the others are alive?' He looked at me and I almost flinched at the raw grief of his expression. 'I don't know. I simply don't know,' he repeated.

'Stanley was backstage, it took a real hit,' he said slowly, indicating the back of the building, onto which a team of fire wardens was now training hoses. 'Florence and JoJo were onstage, and I was in the wings... I don't remember after that.'

He subsided into silence.

I put my arm round him. 'I'm so sorry,' I said inadequately. As I spoke, I looked up to see Lou appearing in the jagged black doorway. Behind him, amongst a gaggle of others, were Josephine and Florence, bedraggled and dust-choked, but alive and being lifted down by burly men in khakis.

'Oh, thank God,' I murmured, pointing so Jack would see them.

At the sight of them, he gave a strangled sob, and put his head in his hands, his body shaking.

Lou looked up at my shout, and as he saw me holding Jack, his face changed from relief to a professional mask.

'I'm going back in,' he shouted over the noise of throbbing engines and water pounding onto the burning interior. 'Sybil and Daphne...'

'Oh God, Syb and Daph...' Jack moaned. 'Our darling landladies.'

'They were sitting next to me,' Marie said, 'but there was no sign of them. Oh, I hope they got out...'

I felt that now was not the time to reveal the likely truth about the darling landladies. I was more worried about Lou and Marple, plunging back into that blackened inferno of collapsing beams and crumbling ceilings.

Florence was still being carefully checked by an Ambulance Auxiliary worker, but JoJo hurried over, her eyes clean and wide with shock in her filthy face. Jack tried to stand, but she collapsed onto the pavement on his other side, and threw her arms around him, as I hastily withdrew mine.

'Oh, Jack,' she said, 'I thought that was it, when the curtain fell, and the flames... Oh, Jack...'

He was clasping her to his chest, murmuring into her hair, and amidst the noise and chaos, I heard him say, 'Darling JoJo, it's always been you – I couldn't bear you not to be in the world...'

I finally saw what a fool I'd been to have imagined that it was me who interested Jack Webb.

CHAPTER TWENTY

'I suppose he was in love with her all the time,' said Marie, after we'd been moved further along the pavement to make space for more casualties. People on stretchers were now being carried out, but there was still no sign of Lou.

'It was Jack who quoted Byron.'

'He had loved her all along, with the passion of the strong,' I agreed. 'But Jack's curse wasn't "The Green Eye of the Little Yellow God",' I added. 'It was Guy – because Josephine was in love with him.'

Marie clutched my arm. 'Edie, you don't think... could Jack have killed Guy, to get his rival out of the way?'

'No, I don't think so,' I said. 'We found some things out...' The horror at Grafton Street seemed a thousand years ago. All that existed now was the burning theatre, and the question of how many had died entombed.

'I wish Lou would appear,' said Marie. 'Should we try to go back in and help?'

I longed to do so, but the fire wardens were having none of it. Unlike us, Lou had the special dispensation of being police.

Turned away, we leaned side by side on a wooden barrier

that had been hastily erected. I was mesmerised by the scene, a moonlit William Blake painting of smoke and fire, silhouetted figures gesturing in the unearthly light.

Time inched by, and our shared concern for Lou and Marple grew. As we gazed helplessly at the yawning hole from which stretchers were emerging, there was a vast, rumbling boom and a further wave of thunderous crashing from the centre of the building.

'That's the auditorium ceiling gone!' a helmeted man shouted, running towards the theatre, and Marie and I clutched each other in icy dread.

There was nowhere to look, nothing else in the world but that terrible dark space, where Lou was not. The seconds and minutes ticked on.

It was only when Marie gave a piercing shriek – 'There!' – and sagged against me that I realised. I had somehow missed the moment. Perhaps I'd squeezed my eyes shut, praying to a God I didn't believe in – but Lou was outside, still standing. There was a stretcher holding a covered body on the ground beside him. A scrap of yellow and white fabric spilled from under the blanket, a soot-stained ambulance worker was shaking his head, and next to him – Sybil. She was wailing, a terrible, ghostly ululation of grief and pain. The sound froze my blood, and Marie gripped my hand.

'Oh, not Daphne,' she whispered. 'She seemed so sweet.'

I ducked under the barrier, and ran. Lou looked up and his face sagged with relief. I wanted to embrace him, but thought he might feel that was deeply unprofessional under the circumstances. Instead, I lightly touched the ripped, grimy arm of his jacket, and quietly said, 'You're alive.'

Briefly, he put an arm round me and pulled me to him, then just as quickly released me. Sybil was now bent over the stretcher.

'My girl!' she wailed. 'My darling girl!'

I glanced at Lou. He looked as puzzled as me, but as Sybil sank to her knees, embracing the prone body under the blanket, I knew.

I turned to him. 'I don't think Daphne was Sybil's sister.'

'What?' he asked. 'Well then, who on earth...'

I looked back at Sybil, now rocking to and fro in a paroxysm of despair, and despite everything, my heart quailed at her pain.

'Lou,' I said, 'I think she was her daughter.'

The night had taken on the eerie, changing quality of a nightmare. Over two hours had passed – Sybil now sat in the back of an ambulance, keening, while Lou, Marie and I did what we could to help the casualties who could move – Manchester Royal was not far, and ambulances came and went, delivering the injured to the emergency department, and the dead to the mortuary.

Army reinforcements arrived, helping to dig in the rubble for bodies or survivors – whenever anyone was found alive, a cheer would go up. The cheers were becoming less frequent, more ragged, as the hours went by. At some point, the air raid ended and the all-clear sounded, but it barely registered. I was running back and forth under merciless arc lights to the emergency stirrup-pump, fetching water to bathe wounds and ease dust-dry throats. How I wished Annie was with me, with all her unflappable nursing experience – but she was, I hoped, safely at home, fast asleep after an uncomfortable few hours crammed next to Mrs Turner in the Anderson.

Lou was now managing the rescue effort, directing men to the areas where people might still be found. There was no sign of Wallis Middleton, and I hoped he had died instantly, in the place where he had always found the most purpose and comfort.

Florence had intended to return to Grafton Street and get

'the first train back to London' in the morning, but Lou was forced to explain that the house was now a crime scene.

'If you can find a hotel,' he said, 'I'll ask a constable to accompany you in the morning, to get your things.'

'But why?' Florence asked repeatedly. 'Why is it a crime scene? For heaven's sake...'

'I can't tell you at the moment,' he insisted. 'Go to the Mitre in Cathedral Gate, they usually have rooms, and it's clean and safe.'

She stamped away, furious and upset, but there was no time to worry further about her. Stanley was still missing, and firemen were clambering over the spilled bricks of the dressing room area like chain gangs, searching for signs of life. So far, all was mute, and despite my personal feelings towards Kerridge, my heart was heavy.

Jack and Josephine were still unaware of what we had found at Grafton Street and, all too soon, we'd have to tell them and spark a fresh wave of grief. They were still on the pavement huddled together, a shared horsehair blanket wrapped around them. Looking at them, at how Josephine had laid her head on Jack's shoulder, and the way they murmured gently to each other, I thought Jack may one day get his wish. He had hoped to make her jealous, that was all. Perhaps it had worked. In time, I might feel foolish and rather humiliated – but examining all that would have to wait. Lou was standing in the stark beam of an arc light, beckoning me over to the ambulance where Sybil sat.

'Look,' he said. His voice was hoarse with dust and exhaustion, his face grimy with soot. 'We need a confession from Sybil, but she's been too upset to speak. Daphne...'

'I know,' I said. 'Can it wait till morning?'

'Not really,' he said. 'If there's a tiny chance she's innocent, I don't want to keep a grieving woman in a cell all night – or what's left of it. It's not protocol, but can you come and help me speak to her? She might be reassured if there's a woman there.'

I nodded. 'Of course. Where's Marie?'

'Looking after Marple, and helping out with the WVS who've just turned up,' Lou said. 'Thank God for the women. Saving the world, one tea urn at a time.'

I smiled. It was so long since I had done so, I felt the coat of dust on my cheeks cracking.

'Come on, then,' I said. 'And please be as gentle as possible with her.'

Inside the ambulance, Sybil sat alone on the pull-down stretcher, her head in her hands. She was silent now, her red hair had fallen loose from its topknot, her gay scarves hung tattered and knotted about her neck, the draped, elegant clothes torn and creased. She reminded me of a biblical painting, a grieving woman lost in a desert.

'Sybil,' I said quietly, climbing in to sit beside her. 'I'm so sorry about Daphne.'

She shook her head. 'It can't be true,' she murmured. 'It can't be real.'

Lou took the stretcher opposite. He leaned towards her. 'I am so very sorry,' he said. 'Truly. But we need to ask you some questions.'

'It doesn't matter now,' said Sybil. 'I've nothing left. Ask anything.'

I glanced at Lou. I had never felt so cruel, and yet she was a murderer. He, too, looked anguished. 'Can we get you a cup of tea from the WVS first?' he asked.

Sybil shrugged. 'Don't care.'

'Perhaps in a bit,' I said. 'Sybil, Daphne was your daughter, wasn't she?'

She nodded. 'But we couldn't say so. The judgement... I

was respectable, I couldn't have gossip...' She began to cry again, and I put my hand over hers. She was so thin, the white of her bones shone through.

'I know it's hard to think about,' I said, 'but Sybil, we found Ginny's body in your garden. And the poison that was used to kill Leonard in the shed.'

She looked up at me for the first time. Her kohl smudged eyes were lightless and defeated.

'Was it you?' Lou asked her, almost kindly. 'We will find out, you know.'

Sybil closed her eyes and laid her head back. She nodded, once, and despite everything, I felt a flare of shock. Three people, all innocent. All dead, because of the broken woman beside us.

'Can you tell us why you did it?' I asked her. 'It might help, to get it off your chest.'

'This isn't a formal interview,' Lou said to me quietly, 'she's in no fit state. But I will take notes as you talk.' He extracted a battered notebook from his jacket and unclipped his pen.

Sybil opened her eyes again, and gazed through me.

'I'll tell you,' she said. 'It makes no difference – I've nothing to live for. Perhaps I'll have that cup of tea now.'

After I had fetched the tea, and Lou had found Sybil a blanket as she was beginning to shiver in the pre-dawn chill, she sighed.

'All right,' she said. 'This is what happened, and I promise it's all true. I'll plead guilty, there's no point pretending it wasn't me.'

'Go on,' I said, as Lou's pen scratched on the paper.

'I was a child star,' Sybil began, the tea trembling in her hand. 'My mother was an actress – people thought they were whores in those days, and when she married my father, she had to give it up. She poured all her hopes and ambitions into me.

She was unwell,' she went on, 'all five of my siblings died at birth, and she was terribly weak. She died when I was ten, but by then, I had already starred in *Alice in Wonderland*, and a few other plays, and everyone thought I was marvellous. I didn't go to school – acting was all I knew how to do, and from the very beginning, I adored it. There was nothing like the applause, the approval – my father was an exacting sort of man, but when wonderful reviews came in, or the audience gave a standing ovation, those were the times when I knew I'd pleased him.'

Sybil looked into the distance, and it was clear she could see her father there in his evening suit, clapping in the front row, his stern face glowing with approval.

'As I grew up, I kept on getting leading roles,' she went on. 'I made great friends in the theatre – really, it was my whole life. I only went home to sleep and eat, I lived for my work – learning lines, the slog of rehearsals, dress fittings, the thrill of a first night, somebody running to the news stand on Shaftesbury Avenue at midnight for the early editions, turning to the reviews...' She pressed a quivering hand to her eyes. 'Glorious days. I was good, there's no point pretending otherwise. I was born to be an actress.'

'What happened?'

'I starred in Shakespeare, modern plays, melodramas,' she said. 'I went all over the world – my father died when I was seventeen and my little theatre family cared for me. I was earning my own money, almost unheard of back then for a woman of my class, and I was a beauty – there were suitors at every stage door, professing their love. But I wasn't interested.' She shook her head, reliving the past. 'I didn't want to settle down, have some dull husband telling me what I could do, or where I could go. I was an ingénue, but by twenty-five, I was just beginning to become a true actress, someone who could master any role. Then I met him.'

She paused. Lou's pen stopped, and I waited. Outside, engines juddered, and men called out to one another. In the ambulance, it was silent as the moment before curtain up.

'Who did you meet, Sybil?' I asked eventually.

'Leonard, of course,' she said. 'He was in *Hedda Gabler* with me, he was a great star by then, crowds flocked just to see him. Every night, a great scrum around the stage door waving autograph books, women thrusting roses at him, fainting with excitement when he appeared. He had a dove-grey evening suit, bespoke, it fitted like an opera glove – he'd always put it on to meet them afterwards. My God, but he was a handsome fellow,' she murmured.

'I had always made it a point never to fall in love with an actor,' she went on. 'Vain, silly popinjays, most of them, no matter how talented.'

I saw Lou raise an eyebrow in agreement.

'But Leonard... he was cultured, intelligent, gentle,' Sybil continued. It was as though she had entirely forgotten her dreadful current situation and surroundings.

'I fell in love with him. And to my astonishment, he seemed to feel the same about me. I knew he was married, but his wife was very rich, and I told myself he had only married for her fortune. I was close to the truth, as it turned out. Besides, she was far away visiting family in New York, and our affair... well, it felt destined, as though we had been fated to be together from the first moment our twin souls entered the world.'

I tried not to look at Lou.

'But then...' Sybil swallowed. 'I had been too reckless in my passion. I found that I was expecting a baby. Leonard was distraught, and so was I. I was touring, starring in productions one after the other... I couldn't keep a child, my career would have been destroyed, as would my reputation. Nobody would employ an actress who had been ruined by a married man.'

She fiddled with the rings on her hand, lost in past sadness.

'He wouldn't divorce Elizabeth for fear of a scandal, he told me, and I realised how stupid I had been. When the baby began to show, I told my agent and friends that I was exhausted and was going to Switzerland for a rest cure. I found a private clinic and told them I was newly widowed, but I'd had to confide in the director, James Lyons-Booth – he had guessed the truth. He told his wife, Agnes, who was a notorious gossip, and within days, everyone knew. It was a scandal.'

I felt a great sadness. Sybil's career and reputation had been destroyed due to love, while Leonard's carried blithely on.

'After the baby was born – my beautiful daughter,' Sybil said, her eyes misting, 'I named her, and I signed the papers and they took her away. I was left alone, looking out at the mountains and wondering why I had done it – I had given up my child for my career, and it was already too late. I could have kept her.'

Silent tears began to roll down her cheeks, clean tracks in the dirt.

'When I returned to England, no theatre would touch me,' she went on. 'I discovered that Elizabeth had contracted typhoid in America and died, and I thought Leonard would send for me, but he never did. A few years later, I heard on the grapevine that he was spending a great deal of time with a man called Toby Beechwood, a very rich playwright who was known for his debauched parties in Hampstead. When Toby was arrested on the Heath, I understood that Leonard's interests... well, that they now lay in another direction altogether.'

I nodded.

'Go on,' murmured Lou, his pen flying across the page.

Sybil pulled the blanket more tightly round her shoulders as if she were a child who needed comforting. In some ways, I thought, she was.

'I missed acting every day,' Sybil continued. 'And I missed the daughter I'd given up for no reason far more. I came to

Manchester for a fresh start and used the remaining money I had to buy number twenty-three. I still had a handful of friends in repertory, and they spread the word that I would take theatrical boarders. As time went by, none of the younger ones recognised me – I could still hear about the theatre, enjoy the company of theatre people, and in some ways, though it was agony, it was comforting, too.'

I wondered if I would feel like that about newspapers, if I were forced to leave the inky clack and bustle of the *Chronicle*'s offices, and watch some other young woman take my place next to Pat... I concluded swiftly that I would.

'Daphne...' I said. 'How did she...?'

'It was a miracle,' said Sybil, her face briefly alight with the memory. 'She had been adopted by a couple from London, and when she turned eighteen, in 1924, she decided to track her parents down. She was so resourceful,' Sybil went on. 'She went to Somerset House on the Underground, all alone, and ploughed through the records. She knew her grandmother had been an actress so she thought I might have been too. She went to the British Library and searched old newspapers for weeks, until she found a reference to "a scandal" in 1906, and from there...'

'She worked it out,' said Lou. 'Clever of her.'

'She was clever. Far brighter than me,' Sybil said. 'She turned up on the doorstep and I knew – I knew instantly that she was my daughter. She had Leonard's eyes, my face shape... I took her in and immediately, it was as though I had been beside her every day of her life.'

'So she wasn't widowed young?'

'No. Daphne never married. That's just what we told people to explain her presence,' Sybil said. 'She moved in with me, and we ran number twenty-three together. She was a godsend and a blessing.'

We were reaching the hardest part now. The tea was cold in

Sybil's hand, and outside, the sound of trucks had died away. It would soon be dawn.

'What happened when Ginny and the others arrived?' I asked Sybil.

She nodded slowly.

'I knew I'd have to tell it all one day,' she said. 'I never thought it could stay a secret. Daphne wanted to confess, but I couldn't see my little girl in prison, could I?' She lifted her wet eyes to me. 'I can go, it's all right for me, I've nothing left now, but it wasn't her fault.'

'Tell us what happened, Sybil,' said Lou.

'I will. It'll be a relief. I hadn't seen Leonard for years,' she said. 'And then in the late twenties, he needed digs in Manchester and the producer wouldn't put up for a hotel, so he came to me. It was a shock to see him standing there, and I still felt very angry, but we had a long talk that night,' she went on. 'He apologised and I told him the truth about Daphne, but she didn't know he was her father. I couldn't bear to let her find out that he hadn't wanted her, or me.

'Leonard wanted to meet her, but I'd only allow it if he kept our secret. Daphne always thought he was an old friend.'

'What did she think had happened to her father?' Lou asked.

'I didn't say. I think she knew not to ask. Leonard would come as a guest occasionally, over the years, and behave as though we'd only ever been friends – he'd go on and on about his 'great pal, Cedric' and expect me to be delighted at his unconventional, happy life. I had lost so much,' she added, 'but I smiled along, and told myself that at least I had Daphne. I still loved him, you see – if he could be nearby, even as a friend, it was better than nothing.'

'I understand,' said Lou quietly. 'So when ENSA arrived...'

'Well, at first, I was braced to see Leonard, and put on a

cheerful face, as usual,' said Sybil. 'But this time...' She broke off.

'Go on,' I said.

'Well, he was such great friends with Ginny and Guy and the others. I could see he'd found a little troupe of real talents, and I felt so old and cast aside. He didn't want to talk about old times with me anymore, he wanted to talk to Ginny about their new show. I knew then that it was all over for me – I was just a deluded old woman, clinging to the past.' She paused, and took a deep breath.

'I'm not proud of what I did,' she said. 'I'm horrified. I wasn't in my right mind. Well, I suppose I've been punished now,' she added bleakly.

'The day of the first show in Manchester, they were all terribly excited. We were in the kitchen. Leonard was talking to Ginny about her career, and Guy was there – it was obvious that he was besotted with her.'

'*The fact that he loved her was plain to all...*' I quoted, and she nodded.

'I was going upstairs later on, with some clean towels for them all, and I overheard Leonard in his room, talking to Ginny. I heard her say, "I can tell you this, because I know you're unconventional too, and you won't judge me." I stopped to listen, and she said, "I think I might be expecting Guy's baby, and I don't know what to do." I almost gasped aloud, but I wanted to hear what Leonard would say. He had been so certain that I must not ever mention having his child, he'd wanted me to go to a backstreet butcher, but I'd seen the results of that with other actresses – some of whom did not survive the procedure – and I refused. But he insisted I give her up at birth.'

Sybil took a long, shuddering breath. 'I listened at the door, and I heard him say, "But Ginny, my dear, of course you must keep the child. Guy will obtain a divorce and marry you – any man who cared a fig for you would do the same."'

Lou and I looked at Sybil. In that moment, I understood why she had done it – and I almost felt I might have done it too.

'So,' she went on, her voice low. 'I dropped the towels and ran downstairs. I thought I might collapse with hurt and rage. I wanted him to suffer – not to kill him, never that, just to make him briefly suffer as I did. I'd had some almond chocolates in the pantry since before the war – a departing actor had given them to thank us, and neither of us likes almonds. I snatched them up and ran to the shed, where I took the bottle of cyanide I keep for garden pests, and the syringe I use for administering fungicide for the potatoes – they can get terrible blight – and I injected a tiny bit into each chocolate. Then I took them to the theatre and dropped them off at the stage door. I thought he'd just have one and feel ill and it might ruin his performance that night and get him bad reviews. It never occurred to me that he'd eat all of them at once!'

'Sybil, a child might have...' I began.

'I know,' she said. Tremors were running through her, and I put my arm round her slight shoulders. 'I'm disgusted at myself. When the others came back and told me that Leonard was dead, I thought I'd pass out.'

Lou was nodding. 'And Ginny...?' he said softly, though the sympathy had drained from his voice.

'Ginny...' Sybil put her head into her hands. 'The day of the tribute, she was so eager to get it right, so desperate to show the world what a wonderful man Leonard had been. She said "he was just like a father to me", and I thought of Daphne, who had been forced to grow up without a real mother or father, who would never know the paternal kindnesses of Leonard Lessiter. The others had all gone off to the theatre, and Daphne had set off for the shops. Ginny was the last to get ready, and she came into the garden where I was digging. I felt very angry and very guilty about Leonard, and I didn't know what to do.'

'Did Daphne know?' I asked.

Sybil shook her head. 'Not at that point. Ginny asked if I would be coming to the tribute, and I said no. She seemed surprised and asked why not, and...'

Sybil covered her face again. We waited, as her shoulders quivered.

'... and I said there were things about Leonard that she didn't know – if she did, I told her, she wouldn't be so keen to pay homage. She scoffed at me. She said, "He's a wonderful man – and just because you're a failed actress, you shouldn't try to ruin his reputation." She said, "Leonard found me the starring role that made my name – and his kindness recently has helped me to make a very difficult decision."'

'I'm afraid I laughed at her,' Sybil continued. 'It was when I was starring with him in *Hedda Gabler* that our own affair began. And then, Ginny lost her temper and said, "What would you know about love or family, Sybil? All you've ever had is your sad old widowed sister," and that was when I... well, I didn't think, I was enraged – I lifted the spade I was holding, and I hit her. I just wanted to make her stop talking, stop saying these terrible things about Daphne, and about me. She had everything I'd ever wanted, everything that had been taken from me.'

I closed my eyes. *Oh Sybil*, I thought. So much hurt and sorrow, turned suddenly to rage, could set the world on fire.

'Ginny...' Sybil swallowed convulsively. 'Ginny fell down on the grass,' she said. 'I was wearing gardening gloves, and I dropped the spade and pulled them off and tried to revive her, but she... she...'

'She was already dead,' said Lou. Sybil was strong and rangy. Wielding a spade at Ginny's head, at close range... I shuddered.

'Yes.' Sybil said. 'I was beside myself. I howled at what I'd done, I wanted to die with horror. When Daphne came home, that's how she found me, in the garden next to Ginny's body.'

'Didn't the neighbours...?' I began, but Lou said, 'You were at the back, weren't you? Out of sight, behind the bean rows?' and Sybil nodded.

'We left her there while we dug her... the...'

'Grave,' said Lou implacably.

'Yes. I dug for as long as I could, and after it was dark, Daphne helped me...'

'To bury her there, and pretend she was missing,' Lou concluded. 'Did it occur to you to confess?'

Sybil nodded. 'Of course it did. I can't tell you how much... I have never played Lady Macbeth,' she said. 'But it's true. All of it. *Will this little hand never be clean?*' She spread both of hers before her, studying her calloused fingers. 'After everything I went through, the guilt I feel now is the very worst thing of all. It's hungry,' she added, her eyes blazing. 'It eats happiness and laughter and comfort and leaves everything inside one empty and cold.'

'And yet,' said Lou. 'You didn't confess. You did it again, when you killed Guy.'

'I couldn't leave Daphne again,' said Sybil. 'I had spent so very long without her. But I didn't kill Guy.'

'Daphne did,' I said, and she nodded.

'I can tell you now she's gone,' Sybil said on a bitter sob. 'Otherwise, I should willingly have hung for it.

'Daphne was struggling with the nature of what she'd helped me to do,' Sybil said. 'I felt dreadful, and I told her to go and clean the rooms to keep her mind off things. Normally it's my job, and she does the cookery. But she did, and while she was in Guy's room, she found some loose papers under the bed and glanced at them. It was clear that Guy had suspicions and was making notes. And he had written...'

'*Ask Sybil and Daphne – Again* – underlined,' I said.

'Yes. She was back in the kitchen when she heard Guy telling Jack that he was waiting for a letter from Rosemary to arrive, and that if it wasn't at the theatre early on, he'd go back afterwards, he was so desperate to read it. I suppose it was about his divorce.'

'Of course,' I breathed. 'Rosemary already knew he was in love with Ginny. She was deciding whether to grant it.'

Lou nodded. 'But she didn't know about the child. He needed the settlement before it became apparent that Ginny was pregnant.'

Sybil sighed. 'I don't know about any of that. But Daphne panicked, she thought he might have guessed the truth, that he would go to the police and they'd – you'd find her body.'

'But the charm bracelet,' I suddenly remembered, 'the one she never took off...'

'Yes. I... well, I removed it before we buried her,' Sybil said. Lou looked disgusted. 'I thought if it was found at the theatre, it would make it look less likely that she had vanished at home. It would seem she'd perhaps left it there and disappeared after being at the Gaiety, due to a row with Guy.'

'And you put it back in her room... why?' asked Lou.

'Daphne took it back,' she said. 'She thought it might cast suspicion on Josephine, who was the last person to see it.'

'And the handbag in Stanley's car?'

'Me.' Sybil gave a brisk shake of her head. 'He's a bloody awful man, and I knew he wouldn't be hung for it, there was no other evidence. I hoped it might divert attention for a while, at least.'

'Yes, it did do that,' Lou agreed coldly. 'Now tell me about Guy's death.'

'I wasn't there,' Sybil said. 'But Daphne... she did it to protect me. That was the only reason, I swear. She wasn't a bad person – she was a good girl.'

Sybil's eyes filled again.

'She slipped into the theatre during the interval, then hid in the powder rooms,' she said. 'After the others left, she went backstage and tried a few dressing rooms before she found Guy's. She was going to talk to him, that's all – explain why it wasn't us, that he had the wrong end of the stick. He turned up eventually, very late, with the letter and was startled to see her.'

'I bet he was,' muttered Lou.

'But she told him she'd come for a chat, and they couldn't talk at number twenty-three in case anyone overheard. He asked her what about, and she said, "I saw the papers in your room, Guy, and I think you might suspect us..." and he said, "Yes, I do." Daphne asked him why and he said that Ginny would never have vanished, that he was waiting for Rosemary to agree to a divorce and he had promised Ginny he would marry her before the baby came... all the things I had once hoped for,' Sybil murmured.

'Daphne said, "But it could have been anyone," and Guy said none of the others would have had time to kill Ginny and get rid of the body. Only Stanley had a car, and there wasn't a trace of Ginny in it, bar her handbag.'

'Sharp man,' said Lou approvingly.

'Daphne asked what he was going to do about it – silly, silly girl, she panicked – and he said, "What do you think? I'm going to the police first thing in the morning." That was when...'

'When she picked up the dagger and stabbed him,' I said.

'Yes. But you must listen, it was the heat of the moment! There was no intention...'

'Just like her mother's murderous rage was the heat of the moment, too,' said Lou. 'But you're forgetting something.'

'Am I?' Sybil looked suddenly imperious.

'You're overlooking the gloves,' he said. 'If it was so sudden and unexpected, such a *crime passionelle*, then why did Daphne take Josephine's gloves and put them on before she entered the dressing room, then stuff them up a bloody chimney afterwards?'

Sybil sagged. 'I don't know,' she murmured, 'I only know what she told me.'

'Perhaps you agreed together to get Guy out of the way,' suggested Lou. 'And having already visited the theatre once in disguise, you felt it had better be your daughter who did the deed. After all, as you're so fond of quoting *Macbeth*, perhaps you both felt, *I am in blood Stepped in so far, that, should I wade no more, returning were as tedious as go o'er.* It was easier to carry on killing than turn back and risk discovery, wasn't it?'

'Perhaps,' said Sybil. She closed her eyes. 'I'm so terribly tired of it all. There's nothing left to say,' she murmured. Sybil held her thin wrists out like a supplicant. 'May I please be arrested now?'

EPILOGUE

Dawn was breaking when we left the site of the bombing. Sunrise gilded the edges of the city's buildings, and the extent of the damage was becoming clearer in the growing light.

'The roads are still blocked,' said Lou. 'I'll walk you home.'

I checked my watch. 'I'm due at work in about four hours.'

'I'll ring Mr Gorringe myself for you,' said Lou. 'You need some sleep.'

'What about Marple – won't he be too tired to walk?' Marie had handed him back to Lou and caught a lift home with a friendly ambulance driver an hour before.

'He's been asleep under the emergency tea-stand,' Lou said. 'He's full of beans, aren't you, boy?'

Of the three of us, Marple certainly appeared the most energetic. Lou had asked another ambulance driver, who turned out to be an auxiliary called Penny, to drive Sybil to Newton Street and book her in.

Penny had saluted smartly. 'What's she done?' she whispered to me. 'She seems a nice old lady.'

I shook my head. 'I really don't know where to begin,' I said. 'But tell them to be gentle with her. She's just lost her daughter.'

Now, as the embers of the Gaiety smouldered behind us, Lou and I walked up to Oxford Road.

'What a night, York,' he said. 'What a bloody night.'

'I can't believe it's over,' I said. 'I suppose they're not going to Africa now.'

'I doubt it,' Lou said, as we walked past an ARP warden, streaked with soot and asleep on a pile of sandbags. 'But it seems Jack has won his prize at last in JoJo. Last seen holding hands, staggering into a cab. I'm sorry, Edie. I know you liked him.'

'He was using me to make her jealous,' I said. Despite everything, I felt a pang of humiliation.

'I think he liked you, too,' Lou said. 'But the heart has its reasons.'

'I wish I understood them.' I shivered in the early-morning cold.

Lou put his arm around my shoulders and pulled me to him for the second time that night.

'None of us do,' he said. 'We can but try. Edie, look – I owe you yet another apology.'

'Do you?' I asked. 'You've already said sorry for the other night, and—'

'Not for that,' he said. He dropped his arm and I immediately missed his warmth, but to my surprise, he took my hand.

'Well, for that, yes, but more generally. I've been difficult and snappish with you lately, and you haven't deserved it. I've come to rely on your help with these tricky cases – I said it's because I'm short-staffed, which I am, but quite frankly, Sergeant Beeston does not have your delicate touch when it comes to questioning suspects. Or your strokes of genius,' he added.

I was speechless – partly through sheer exhaustion, partly because Lou's hand felt so reassuringly right holding my own –

but mainly because he had never in all our friendship been so fulsome in his praise.

'The thing is,' he went on, as we crossed towards the junction, where an exhausted constable was redirecting a trickle of cars, 'it's... well, in truth, I was jealous of Jack. I could see that you liked him, he's a handsome bugger, and I was worried. I thought he might carry you off to London.'

I looked up at him.

'Me?' I said. 'Go off to big London, with one of them theatricals?'

Lou laughed. 'I was concerned. And as Marie will tell you, I don't handle things terribly well when I feel upset.'

'Oh, she already has,' I said, and he rolled his eyes.

'Of course she has. She adores you, by the way. And the thing is Edie,' he said, as we picked our way past another landslide of rubble and collapsed beams, 'I'm terribly fond of you, too.'

There was a silence.

'As a friend?' I asked. My heart was racing and my palms felt cold, despite his firm grip.

'No,' Lou said. 'Well, yes, but not just as a friend. As... I don't know what else. Something.'

'I think I'm very fond of you as well,' I said. My words seemed to be emerging without my brain directing them. 'When I thought Marie was your girlfriend, I... well, it wasn't a terribly nice feeling.'

He squeezed my hand. 'I've always sworn I'd never get involved with a journalist again,' he said. 'After Lorna – she thought nothing of hurling herself into danger, and she ended up dead. I still believe it was my fault, and I always will,' he added, as I began to speak.

'You're just the same,' he said, 'although looking back, Marie was right – she didn't have a very good sense of humour. Unlike you.'

'Well then...' I said, as the horse chestnuts of Alexandra Park appeared in the distance, all their white candles illuminated in the early-morning glow. 'Now what?'

Lou looked down at me. 'I don't know,' he said. 'We work so well together and I'd hate to ruin it. I'm grumpy, I like my own company, I'm not the marrying kind, I work all hours...'

'And I take unnecessary risks, and fly off the handle, and shout in the street,' I said. 'I like living with Annie and I'm horribly ambitious for a woman. I can't cook or sew to save my life, and I don't think I want to have children.'

Lou nodded, then broke into a smile so large and joyful, I couldn't help but smile back.

'I know all that,' he said. 'But I have the solution.'

'What?'

'Let's wait and see what happens.'

'That's a wonderful idea,' I said, and still holding hands, Marple trotting beside us, we walked on, towards home.

A LETTER FROM F.L. EVERETT

Hello,

Thank you so much for reading *Murder on Stage*. Please do sign up to my newsletter for more information on my books. Your email address will never be shared and you can unsubscribe at any time.

www.bookouture.com/f-l-everett

Of all three Edie York novels, this is the one that came to me most easily. Once I'd done most of the research, I started writing and couldn't stop. I felt I was there at the Gaiety, popping into Florence's untidy dressing room, waiting in the blue and gold foyer in an Art Deco chair and sitting in the stalls waiting for the show to begin as the audience murmured in anticipation; or sitting at the Grafton Street kitchen table eating a bowl of homemade soup and rolling my eyes at Stanley's terrible jokes.

Manchester is my home town, and it was a joy to write about the city in summer, too, when gardens were blooming and people could wear frocks and shirt-sleeves, rather than in the damp and cold of a wartime winter.

If you'd like to know more, there's a wealth of information about ENSA out there, and any liberties I've taken are entirely my own, to serve the story. I loved the idea of actors volunteering to entertain the troops, and of how close a rag-tag little theatrical troupe could become when bombs were raining down and they were all forced into digs together, stars and hopefuls alike.

Best of all was the opportunity, finally, to offer Edie and Lou a future together, however uncertain it may look. It's been clear from the moment they met that they're made for each other – at least, it has to me and Annie!

I'd love to hear what you thought of the book.

If you've missed the first two Edie books, do catch up with *A Report of Murder*, which launches her crime-solving career, and *Murder in a Country Village*, in which our girl heads to the hills to investigate the mysterious death of an artist.

If you did enjoy *Murder on Stage* even a fraction as much as I enjoyed writing it, I'd be so grateful if you could write a review. It makes a huge difference in helping new readers to discover my books.

I love hearing from my readers, wherever in the world you may be – you can get in touch through social media or my website.

Thanks again for reading,

Flic x

www.fliceverett.com

X x.com/fliceverett

instagram.com/fliceverett

ACKNOWLEDGEMENTS

Thank you so much for reading *Murder on Stage*. The majority of my gratitude goes to everyone who has made the time to enter Edie's wartime world, and follow her adventures in crime-solving. I truly hope you enjoyed it there.

I must also once again thank brilliant historian Catherine Pitt and my tirelessly insightful editor, Susannah Hamilton. Thanks also to the meticulous copy editors and proof readers who have pored over the manuscript, filleting out my random punctuation, and to Zoe Mills, who does such a wonderful job of reading the Edie York audiobooks.

Finally, thanks to my fellow writers who amuse and reassure every day, on and offline, (particularly Eleanor Bailey), and to my lovely family, who are extremely supportive of me staring into space and ignoring them while I make things up. And of course, to Ellroy, Larkin and Marlowe, who always make sure I have some structure to my day, and get outside once in a while.

PUBLISHING TEAM

Turning a manuscript into a book requires the efforts of many people. The publishing team at Bookouture would like to acknowledge everyone who contributed to this publication.

Audio
Alba Proko
Sinead O'Connor
Melissa Tran

Commercial
Lauren Morrissette
Hannah Richmond
Imogen Allport

Cover design
Emily Courdelle

Data and analysis
Mark Alder
Mohamed Bussuri

Editorial
Susannah Hamilton
Nadia Michael

Copyeditor
Faith Marsland

Proofreader
Catherine Lenderi

Marketing
Alex Crow
Melanie Price
Occy Carr
Cíara Rosney
Martyna Młynarska

Operations and distribution
Marina Valles
Stephanie Straub

Production
Hannah Snetsinger
Mandy Kullar
Jen Shannon

Publicity
Kim Nash
Noelle Holten
Jess Readett
Sarah Hardy

Rights and contracts
Peta Nightingale
Richard King
Saidah Graham

Milton Keynes UK
Ingram Content Group UK Ltd.
UKHW012247110624
443988UK00004B/241

9 781837 904686